REMORSE BY DEGREE

Keith Julius

Published by Keith Julius

Temperance, MI 48182

First edition - December 2015

www.KeithJulius.com

ISBN: 978-0-9969607-1-7

Printed by CreateSpace

Cover used with permission of Třinec Iron and Steel Works (Třinecké železárny)

This book is dedicated to Monica R. Sholar. Without your enthusiasm and encouragement this story would still be hidden away on my computer. Thank you so much for the push.

Prologue:
Monday, December 7, 2015

THE 24-HOUR CONVENIENCE STORE IS A beacon of light in an otherwise darkened neighborhood. It faces Route 31 in Roseland, Indiana, a northern suburb of South Bend. A gentle snow falls around the structure, the flakes drifting lazily on the westerly breeze that sweeps across the parking lot to swirl the accumulation of white.

Zak Tyler sits alone in the store, perched behind the counter on a high stool. To his left is the cash register, a display of astrological scrolls sticks out from a cardboard holder on his right, and behind him a backdrop of lottery tickets lines the wall. The clerk's attention is focused on his cellphone, his fingers manipulating the tiny creatures on the screen as they cavort through the world of the video game he plays. The store is quiet save for the pings and beeps that accompany the animated action.

At 2:53 AM the sapphire blue Camaro pulls into the parking lot. For thirty seconds no motion follows, then the driver steps out to enter the store. A blast of wintry air follows closely on his heels, to be snuffed out with the slamming of the door behind him. A small bell sounds as the glass panel vibrates shut.

Zak looks up briefly, acknowledging the customer with a brief nod of his head, then returns to his game.

The new arrival appears to notice none of it as he walks leisurely toward the back, his eyes surveying the layout of the store. He stops at the pyramid of Budweiser 12-packs rising in the corner. The display is decorated in bold red ribbons, as an apparent reminder not to forget the spirit of the holidays. He spends less than twenty seconds deciding on his purchase, grabbing one of the cartons and taking it with him to the front counter.

Zak, once again engrossed with his cellphone, looks up from his gameplay with a bothered expression on his face. "Will there be anything else, Sir?" His tone fails to match the politeness of the words.

Pausing for a moment, pondering the question, the customer fumbles in the pocket of his coat. "Yeah," he says at last. "Gimme a pack of Marlboros. Regular."

A shelf along the back wall, conveniently located beneath the lottery tickets, holds the cigarettes and tobacco products. With a minimum of effort the clerk spins half-around on his stool to grab the item. "Anything else?"

"Yeah. All the cash from the register."

Zak looks up, his eyes opening wide at sight of the .45 automatic leveled in his direction, the blue-steel of the barrel gleaming dull under the bright lights.

"No funny moves," the gunman prompts. His arm holds steady as a rock, the features of his face impassive and uncaring, his gray eyes disturbingly emotionless. "Just hand over all the money. Understand?"

"Yes, Sir."

Zak becomes more animated. He jumps off the stool, punching open the cash drawer and removing the tray of bills, which he places on the counter.

There isn't much. The gunman counts as he withdraws the money. "There's only sixty-seven dollars here. This can't be all of it?"

"Sure it can. I mean.... That's all of it. Honest."

"Cut the crap." The gun motions to the left. "Back away from there, so's I can see for myself."

Zak allows him plenty of room as the gunman slides behind the counter, running his free hand beneath the shelf, searching. A disbelieving expression crosses his face. "What the hell? There's got to be something else."

He twists around, examining the wall behind the counter. His search stops at sight of a small panel near the floor, secured with a lock. "Open it!"

Zak shrugs. "I don't have the combination."

"Wrong answer." The gun lifts, swinging in a deliberate arc.

The movement is half-completed when Zak takes his cue. "Don't shoot!" He lunges toward the knob. "I'll see what I can do."

A sound, of a car slowing down, drifts in from the street outside. The gunman takes a step toward the front window, holding his breath until the vehicle resumes its motion past the store.

A metallic scrape sounds from behind him. He turns, watching as the clerk pulls a silver-plated .38 revolver from a drawer beside the safe. Zak fumbles with the mechanism, his thumb slipping on the hammer. Fear controls his motions. His movements are erratic. Anxious.

There is no hesitation from his assailant. The automatic in the robber's hand barks three times in quick succession, the explosive blasts blending to a single deafening burst.

The youth's chest develops a pulpy cavity, the force of the blast spinning him about and hurling his body against the wall. A red spray ejects from his back, the blood showering a glass display case holding deli items. The body thumps to the floor as rivulets of red run slowly down to blend with potato salad and coleslaw and cold baked beans, the deep red diluting to a pale pink at contact with the food.

The customer kicks the .38 from lifeless fingers and spits on the floor. "Bad move, asshole."

The body is discovered eighteen minutes later. By then the blue Camaro is cruising down the highway, seven miles away, the driver swigging his second can of beer.

Chapter One: Wednesday, December 9, 2015

"I TELL YOU, DANNY BOY, THE WORLD'S going to hell, and there ain't a damn thing we can do about it."

Daniel Jameson looked up from his desk. "What's that, Ed?"

"World's going to hell," Eddie Boyd repeated. "Take that thing the other night. You know. That kid shot in the convenience store."

His mind preoccupied with the figures on the requisition form on the screen in front of him, Daniel found it difficult to follow what was being said to him. He knew an answer was expected, so he offered a meek reply. "I'm not sure I follow you."

"Sure you do, Danny Boy. Over In Indiana. South Bend. Young kid. Only twenty-one, the papers said. Snuffed out. Bam!" Boyd slammed the fisted knuckles of his right hand into the open palm of his left to emphasize his words. "Just like that. One minute he's here. The next...."

Boyd stopped in mid-sentence, a startled expression on his face as he continued. "Hell, Jimmy will be twenty-one next July. That could have been *my* son."

Daniel remembered it, then. The story had been all over the front page of *The Toledo Blade* on Tuesday, with additional coverage this morning. Daniel hadn't paid a lot of attention to the item. It just got too depressing to follow all the bad things going on in the world. Sometimes it just seemed easier to ignore what was happening around you. He had enough problems in his own life without getting involved with somebody else's.

"It's a shame, all right," Daniel finally agreed, feeling it was necessary to say something. "Think they'll catch the guy that did it?"

"I sure hope so. And I tell you what. If that had been my son, I'd be out right now, buying a gun, goin' after the bastard that done it. Know what I mean?"

"That won't bring the boy back."

"Maybe not, but it sure as hell might save some other poor kid's life. I tell you what. When they do catch him, they should just haul the son-of-a-bitch off, stick him in front of a wall, and plant a bullet right here." Boyd tapped the center of his forehead with a beefy finger. "Right between the eyes."

"And who would they get to do that?"

"I'd do it. Be glad to. Hell, they could probably even sell tickets for it. Now there's an idea...."

Boyd wandered off, muttering to himself.

Daniel shook his head and returned to work. He could never understand the Eddie Boyd's of the world. He hoped he never would.

The sharp tap-tap of heels crossing the room intruded on Daniel's concentration. He tried to ignore it, but as the sound drew closer his hand stopped in its motion and his head lifted. His eyes took in the approaching figure.

He noticed the legs first, or at least what was revealed of the legs between the top of the no-nonsense shoes and the hem of the mid-length skirt, and realized it had to be Teri Stone. No one else in the office had legs like hers.

"Morning, Dan," she smiled.

He assessed her body, not for the first time, in the few seconds it took to lift his head. She had a Barbie-doll figure, thin-waisted, with a more than ample bust line - a fact most men found not-at-all unattractive.

"How's it going, Teri?"

"Couldn't be better." Moving aside a stack of reports, she sat down on the edge of his desk before continuing. "Finally got my Christmas tree up last night, and all the outside lights."

"Wasn't it sort of cold for that?"

"Actually, it was kind of nice. The snow made everything feel sort of comfy. The kids tried to help, the little darlings, but didn't manage to do much more than get in the way."

"I know what you mean." Daniel slid his mouse forward, removing the cursor from the screen's image, then swiveled around in his chair. It was obvious he wasn't getting any work done in the next few minutes, anyway. "Lisa and Jeff were the same way when they were younger," he remarked. "It's not too bad now, of course."

"How old are they?"

"Lisa's thirteen. Jeff will turn ten in two months."

"Lisa's a teenager already?"

"Oh, yeah! Just try calling my home sometime. I swear that girl spends more time on the phone than you do."

"All part of the job, Dan." She leaned forward, depositing a folder on the desktop.

"What's that?" Daniel asked.

"Shippers for the Berkley order. Three hundred fifty parts. Jack says they have to go out by Friday."

"Tomorrow?"

She nodded.

"He's got to be kidding. Hell, we'll be lucky to have half that many by then."

She merely shrugged.

Daniel lifted a corner of the folder, glancing at the forms inside, then turned back to Teri. "If Jack wants those parts that bad, let him go out and run the molds himself."

"That will be the day!" Her laugh was infectious, and Daniel found himself chuckling along with her. "Just see what you can do. Okay?"

"All right. I'll get on it in a bit."

Teri shook her head. "Sorry, Dan. Jack wants to know right away how things look. He's waiting for an answer."

She shrugged in resignation and turned away. After two steps she turned back toward him, a mischievous grin on her face. "And Dan. Quit being so old-fashioned. Get Lisa a cell phone, for heaven's sake."

Daniel sat for a moment, watching her cross the office to return to her cubicle by the front windows, before pushing himself away from his desk. Grabbing the folder Teri had left and his safety glasses from the top right hand drawer of his desk, he headed toward the door. A row of wooden pegs on the wall beside the shop entrance held an assortment of hard-hats. Daniel latched onto one on his way out.

Stepping into the shop was like entering another world. The first thing Daniel noticed was the change in temperature, easily a twenty-five degree variance within a few steps. It was like walking into a sauna. As the heat assaulted him Daniel had to remind himself it was the second week of December. Outside snow lay on the ground, while the wind-chill factor hovered in the single digits, but winter weather seemed like a world away at the moment.

The odor of the foundry no longer disturbed him. At one time it had. The nauseating mixture of sand and reactant agents and molten metal and, of course, human sweat, lingered everywhere. The smell was so ingrained into the structure that, even during the annual shut-down in August, the place still reeked. Daniel Jameson had no idea what brimstone smelled like, but he was certain it couldn't be any worse than this.

Just a typical day at CONSOLIDATED CASTINGS, INC.

Across the vast room the furnaces blared with heat and noise, the light from the molten metal bathing the entire building. It was nearly time for the pour, the iron having been heated to well over a thousand degrees by now. He could see faceless men in metallic, heat-resistant overalls, directing the ladle supported by the overhead crane.

It was always interesting to watch the pour, to experience the raw energy of the molten metal as it was being tapped to serve man's needs. Often he found himself pausing, mesmerized with the sight, witness to an event that had been going on for centuries now, dating back in its simplest form to the start of the Iron Age.

Too much to do. Daniel forced himself away from the sight as he circled the last row of conveyor belts and approached Michael Blake. Blake had been a molder at CONSOLIDATED for over twelve years now, and he was good at what he did.

Daniel paused to watch as Blake finished scraping the top of the mold level, then lifted the cope to reveal the dingy aluminum match-plate that seconds earlier had been covered in the black, sticky sand. The metal pattern was removed next, which left the drag, or bottom half of the mold, exposed. Replacing the cope completed the job, comprising a block of sand with a cavity in the shape of the part to be cast. A wooden jacket held the two halves in place. With a casual push, Blake sent the finished assembly along its way down the conveyor system.

Blake turned around, brushing sweat-drenched hair from his eyes, and noticed he was being watched. Only then did Daniel step forward, waving with the folder in his hand at the tail of hair draping halfway down the other man's back.

"When you going to get a haircut?" Daniel asked, his voice raised above the ruckus about them.

It was a running joke, and Blake answered as he invariably did. "Go to hell!"

Both men laughed as Daniel stepped forward. "How's it going, Mike?"

"Can't complain. Wouldn't do any good if I did."

"Probably not."

"So what brings you out into the real world? Don't tell me they're gonna make you work for a change?"

"Not if I have anything to say about it. It's Baker again. He wants to know about the castings for the Berkley order. Says we need three hundred fifty by tomorrow."

"Can't you find somethin' to keep him off our backs?"

"Hey! My hands are tied! So how about it? How many we got so far?"

"I don't know. Paul's been taking care of that one."

"Where can I find him?"

Blake looked around as he rubbed his hands on his shirt. They didn't look any cleaner when he was done, the motion accomplishing little save to redistribute the dirt. "I don't see him right now. How soon do you need to know?"

"Baker's waiting."

Blake lifted a hinged section in the conveyor behind him and passed through to the other side. "Wait here. Be right back."

"Gotcha."

Daniel opened his folder as Blake walked away, looking again at the figures Baker had requested. The guy was nuts. That was all there was to it. There was no way they could get that many parts by Friday. If it was a simple squeeze mold, that would be different. But the parts he was talking about required a three-part mold, with nearly a dozen cores. It just couldn't be rushed.

There was always a great deal of noise in the foundry; of necessity, foundries are not quiet environments. But something about the sudden metallic grinding sound, something unusual, caused Daniel to look up. The ladle of molten metal dangling from the overhead crane groaned a second time, shifted further, and revealed a white-hot flow that began to pour from the container.

But something wasn't right.

The ladle wasn't anywhere near the proper location.

Even from the other side of the vast room Daniel felt the searing heat. He held his hand up as protection against the glare. It was only then, with his eyes shielded, that he could fully take in the present situation. It was only then that he could detect the figure of Michael Blake, less than forty feet from the spot the pouring metal sought as it slipped from confinement. Already the flow had struck the dirty floor, splatters of molten liquid coagulating in random splotches wherever they landed.

Blake spun about, took two panic-driven steps, and slammed against a section of conveyor belt. He went down hard, but only for an instant, managing to drag himself back to his feet. Blood flowed from the gash in his right leg as he hung on the railing and stared behind in horror.

Slowly, like a flow of lava from some primeval crater, the metal oozed toward him, hissing as it spread across the floor. Occasionally something in its path would explode, emitting a jet of moisture or a plume of smoke. But nothing could stop its progress.

"No!" Daniel Jameson screamed the word without realizing it, bolting into motion at the same moment. Perhaps, if he had stopped to think about it, he wouldn't have acted so swiftly, but by that time the adrenaline coursing through his system had taken effect. He could no sooner stop his present actions then he could the advancing metal.

His folder fell to the ground, pages scattering in all directions, as Daniel vaulted over the first row of conveyor belts. It was an ungainly maneuver. He nearly lost his footing in the process, but he recovered sufficiently to continue in his dash.

Running parallel to the rows of molds stacked upon the conveyors, he could feel the heat increasing with each step he took. He kept his eyes locked on the figure ahead. Michael Blake dragged himself along inches at a time using only the strength in his two arms, the ragged tear in his leg leaving a trail of blood on the dirty shop floor. The agony on his face was obvious even from a distance.

Daniel's gaze locked on the stricken man, and for an instant eye contact was achieved.

Blake stopped. For a moment the pain seemed lifted from his face. His eyes turned soft. The corners of his mouth relaxed.

But then the instant was gone.

"Get out of here!" Blake motioned with his left arm as he

yelled.

"The hell I will!" Daniel countered.

"You damn fool...."

His next words were lost in an ear-splitting scream of pain. The molten metal had found him.

Daniel lunged forward, landing on top of the conveyor inches from the stricken man, flailing his arms wildly to grab anything he could find. His fingers clenched material and Daniel yanked with all his might. It was like pulling against a dead weight. There was no movement, no help, no sign of anything from the figure sprawled against him.

Daniel continued with his struggles, dragging his arms across the metal railing of the conveyor belt. He felt the ripping of skin. Part of him was aware of the blood that began to flow from his left elbow, but there was no indication of pain. He felt detached. Distant. The red flow running across his skin could have been an image on a screen, and not something leaking from his own body.

Oh, God, no! Oh, God, no!

The same three words kept repeating themselves in Daniel's head. He was uncertain where they came from. Were they Michael's? Or his? Or merely thoughts flashing through his head?

It was difficult to see. His eyes ached from the glare of the molten iron. Perspiration drenched his body. Several of the wooden mold jackets, ignited by the hot metal, burned nearby, adding an offensive black smoke to the surroundings. The vapors hurt his nostrils. His chest stung. His throat was inflamed and raw, and repeated coughing only prolonged the agony.

"Hang on, Mike! Hang on!" Daniel failed to recognize the raspy voice shouting encouragements as his own, his body by now performing in automatic mode. "You're gonna be okay!"

Still Daniel continued to pull.

By this time Blake was off the ground and onto the conveyor belt. Daniel could feel the heat beneath him. Could smell burning shoes. Singed hair. Incinerated flesh.

Then he felt it. A definite pull against him. The first sign of resistance.

Daniel forced his eyes open.

A giant metallic figure, like some otherworldly creature, stood motionless in front of him, staring down at them. Daniel blinked, forced his mind to reason properly, and came finally to the realization that it was one of the furnace attendants.

"Get out of here!"

Daniel stared at the speaker, his mind failing to comprehend the words.

A hand clasped his shoulder. "Get out of here!"

What did he mean? What was he trying to say?

"Are you deaf! Get the hell out of here! We'll take over!"

Finally understanding came to Daniel, who slowly nodded his head, acknowledging the wisdom of the advice. His hands went limp as he felt a weight being lifted from him. Rolling onto his back, he lay for a moment, taking in a deep breath, aware for the first time of the exertion he had gone through. The gulp of air brought searing agony to his lungs, and he coughed as he forced himself to a crawling position.

He knew he couldn't step onto the floor, the metal beneath him sending shimmering waves of heat which warned of the foolishness of getting off the conveyor system. He pushed himself along on hands and knees, favoring his left arm, which was beginning to ache fiercely now.

Several times he encountered molds in his way, stacked upon the conveyor and awaiting the pour. He bypassed the objects in the most simple and straight-forward manner he could conceive of, pushing each mold off the edge. In his wake he left a series of mounds of black sand on the floor.

Realizing at last that it was safe to step down, he slid off the conveyor belt and began trudging along, heedless of where he was going other than the fact that he was leaving the molten metal, with its awesome heat and glare and destructive power, behind him.

Chapter Two:

A BLUR OF HECTIC MOTIONS AND VAGUE sensations followed. Daniel could remember a white cloth being wrapped around his arm - the pressure against his torn elbow was excruciating - and obviously someone must have put it there, but he couldn't recall the incident taking place. One minute he was bleeding, red drops running from the tear in his skin, down his arm, and leaking at last off his fingertips. The next moment he was bandaged.

His body felt numb, like he had lost control. Hands led him on, and he marched blindly forward. Somewhere in the back of his mind he knew where he was going, as he shuffled between the rows of stacked molds, past the blast furnace, and finally through the man-door that led to the shipping department and eventually to the exit. But his consciousness registered none of it.

The blast of cold air as the overhead door opened hit him hard, slamming against his chest, and he found himself gasping for breath. A mad bout of shivering overcame him which failed to abate even after someone threw a blanket over his shoulders.

An ambulance poised at the doorway, snout pointed into the wind, anxious for a hasty getaway. Daniel could see the red and blue lights swirling through the driving snow, but no sound reached his ears. Either the siren was silent or the wind was stealing the undulation before it could reach him.

Then it struck him that everything was silent. People scurried about haphazardly. A form lay on a stretcher, bodies huddled over it, working furiously away at their revival techniques. A crowd had gathered on the sidewalk outside, hearty souls more than willing to brave the elements for the opportunity to catch a glimpse of human tragedy.

But all was quiet. It was like watching a silent newsreel of somebody else's disaster. Too many senses had been assaulted at once for his mind to comprehend it all.

Daniel felt motion again as he was escorted into the back of the truck. A figure in white stood before him mouthing soundless words, their faces only inches away from each other. Daniel wished he would just leave. He considered pushing the intruder away, but, lacking the energy to respond, he sat instead in silence, mesmerized with Michael's form, pale and seemingly lifeless on the stretcher before him.

Blake's cheeks were collapsed and withdrawn, his lips cracked and bleeding. A white cloth soaked with red wrapped around his legs. An intravenous tube led from his arm to a sack of clear liquid supported by a metal hanger.

A trio of attendants swarmed about, one of them speaking into a 2-way radio. Instructions were shouted back and forth, a quick staccato of orders assessing pulse rate, blood pressure, and other vital signs, while an oxygen canister was prepared to assist in breathing.

The paramedic manning the radio took time to shout out in frustration. "What's the hold-up?! This guy needs to get to the hospital. And I mean NOW!"

His attention returned to the radio, as he continued to relay information from the physician at the trauma center.

As Daniel continued to stare the image began to swirl in and out of focus. A weakness developed in his stomach. His mind felt weary while his eyelids grew heavy, and as the ambulance pulled away the motion of the vehicle lulled him into an uncomfortable sleep.

"Are you feeling better now, Mr. Jameson?"

Daniel opened his eyes. He turned from the counter

beside him, away from the clutter of medical implements and bottles of Band-Aids and cotton swabs and alcohol, and sought the voice. The young man walking toward him in the antiseptically-white lab coat looked barely out of his teens. He sported a smile meant to offer reassurances.

"Where am I...?

"Riverside Hospital Emergency Room."

Turning his head from side to side, Daniel realized for the first time that he was lying on a cot. A flimsy plastic curtain wrapped three-quarters of the way around the bed - the headboard rested against the compartment's only real wall - and forms could be seen moving on the other side. Faint traces of conversation reached into the enclosure as two uniformed nurses passed by. In spite of himself, Daniel found himself listening to the talk.

"... so Dr. Jensen says, up the dosage to 150 CC's."

"Isn't that a lot?"

"Well, that's what I thought! But I couldn't be telling him that, now could I?"

"Not if you want to keep your job, anyway."

The voices mingled in a giddyish bout of laughter as they faded away, leaving silence in their wake.

Attempting to raise up on his elbows, a stabbing pain shot through Daniel's left arm. He collapsed onto his back, a bleat escaping his lips.

"Steady there, Mr. Jameson. It might be a good idea to just take it easy for a while."

Daniel shifted to face the speaker. "Mike...?"

"That would be Mr. Blake, right?"

Daniel nodded his head.

"He's in surgery right now."

"How is he?"

"Too early to tell. But there's a good team working on him. I'm sure he'll be okay."

"God, I feel awful. And my tongue feels thick."

"That's probably from the shot they gave you."

"Shot?"

"For the pain."

"Of course."

A metallic voice, from a loudspeaker somewhere outside the enclosure, intruded. "Dr. Savage. Paging Dr. Clark Savage. You're wanted in O.R. #3, Dr. Savage."

Daniel Jameson turned back toward his visitor. "Doctor...?"

The attendant shook his head. "Nurse. Jim Stacey. Just ask for me if you need anything." As he talked the young man manipulated instruments on a cart, which he then rolled over beside the cot.

"What's that for?" Daniel asked.

"From the looks of that dressing, and the amount of blood, I'd say that's quite a gash on your left arm. When did you have your last tetanus shot?"

"Tetanus shot?"

"Yes. Have you had a tetanus shot lately?"

"I don't think I've ever had one."

"Well, you'll be getting one today." He seemed to be finished with whatever he was doing on the cart. "The Doctor will be out in a few minutes. Don't go anywhere."

"Yeah. Right."

Time is a strange commodity. For Daniel Jameson, cloistered behind the flimsy curtain, the seconds dragged by with an incredible slowness. He became aware of minute details - the soft hum of the fluorescent lights above him, the complaining squeak of a cart being pushed down a hallway, the murmur of indistinct voices from the nurses' station. As he lay on his side he stared at the pattern in the linoleum, counting the colored dots and following the various patterns in the vinyl. Eventually he wearied of the activity, and his eyes searched for other diversions.

A laminated poster on the wall by his head depicted a standing figure. Half was a skeletal representation, while the other side sported a confusing jumble of red and blue muscle and ligaments. Daniel found little comfort in the picture, and quickly turned away.

His arm was beginning to ache. It throbbed with each beat of his heart, not really so much in pain, but more with a nagging pressure that refused to go away. He caught himself holding his breath several times, as though the action would delay the sensation, but the more he struggled to ignore it the more intense the feeling became.

After a seeming eternity the doctor entered, an elderly man with a trim black beard spotted with flecks of gray. He looked up from the iPad in his hands as he walked over to Daniel.

"How's the arm?"

"Hurts a bit."

"I'm not surprised." A few more notations were entered on the iPad before the doctor set the device down. He then removed a scissors from the cart and began to cut through the gauze around Daniel's elbow. The cloth fell away to reveal a ragged tear in the skin, black with dried blood. "That doesn't look so bad."

"Looks like hell," Daniel commented.

"I've seen worse. Here, put this under your arm."

Daniel slid the plastic basin under his arm as the doctor approached with a bottle of red liquid. "First we have to clean the wound," he explained, attacking the tear with a vengeance Daniel found all too unnecessary. Daniel gripped the edge of the cot with his good arm and closed his eyes, hard, to fight the pain, and at last the scrubbing was complete.

"That's the worse of it. A few stitches and you'll be home free."

"Have you heard anything about Michael Blake?" Daniel asked.

"Michael Blake?" The doctor turned toward the nurse, Jim Stacey, who stood at the foot of the cot.

"You know," Stacey answered. "The other one that came

in with Mr. Jameson." He paused, uncertain what to say next.

The doctor faced Daniel again. "Oh, yes. Yes. I understand there's a team working on him right now. A friend of yours?"

Daniel nodded. "Yes he is. Is he going to be okay?"

"Don't know. What happened?"

"Accident. In the foundry. One of the chains broke on the ladle. I think." It seemed so long ago now, like part of a bad dream. "Yeah. That must have been what happened."

Silence invaded the room as the doctor worked on. Daniel found himself more relaxed now, almost calm, and wondered why. How could he be feeling like this after what he had just gone through? What Mike had just gone through?

His eyes remained closed, and he found himself listening to his own breathing, a steady motion that brought a semblance of sanity to a crazy situation.

Daniel realized that accidents happened, especially in a shop environment. He had heard of people losing fingers before, and a while back a casting had fallen off a skid and broken Larry Matthews' foot, but in more than twenty years of working there, Daniel had never heard of anything serious - anything approaching life-threatening - happening at CONSOLIDATED. But this was something else. It made him view the foundry, and the hazards prevalent within the system, from a different perspective.

"There. All done."

The doctor's voice broke Daniel's concentration. "What's that?"

"All done with the stitching. We'll get a bandage on it, and you'll be ready to go home as soon as you've had that tetanus shot. We want to see you back here in three days, to take a look at things."

"Right."

The doctor retrieved his iPad, manipulating some figures. "I'm sending in a prescription for you. What pharmacy do you use?"

Daniel named the location, the local Kroger they shopped at on a regular basis.

"You'll want to take two of these, every four hours," the doctor advised. "For pain."

"It doesn't feel so bad."

"Oh, it won't. Not for a couple hours, anyway. Believe me, by tonight you'll be wanting a dozen. But no more than two at a time. Got it?"

"Got it."

The doctor continued, with further instructions regarding the medication, but Daniel only half heard, his mind wandering once more as the weariness returned.

Chapter Three:

"GOD. THIS PLACE SUCKS."

Rachel Keller took a drag from her cigarette, expelling a pale blue plume from between her brightly painted lips. The smoke hovered above her a few seconds, then slowly spread across the low ceiling of the room to mingle with the dim haze that was the accumulation of other people's exhalations. "Have we hit rock bottom or what?" Rachel continued.

"Oh, I don't think it's that bad," Jackie Somerset replied, ever optimistic. "If you weren't here you'd probably just be sitting at home, watching something stupid on TV."

"Right. Instead we get to watch somethin' stupid in the next room."

Jackie rotated her chair in a casual half-circle until she was facing the other direction. Through the door to the back room she could see the two men playing pool. The clunking of colliding ivory carried to the two young women, the sound occasionally accented with a cheer from one of the players.

Jackie took a swig from her Bud Lite. "I don't understand those boyfriends of ours'. What do they see in that game?"

"Well, you know guys and their balls...." Rachel left the statement incomplete as she reached for her drink. She tipped the bottle quicker than she had anticipated, resulting in a stream of beer that ran down her chin and dribbled onto the front of her sweater.

"Damn!" Rachel grabbed a napkin and began sopping up the excess, abandoning the attempt after several swipes. "What the hell. It needs to go in the wash anyway." She threw the napkin down and turned away from the bar. "I can't believe it's so dead in here."

"What do you expect for a Wednesday?"

"I don't know. Maybe another living person. God, I feel like I'm in a morgue or somethin'."

Jackie leaned back against the bar, her eyes surveying the room. It wasn't even that she was interested in what was going on around her, but, after all, you had to look at something. Most of the tables were empty. Two middle-aged men sat at the other end of the bar, one puffing on an oversized stogie that emitted thick puffs of black. It reminded Jackie of a steam locomotive, belching smoke as it hurtled down the track. Come to think of it, it sort of smelled like a locomotive as well.

A young couple had chosen a booth in the corner, removed from everybody else, where they could slump down in their seats and share their secret thoughts away from prying eyes. Jackie wondered for a moment if they were even old enough to be drinking, but the question quickly vanished from her mind. What business was it of hers, anyway?

The lack of activity in the place didn't really surprise her. Wednesday nights were generally dead at *Papa Joe's*. Saturdays were the big nights, when the weary many, standing with their drinks and nachos and whatever else they could hold onto, shot envious glances at the fortunate few, those who managed to find a seat at one of the tables. It almost got to be a competition. Just last week a fight had nearly broken out when one of the regulars, coming back from the rest room, found someone in his seat. The owner - his name really was Joe - had to threaten to throw them both out before he could get things settled down.

Jackie always felt sorry for Peggy and Linda on those nights, weaving their way as best they could through the tables as they took orders, dealing with the occasional rough comments from the inebriated, calculating tabs and organizing orders in an endless stream that never seemed to let up. She wondered if the tips really made up for the abuse they took.

Once, on a day much the same as this one, when things were so dead you almost felt like screaming, she had talked to Peggy about it. "I don't know if I could waitress in a place like this. Doesn't it bother you, the way these drunks come on to you?"

"Nah. They're harmless. Most a the time, they don't even know what they're sayin'. Besides, you get the best tips from the ones that are the most sloshed."

But Peggy was different than Jackie. So calm about things, and so certain of herself. Jackie knew she could never handle things the way Peggy did.

A middle-aged woman passed by on her way to the jukebox. She tended to flab, the excess baggage hanging from her bare arms and swaying back and forth as she swung her ponderous hips. Her eyes were small little specks buried beneath excess flesh. Her face portrayed neither joy nor sorrow, but rather a blandness, as though she had long lost any expectations of a better life. She forced her hand into the pocket of her too-tight jeans, fishing for coins.

As the woman stopped at the music machine Rachel laughed, lifting her voice to be certain it was heard from across the room. "What's it gonna be tonight, Marge?" Turning toward Jackie, she acquired a whisper. "As if we didn't know."

"If I have to listen to Billy Ray Cyrus one more time...."

The rest of Jackie's words were drowned out by a familiar guitar intro.

Rachel slammed her drink down on the bar. "Don't you ever get tired of that shit?"

Marge didn't even bother to turn around as she flashed her hand gesture. "Go to hell," she spouted. Within seconds she was lost in the music, oblivious to everything around her, her body making rhythmic movements approximating the tempo of the song as the swollen limbs shook grotesquely.

It wasn't a pretty sight, and Jackie turned away. "Leave her alone, Rachel."

"You said yourself you didn't like the song."

"I know. I just don't think it's worth raising a fuss about, that's all."

"Of course it's worth raisin' a fuss about. Hell, what fun would it be if we couldn't stir things up once in a while. Speakin' of which.... What are you and Brad doin' tonight?"

Jackie glanced again toward the back room, then returned to her drink. "From the looks of it, we're playing pool."

"That's a bitch, ain't it?" Rachel stubbed out her cigarette. "Why don't you say something to him?"

"I don't want to be a bother."

"A bother?"

"Hey, Brad works hard all day. He needs the time to unwind. I figure he'll get to me when he's ready."

"Honestly, Jackie, I don't see why you put up with him."

"I don't see Jeff out here."

"That's different. Jeff and me got an understanding. I give him time for the things he enjoys, but I get to do what I want, too."

"Maybe Brad and me got an understanding?"

"The only thing Brad understands is using people. How 'bout that Chevette he sold to Pete Winters?"

"That wasn't Brad's fault! How was he to know the transmission was gonna go?"

"Wake up and smell the shit, girl. Brad knew that car inside and out. Hell, he works all day in a body shop, don't he? And half the time when he's not at work he's out in the garage screwin' around with somebody's engine."

"So he's a hard worker. What's wrong with that?"

"He's a hard worker, all right. As long as there's somethin' in it for him."

"I don't want to talk about it."

"You never want to talk about it."

"This from the authority."

Jackie swiveled on her stool, turning her attention away from the conversation and back to her drink. Rachel had been her best friend for eight years now, ever since their senior year in high school, but sometimes she got this holier-than-thou attitude that really infuriated Jackie.

A silence fell between the two as Jackie considered her friend's words. She knew Brad wasn't perfect, but to listen to Rachel talk he was one step away from the dregs of the earth. Was she seeing something Jackie couldn't?

No. That wasn't it. Rachel just didn't know Brad good enough. There was another side to him, a side the two of them shared when no one else was around.

Jackie attempted another swig from her beer, realized it was empty, and set the bottle down.

"Want another?" Rachel asked.

"No. That's enough for tonight. I got to work tomorrow, you know."

The jukebox behind them quieted at last, the last notes of "Achy Breaky Heart" fading away. Moments later the machine blared back to life, as the song that had just played began to repeat itself.

"Not again." Rachel slid off her stool. "I think I've had 'bout enough of this place for one night. Let's see if we can't get them lowlifes in the back room movin'."

Chapter Four:

AS THE TWO WOMEN WALK IN THE ROOM Brad Wilkens leans over the pool table, concentrating on a difficult shot. With practiced ease he sends the cue ball sailing. It taps the seven, nudging it toward a side pocket, where it hesitates for a moment before disappearing down the hole.

"All right!" Brad shakes his fist in apparent ecstasy over the shot, then looks up at Jackie. "Did you see that shot, baby? That was one in a million."

She fails to comment on the observation. "When are we leaving, Brad?"

"I can't leave now. I'm on a roll." Brad bends down, eyeing the next shot.

Jackie stands in the doorway. Rachel floats away from her, to move over beside Jeff Black, who stands with one leg propped up on a chair as he chalks his pool stick. Rachel removes the cigarette from Jeff's mouth, takes a short drag, then replaces it. Jeff never bothers to look up.

Jackie swallows before speaking again. "I think we've been here long enough, Brad. Let's leave."

Brad turns toward Jeff, a smile on his lips. "What did I tell you? She just can't wait to get me alone. Sounds like she's hungry for somethin' tonight, and I ain't talking food."

The two men laugh at the comment, as though it's the funniest thing they've ever heard. Rachel, careful not to look at her friend standing in the doorway, laughs as well, but with less exuberance.

Jackie shifts her feet in obvious embarrassment. Without a word she turns to walk back to the bar.

Brad's voice carries clearly across the room. "Women. What you gonna do with 'em?"

His last words are cut off with a sharp crack from the pool balls as he takes his next shot.

Chapter Five:

AS SOON AS HE ENTERED THE WAITING room Daniel Jameson saw them, the two women sitting beside each other in the hard plastic chairs hospitals invariably provide for their visitors. Teri Stone was reading *Cosmopolitan*, the brunette on the cover of the magazine glaring from above her ample cleavage with a smug look of satisfaction.

Amy Blake - Michael's wife - sat beside Teri, alone in her suffering in a crowded room of fidgeting people. Her hands made slow circular motions in her lap, the fingers twisting and grinding against one another in random patterns. No doubt she was unaware of the movement.

Daniel stood for a moment, staring at Amy. They had met half-a-dozen times before, so there was a certain familiarity about her, yet he found himself examining her features more closely. Something seemed different than he remembered; some quality in the texture of her face, and a glow in her green eyes, surfacing even beyond the anguish, reminded him of something he had seen before.

It took Daniel a few moments to isolate the look.

When Becky had been expecting Lisa fourteen years ago, and again with the coming of Jeff three years later, she had complained with each pound she put on, bemoaning the new shape her body was thrusting upon her. But as the months progressed Daniel had noticed another change, something inward, that his wife wasn't aware of. She grew with a beauty that brought a radiance to her features, regardless of the physical alterations she was experiencing. In all their years of marriage he couldn't remember his wife looking any more beautiful than when she was with child.

Since that time, Daniel had noticed the same look, the same glow, in other women. Standing now in the waiting room, looking over at Amy Blake, he saw once again the inner beauty of approaching motherhood.

Now that he was aware of her condition, he became more discriminating in his perusal. He could detect the beginning of a bulge in her belly, and the swelling of the breasts, and a slight puffiness in her cheeks. All things he had missed at first glance.

But there was more to it than physical change. That she was distraught was obvious. Concern for her husband enveloped her. Yet through it all the radiance remained, the promise of the future heightened in her physique.

Daniel couldn't help wondering what that future would bring. He swallowed the lump in his throat and walked slowly into the room.

Teri noticed him first. She motioned to Amy Blake to remain where she was, then got up and intercepted Daniel as he approached. She kept her voice to a whisper, as though afraid to speak louder lest she upset some unspoken rule of the hospital. "How you doing?"

"All right, I guess."

"How's the arm?"

His good hand strayed to the damaged limb, the fingers playing over the wrapping. His skin beneath the cloth felt dry and rough; it was beginning to itch, like someone had shoved a piece of sandpaper beneath the bandage. But there was no pain. Only a strange numbness that extended down to the joints in his left hand.

"Doesn't feel too bad," he answered at last.

His reply failed to convince her. "Really?"

"Really. I guess they got me doped up or something, I don't know. Probably hurt like hell a little later, I suppose."

She reached out, as though to touch his arm, then withdrew the motion. "I tried calling your house, but I didn't get any answer."

"Becky's been out of town the past couple days. Some sort of seminar in Baltimore. Her plane's due in later this evening."

"And the kids?"

He was finding it hard to concentrate, the routine questions requiring more of his brainpower than they should have. There were just too many things going on; too much distracting activity around him. Either that, or the medicine he'd been given was more potent than he had realized.

"The kids." He considered a moment longer, forcing himself to think. "They're getting older now. Sometimes they'll stop at a friend's house, especially when they know Becky and I will be late getting home."

His hand gravitated to his pocket, but reaching in found nothing. "Damn it."

"What's wrong?" Teri asked.

"Must have left my cellphone at work," Daniel explained. "I usually put it in my desk so I don't lose it." He shrugged. "I'll have to call Becky later."

Teri snapped open her purse, rummaging through the contents. "You can use my phone."

He shrugged the gesture off. "Wouldn't do any good. I don't know her number."

"You don't know your wife's phone number?"

"I don't know *anyone's* number anymore. That's the trouble with technology. You rely on it too much. I'll fill her in later, I guess."

"You sure?"

"Yeah. Don't worry about it."

The words faded away, as he lost interest in what he was saying. His eyes remained locked on Amy Blake. She seemed to be fascinated with some spot on the floor at her feet, for during the entire conversation there had been no movement from her.

Instead she slumped forward in her chair, as though exhausted.

Daniel turned back toward Teri, lowering his voice. "How's she taking it?"

"Pretty good, really. God, if that was Joe in there I'd probably be a nervous wreck by now."

"Have you heard anything yet?"

"Not a word. Poor thing. You'd think they'd at least have the decency to let you know what's happening."

"Yeah."

For a long moment neither spoke. It was an awkward situation, standing together in the middle of the room. Uniformed workers hustled by from time to time, escorting injured people to the netherworlds of the examination rooms, while concerned family members paced or talked or - like Amy Blake - sat helplessly by and waited. Somewhere a phone buzzed, a shrill cacophony that somehow seemed out-of-place considering the surroundings.

From behind them, in one of the examination chambers, came a hoarse coughing, followed by a mother's soothing words. "It's all right, dear. Once the doctor sees you you'll feel a lot better."

"I hope so, Mom," a meek voice answered.

"I really should head back to the office," Teri said at last, jolting Daniel back to his present situation. "Do you need a lift?"

"I think I'll stick around for awhile. You know...." His eyes remained locked on Amy.

"Yeah. I'm just glad to see you're okay. I hope Mike...." The tears caught in her throat, and she spun away from him. She was more composed when she turned around. "I'm sure everything will be just fine. Don't you think?"

He failed to answer, though it was probable she didn't notice. She began again, her nervousness not allowing another pause in the conversation. "I imagine you'll want to take a couple days off?"

The suggestion took him by surprise. "You know, I hadn't really thought about it."

"Think about it. You earned it." She flashed a reassuring smile. "I'll clear things with Jack. Just take whatever time you need. And I'll see you back at the office."

"Right."

He watched her walk over to the waiting room chairs, and exchange a few quick words with Amy Blake, then she was gone.

He approached the row of seats, uncertain what to do next. As he drew closer Amy stood. "Hi, Dan."

"Hi, Amy." The words hurt coming from his throat, but not from any physical pain.

"How's the arm?"

"Don't worry 'bout it. A few stitches, that's all. I've had worse." Though he hadn't.

"I'm glad you're doing okay." She sat down, her motions slow and deliberate, as though not trusting her body to perform the movements properly. Her hands remained clasped to the metal arms of the chair even after she was seated. He waited, then sat down beside her. He could think of dozens of things to say, but none of them seemed like the right thing, so instead he sat there in silence, waiting for her.

"Teri says you're going to stay here at the hospital for a while," she finally commented.

"I thought I would."

"Thanks. I appreciate that." She managed a smile. "If you need a ride later...."

"I just might. I suppose my car's still back at the shop."

"Probably." She took a deep breath, no doubt to steel herself for the next words. "Teri told me what happened. About everything you did. I don't know how to thank you."

"You don't have to. Really."

"I just want you to know I appreciate it. We.... Mike and I...." Her gaze fell to her hands as she stumbled with the words. "I appreciate everything you did for Mike. I'm sure he'd tell you the same thing, if...." The words stopped abruptly. She looked up from her hands, which became motionless now that she no longer watched them.

For a moment she seemed fine, as she drew a deep breath. Then the tears came. "Oh, Dan...!"

She fell against him, burying her face in his chest as her anguish revealed itself. Daniel's good arm went around her - patting her shoulder, stroking her hair, hanging awkwardly against her - until she regained control and sat stiffly erect, sniffling back the last of the tears.

She attempted to compose herself. "I'm sorry."

"Why?"

"For behaving like such a baby. I don't know what came over me. I thought I got all this foolishness out of my system earlier."

He patted her hand in a reassuring way. "I'd say it's a pretty natural reaction, under the circumstances."

"Thanks." She rummaged through her purse and finally came up with a Kleenex, which she used to dab lightly at the corners of her eyes. "I couldn't believe it when they called me. I thought it was all some sort of horrible mistake. That this couldn't be happening to me.

"But here I am." She laughed, a shrill little sound that caught in her throat, but there was no trace of humor in the outburst. "I know I should be strong. For Mike's sake. But it's so hard."

"I'm sure everything will be fine." Though he couldn't help wondering if that would really be the case.

"I hope so. I just don't know what I'd do without him." Her voice faltered once again.

"So when's the baby due?" Daniel blurted out, hoping to keep Amy's mind off her more immediate problems.

A smile touched the corner of her mouth. Amy's hand strayed to her belly, stroking tenderly at her shirt. "Do I show that much already?"

"No. Of course not."

"You're a dear for saying so, anyway."

The smile deepened. "May 15th," she continued, warming

up to the topic. "It seems such a long time away, doesn't it? But there's so much to do. Mike's been fixing up the nursery already. We got the most adorable wallpaper, with pink giraffes and blue elephants. The crib's on order from Sears, with a matching changing table. I just can't believe all the things you need for one little baby."

"It gets worse, believe me. I swear, Becky did four loads of laundry a day when the kids were little. And half of that was diapers."

"No thanks. I think I'll stick with disposable, if you don't mind. I've got better things to do with my life than to live in the laundry room."

She laughed - a weak little laugh of release - and he tried to join in, but the time just wasn't right. The moment ended abruptly, as the waiting began anew.

Chapter Six:

THE LOW DRONE OF THE PLANE'S ENGINES insinuated itself into her head. For the last thirty minutes she had fought against it, trying to block it out, hoping to get at least a bit of sleep on the trip home, but at last she realized the futility of the idea and gave up altogether. The throbbing power of all that horsepower pushing them along was just too much of a sensation to ignore.

Her eyes sprang open. Carole Rosetti sat beside her, leaning against the window. The young woman's face, reflected in the glass, was aglow with excitement as she watched the ever-changing panorama beneath them. From time to time Carole placed her hand against the window, as though attempting to touch what was just outside the glass, forever out of reach. Carole made no attempt to disguise the fact that this was her first flight. Her enthusiasm concerning the novelty of the event was obvious to all.

Becky shifted in her seat, trying to find a more comfortable position, but the cramp conditions inherent in air travel didn't allow for much maneuvering. Relaxing was not even one of the considerations. It was more a question of finding the uncomfortable position that was least objectionable.

Carole turned her way. "You okay, Mrs. Jameson?"

"I'll be better when we touch ground. Who designs these things, anyway? Herve Villechaize?"

"Who?"

"You know. The little guy from *Fantasy Island*."

Carole said nothing, her blank expression indicating her lack of knowledge on the subject.

"*Fantasy Island*? With Ricardo Montalban?"

Still no sign of recognition.

"Forget it. It wasn't that funny, anyway."

Carole shrugged and faced the window once more, the matter forgotten, exuberance in her voice. "I think this is all so neat, watching the lights and things down there. Look! Doesn't that look like a river?"

Becky leaned closer. Night had settled, sealing the aircraft in a cocoon of black. Off in the distance ahead of them a glow could still be detected, blazing the upper atmosphere on the western horizon, but below she could see nothing, save an occasional scattering of lights indicating a city or, when the illumination was more sparse, a small town.

"All I see is dark," Becky answered at last.

Her lack of interest failed to disturb Carole, who returned to her observations, anxious not to miss a thing. "Oh, it's a river, all right. You can tell by the way the moonlight reflects off it." Her voice acquired a dreamy inflection. "Just think of all the people down there. All the life going on below us."

Becky Jameson closed her eyes once more, hoping for sleep but doubting it would come. Carole's enthusiasm astonished her. The young woman, a second-semester student at Monroe County Community College, had exhibited from their initial meeting a zest for learning and a desire to achieve. She was one of those model students that show up so seldom in an instructor's life, and Becky was glad to offer what guidance and encouragement she could.

The seminar they were returning from - a two-day conference in Baltimore - had featured noted authors and educators from around the country, extolling the latest open-classroom teaching techniques and strategies. Five instructors and three students had attended from The Community College. The others were scattered about the plane, each of them - except for Carole - exhibiting the fatigue of back-to-back all-day sessions.

In many ways, thinking of Carole reminded Becky of her own younger days. When she and Daniel had first gotten married life had seemed full of possibilities. They had grown together, supporting each other with each new struggle they faced. Those had been the best years of her life.

But somewhere along the way something had changed. The children were certainly part of it. Being mother and father left little time for being wife and husband. Daniel started spending more time at work. And Becky, returning to teaching once Jeff was in grade school, found the college occupying more and more of her life. The distance between her and Daniel was growing wider all the time. They were becoming strangers to one another, occupying the same house - the same bed - but sharing nothing else.

The most frightening aspect of the entire situation, the thing that worried Becky the most, was the fact that she found herself hardly caring anymore.

The flight seemed to last an eternity. It certainly took much longer than the trip to Baltimore had taken. At last an authoritative voice spoke to them over the loudspeaker.

"Your attention please, ladies and gentlemen. This is the captain speaking. We will be arriving in Toledo in approximately fifteen minutes. Please return all chairs to an upright position and fasten your seatbelts for the remainder of the flight. Once again, please refrain from using any cellphones or other electronic devices until after we reach the terminal. Thank you for flying with us, and we hope to see you all again soon."

Becky breathed a deep sigh of relief. Fifteen more minutes in the air, another twenty minutes or so to claim her baggage, and then the trip home. In a little over an hour she'd be back in her own house again. She could think of nothing better than to prop her feet up and delve into a good book. Some Steinbeck, maybe. She hadn't read *Of Mice And Men* in a while.

A few minutes later Becky detected the change in speed

and altitude preparatory to landing at Toledo Express Airport. It felt good to be back in familiar territory, even if it was only flying over it.

The plane unloaded without incident, and Becky and Carole collected their luggage. The student was still enthusiastic over the recent excursion, which was evident in her voice as they headed toward the exit. "I'm really glad I had the chance to go to the seminar. Those speakers were just awesome."

Becky smiled inwardly at the choice of words. Though Carole attempted to act mature, to fit in with the instructors, some of whom were twice her age and then some, occasionally she would slip-up, resorting to vocabulary from a younger generation. It made Becky feel suddenly old.

"They put on a good presentation," Becky agreed.

"And I want to thank you again, Mrs. Jameson, for giving me a ride home. I really appreciate it."

"My pleasure." Becky smiled at her companion.

A moment later the expression turned to a frown. Walking through the sliding glass doors that led outside, they were assaulted with a blast of frigid air. Becky hugged her coat tighter, accomplishing little as the shivering began. Instantly, she felt chilled to the bone. "I remember now why I hate winter."

"Not me." Carole took a deep breath. "I love the freshness of winter air. The way the cold takes your breath away when you step into it. It's so invigorating, don't you think?"

Becky refused to comment, trudging the slippery sidewalk that led to the long-term parking lot. It took ten minutes to scrape the ice that had accumulated on the windows the three days the car had sat out, and another five minutes of driving before the air blasting from the vents was approaching anything remotely warm by Becky's standards. Taking Airport Highway toward Toledo, they soon came to the 475 Interchange. Becky maneuvered into the right hand lane to merge with the haphazard line of cars heading north on the expressway.

Carole fell asleep somewhere between there and the Alexis Road exit, having apparently reached the limit of her seemingly endless energy. Becky liked Carole, and it was nice having someone along on the trip she felt comfortable with, but it was a pleasure to have a few minutes of silence. She almost switched on the radio, but decided even that distraction would be too much. Savor the moment, she told herself.

It didn't surprise Becky to see the house lit up like a Christmas tree. It wasn't just the outside lights, or the tree in the front window, the multi-colored lights twinkling irregularly. It seemed every light in the place was on. Which meant only one thing.

Lisa and Jeff were home.

What did come as a surprise was to see the empty garage. Daniel's car was nowhere to be seen. Becky glanced at the dashboard clock. 8:47. This was late, even by her husband's standards.

Jeff, still too young to hide his emotions, greeted her as she walked in the door, throwing his arms around her and offering up a substantial hug, which Becky was more than happy to accept. "I missed you, Mom!"

"I missed you, too, Dear." She planted a kiss on his forehead.

Lisa, having entered the reserved years of the teenager, sat at the kitchen table with a school book in front of her. Her voice betrayed no emotion, though she failed to keep the smile off her face. "How was your trip?"

"Just fine. How have things been here?"

"Same as usual," Lisa admitted. "You know nothing ever happens in this place."

"Where's your father?"

"I don't know." The teenager set her pencil down, devoting full attention to her mother. "He called a while ago, to say he'd be late."

"Did he say how late?"

"Nope."

"Did he say where he was?"

"Nope."

"Well, what *did* he say?"

"Just that he'd be late, and not to wait up for him." Lisa hesitated a moment, considering. "He sounded a little strange, though."

"Strange?"

"Yeah. I sort of got the idea something was wrong, but he didn't say what it was."

"Mom?" Jeff, tugging on Becky's arm, pulled her attention away from the conversation.

"What is it, Jeff?"

"I'm hungry. Can we have supper?"

"You mean you two haven't had anything to eat yet?"

"Just a snack after school."

"I offered to make him something," Lisa jumped in, "but he refused it."

"Why would I want to eat *your* cooking?"

"Why would I *want* you to?"

Becky wondered if this exchange was an indication of how the evening had gone with the two of them. Hoping to forestall any future arguments, she stepped in before things could escalate further. "Come on. I'll make you something."

She approached the kitchen cupboard. As she looked over the shelves, searching for something quick and easy to make, one notion dominated Becky's thinking. Daniel better have a damn good reason for being so late tonight.

Chapter Seven:

THEY SIT ACROSS FROM ONE ANOTHER, Brad Wilkens nursing his beer while Jackie Somerset munches on a ham and cheese sandwich. They haven't spoken much since leaving *Papa Joe's*, and they eat now in silence. Jackie appears withdrawn, locked in her own thoughts.

Brad pulls a pack of Marlboro's from his coat pocket, taps it twice on the edge of the table, and thirty seconds later is leaning back in his chair, smoke curling from the tip of the cigarette in his mouth. He looks around, apparently bored.

It's late, and the restaurant is nearly empty. The few customers in attendance represent the late-night crowd that shows up after everything else has closed down, talking in low voices as they await with trepidation the ending of this day and the start of the next.

A pimply-faced man of about twenty works at a salad bar in the center of the main room, washing down the counter then running the soiled dishrag over the protective glass shield. He hums quietly along with the muzak drifting through the establishment, oblivious to the occasional jeer cast in his direction.

A waitress, a young blonde with a weary expression enveloping her features, approaches the table where Brad and Jackie sit. "Would you like another?" she asks, fatigue in her voice.

Jackie looks up, a confused expression on her face. "What's that?"

Brad stares across the table at her, finishing his beer in a single gulp. "It's a simple question, Jackie. You want another drink or don't you?"

"Yeah. Sure. Another Coke would be fine."

"And bring me another Bud," Brad adds.

The waitress flashes a tired smile. "I'll be right back with those."

She turns and walks away, her feet barely managing to lift off the floor. The day's strain is evident in her every move. Brad makes no attempt at discretion as he watches her crossing the room, his attention focused on the worn creases in her pants.

Jackie leans across the table. "Brad?"

"What?" His eyes never waver until the server passes out of sight, and even then he continues to look in the general direction of her departure.

"You're staring."

"So what?"

"Stop it."

He turns to face her. His smile evaporates, pale gray eyes exhibiting a scathing coldness. "What did you say?"

"Do you have to be so obvious?"

"What's wrong with checking-out a nice piece of ass? It's still a free world, ain't it?"

Jackie turns away, not bothering with a reply. Brad laughs and shakes his head in apparent bewilderment. The coldness leaves him, replaced with a smug self-assuredness. "So now you're mad at me."

"No. I'm not mad. I just don't think you need to be so blunt about things, that's all."

"Hey, baby. That's my style."

Again she makes no reply, returning her attention to the half-finished sandwich on her plate.

Brad waits perhaps fifteen seconds before continuing. "You know, Jeff and some of the guys were talking 'bout going skiing this weekend."

Jackie, about to take a bite, pauses with the sandwich

several inches from her mouth. Brad has ceased talking, awaiting her reaction. The trace of a smile flirts across his face.

She takes her time, pondering her words, setting the food on the table and dabbing lightly at her mouth with a paper napkin. She barely manages an answer, the single word coming as a whisper. "And...?"

"And what? I told him I was going."

"This weekend?"

"Yeah. We're gonna leave Friday, right after Jeff gets out of work. We want to make sure we can get a room, so we'll be ready to start first thing Saturday morning."

The napkin on the table draws her attention, as though it's the single most important item in the room. Her finger rests on a corner of the paper and begins a series of lazy circles across the tabletop, her eyes riveted to the action. "When will you be back?"

"I don't know. Sometime Sunday."

"Do you think that's a good idea? With the weather and all?"

"What about the weather?"

Jackie looks up, the anguish in her eyes unnoticed by Brad. "You know I worry whenever you're on the road. Like that trip you took to South Bend the other day. I still don't understand why you had to stay overnight."

Brad shakes his head in exasperation. "You know, Jackie, sometimes you're just so fucking-stupid I can't believe it."

She looks around in embarrassment. "Please, Brad...."

"I explained all this the other day," he continues. "When you're dealing with customized cars, it's not like you can just walk into K-Mart and pick up a part. There's not many people that do that type of work. That joker in South Bend may be a pain-in-the-ass, but he knows his stuff. That's why we go out of our way to deal with him. Hell, it's for sure he's not coming here to Toledo."

"The shop could have at least lent you a car."

"No way. I drive my Camaro, or I don't go at all."

"Besides, I thought we were going to the movies this weekend?"

"Hell, we can go to the movies anytime. Right?"

Jackie pauses. It is obvious she's uncertain how to react next.

Obvious to everyone except Brad, who gets up from his chair before anything further can be said. "I'm glad that's settled," he remarks, effectively putting an end to the conversation. "I'll be right back. Got to take a piss."

She leans back in her chair, watching him as he swaggers to the restroom at the back of the restaurant. Her breath escapes in a slow sigh. She reaches for her Coke, to take a quick swallow, then realizes the glass is empty.

"Damn."

Jackie wipes the corner of her eye with the back of her hand.

Chapter Eight:

THE TRAUMA ROOM AT RIVERSIDE Hospital bustled with activity. Such had been the case since 4:35 in the afternoon, when Michael Blake was wheeled in on the gurney with a pair of paramedics in attendance. A team of doctors and anesthetists and nurses had attacked him the moment he arrived, prepping him for the ordeal to come.

The first priority was to stabilize his condition. He had lost a substantial amount of blood from the gash in his leg and was still in shock. His skin had blistered and burnt over a great portion of his body, the majority of the damage localized in his legs, which still contained telltale traces of metal that had fused to the flesh. The acrid smoke of the foundry had invaded his lungs. Even after hours at the hospital his breathing was still labored.

Blake's skin was bathed in a cold sweat, his body's defense mechanism working to maintain blood to the vital organs - the brain, the heart, the lungs - at the expense of the less crucial components.

Considering the severity of his condition, many of those present doubted he would make it through the night.

Daniel Jameson looked once more at the clock. It was nearly midnight. He had spent over seven hours at Riverside, the last four and-a-half at Amy Blake's side. She was sleeping now, leaning against the hard plastic of her chair, her position looking to be anything but comfortable. He could hear her breathing, a troubled sound that betrayed her inner worries. He was exhausted, and could think of nothing better than to be home in bed, sleeping the whole thing off, but the pain from his by-now throbbing arm was sufficient to keep him from nodding off. He couldn't help wondering what it would be like if they hadn't given him the pain medication.

The sound of footsteps caught Daniel's attention, and he turned to face the approaching figure. Amy, through some inner sixth-sense, chose the moment to awaken, her eyes snapping open.

Dr. Lois Tyrone stopped before the two of them. Dr. Tyrone had been on duty when the ambulance first arrived with Michael Blake, and even though her shift had ended hours earlier she had remained at the hospital. She had talked to them several times during the evening, with words of encouragement and support, but had as yet offered nothing substantial to reassure them.

Everything about the woman spelled fatigue. Her eyes appeared dull. Her face was etched with lines of weariness, the wrinkles eroding her features. Her clothes looked like they'd been slept in. Her stethoscope hung limp against her, swaying lazily with each step she took.

She pushed back an errant strand of hair as she began. "Mrs. Blake?"

"Yes?" Amy was wide awake now, all senses on the alert.

The doctor stumbled for words. "Do you mind if I sit down?" she finally managed. "It might make this easier."

"Please...." Amy made a barely perceptible motion of her hand toward the chair across from her. "How is my husband?" she continued, before the doctor was even seated. "When can I see him?"

"I'm afraid you'll have to wait a little while longer. He's stabilized, at least for now, but there's no telling how long that will last. We'll be moving him to IC after he comes out of surgery."

"IC...?"

"Intensive Care. We need to monitor him carefully for a while. You must understand, he's gone through a lot. On top of the loss of bodily fluid and the shock to his system, his upper legs have extensive third-degree burns. What this means, Mrs. Blake, is that the skin is damaged down to the subcutaneous tissue below the epidermis and dermis. He'll be requiring multiple skin-grafts, most likely over an extended length of time."

Daniel leaned forward, touching Dr. Tyrone lightly on the sleeve to draw her attention. "You said upper legs...?"

The physician nodded slowly and turned back toward Amy. A disturbed expression crossed her face. "This has to be the hardest part of my job. There's just no easy way to say it." She took a deep breath, as Amy and Daniel hung on her every word. "The damage to your husband's lower limbs was too extensive to be repaired. We had to amputate both legs just above the knees. I'm sorry."

"Oh God, no!" Amy started to rise, then grabbed her stomach and fell back into the chair. As she bent forward a gagging came from her throat.

Dr. Tyrone stood and moved to her side. "Are you all right, Mrs. Blake? There's a bathroom right around the corner...."

"No. No." She waved the suggestion off. "Just leave me alone. Leave me alone."

Amy's face remained buried in her hands as convulsive sobs shook her body. It was a helpless moment for all of them, the three participants locked in a struggle that offered no easy solution.

The doctor motioned to Daniel as she backed away, and he followed her to the nurse's station. He waited for her to begin, a task she obviously found difficult.

"It's been a long day," she said at last. "For all of us. I think it would be best if you both just went home. There's nothing more that can be done now, anyway."

"I'm sure she'd like to at least see her husband."

Dr. Tyrone shook her head. "I don't think that would be a

good idea. It might be too much for her."

"So you're going to leave her like this?" Daniel felt anger rising within, a frustration both at the injustice of the entire incident and his own helplessness in dealing with things. "Can you imagine what she's going through right now? The thoughts floating through her head? She needs reassurance. If she could just see her husband...."

"It wouldn't do either of them any good, Mr. Jameson. Michael Blake is in no position to receive visitors. And, no matter what she is imagining, I doubt it would prepare her for the reality of the situation." A harshness entered her eyes. "I can't ever recall seeing someone in his condition before. The abuse his body has taken. Believe me, it's not a pleasant sight."

Daniel felt the weight of failure upon his shoulders. "Then everything I did was a waste. It was all for nothing."

"I'd hardly agree with that. A man lives and breathes, at this very moment, because of your actions. I hardly feel that qualifies as a waste. Do you?"

Daniel found no reply he could offer.

The doctor reached out, touched him lightly on the arm. "See that she gets home. You both need the rest. I'll let her know as soon as she can get in to see her husband. That's the best I can do."

She turned to leave, took a quick step away, then faced him once more. "I'm sorry. Believe me. There was nothing else we could do."

Chapter Nine:
Thursday, December 10, 2015

BECKY JAMESON LAY IN BED, FLOATING through the vague time between sleep and consciousness. The plane trip had worn her out more than she realized. She had expected to drift off the moment she hit the pillow, snuggled beneath her quilt in the familiar comfort of her own bed, but that hadn't been the case.

She stayed up later than she should have, though if pressed for an answer, she would have had a difficult time remembering the title of the book that had occupied her. While she usually enjoyed reading, she had found it a particularly trying task this evening. Concentration eluded her. Her mind wandered.

She felt on edge, as though there were things left unattended to. Part of it was no doubt a consequence of all the activity the last few days - the discussion groups and lectures and late-night sessions with the other faculty members. Becky had always had a zeal for learning, and it was a pleasure to spend time with others who shared a similar interest.

Her mind toyed with ideas that had been tossed about in Baltimore, contemplating how best to implement them when the new semester began after the Christmas Break. She had always been a vocal proponent of open classroom techniques. Much of what she had witnessed the last few days justified her convictions. It made her consider once more what had attracted her to teaching in the first place. So many fresh minds, with so many energetic ideas, just waiting to be cultivated, nurtured by an instructor caring enough to take an interest in them. It felt good to be needed.

It was a feeling she hadn't experienced enough of lately with regards to her family.

She realized her time at home was important. Her family meant everything to her. But she couldn't deny the inescapable fact that the children were growing older. They were more involved with friends and school activities now, pursuing their own interests. It seemed they did less as a family every day, each member content to go their own way.

Then there was the problem of Daniel. Ordinarily he was the most considerate husband a woman could ever ask for, a hard worker who had sacrificed much over the years for his family. He always thought of them first. He made certain the children got anything they needed, to the point of nearly spoiling them at times. Becky, as well, had never wanted, except during the lean years of their early marriage. And even then, Daniel had provided what he could.

Maybe that's why it seemed all the more strange when something unusual came up.

Like tonight.

Where was he, anyway? To be out this late, and not even offer an explanation, just didn't make any sense. And as bad as it was for him not to think of her feelings, he could have at least considered Lisa and Jeff. They had a right to know where their parents were.

Explanations were due, and she would not be put off.

With these thoughts uppermost in her mind Becky drifted finally into an uneasy slumber.

She wasn't aware of waking up, but there was no denying the fact that she had been disturbed. A sound had intruded, alerting her senses to something out of the ordinary.

Becky opened her eyes, staring in darkness at nothing. A

dim light filtered in through the window, reflected off the whiteness blanketing the yard outside, allowing her to make out vague shapes around her - the outline of her dresser, the night stand at her side, the patch of darkness that signified the doorway leading to the hall. She always left the door open at night, a habit she had developed when the children were young, and tonight had been no exception.

Turning, she spotted the digital read-out of the alarm clock on her dresser. 1:37.

Her senses concentrated. Voices reached her, from somewhere outside the house. Becky leaned toward the window, surreptitiously drawing the curtain aside for a peek into the night. The back end of a car could be seen, parked in the driveway, but she failed to recognize the vehicle. Or, for that matter, its occupants.

Someone spoke again. She recognized the man's voice then.

Daniel's words carried clearly in the crisp December air. "I appreciate the ride home, Amy."

The next speaker was unfamiliar, though definitely female. "It's the least I could do. I don't know how I would have managed through tonight without you."

Becky squirmed for a better view. Damn! Who was she?

The woman’s voice continued. "So what are you going to do about your car?"

"I don’t know. Guess I’ll have to get a ride into the shop later to pick it up. It wouldn’t have done any good getting it tonight, anyway. The way I feel right now, I’ll be lucky to make it across the driveway."

They both laughed, though in a manner that seemed to Becky somehow artificial, and Daniel continued. "Just let me know how everything turns out. Okay?"

"I'll do that. Are you sure you won't have a problem getting in?"

"I have a key to the front door." A pause. What were they up to? "Becky should be home by now, and I wouldn't want to wake her."

"Thanks again, Dan."

"Take care, Amy. Call if you need anything."

"I'll do that."

The car pulled out of the driveway, the tell-tale sound of crushing snow beneath the tires advertising the direction as it drove away. Somewhere a dog barked, a lonely wail in the dark, as though lamenting the vehicle's passing. Becky could hear the front door open and then close, and moments later Daniel's footsteps sounded as he made his way through the hallway and to the bathroom. The door closed behind him, the sound of water running in the sink reaching in to her.

Becky rolled over to stare at the ceiling. Her chest expanded in heavy breaths. She considered doing nothing, feigning sleep at his arrival, but as quickly as the notion arose she dismissed it.

What was he trying to pull, anyway?

Stepping out of bed, she padded across the hallway and toward the bathroom. She wasn't about to give him a chance to duck out of *this* one. Her questions started even before she shoved the door open. "Do you have any idea what time it is? What kind of stunt do you think you're pulling?"

She stopped abruptly at sight of her husband. The anger evaporated with the next words. "What happened to you?"

Daniel looked worn and haggard, his skin pale. His shirt was off, and he struggled with a scissors to remove a bloody white cloth wound around his left arm. He didn't bother to look her way as he answered. "This damn thing itches like hell. I thought taking it off might help some."

Becky hesitated for exactly three seconds before entering the room, closing the door softly behind her so as not to disturb the children. She grabbed the scissors, forcing his attention toward her. "What happened?"

"There was an accident this afternoon. In the foundry."

"Good Lord! Was anyone hurt?"

He flashed an incredulous expression, and she began

anew, her voice flustered. "What am I saying? Of course somebody was hurt. Just look at you! Are you okay? What happened?"

"I'm all right. Just got my arm scraped up, that's all." He paused. "I was the lucky one."

The import of his words struck Becky immediately. She walked to him, planting a kiss on his forehead. His skin felt warm, as though he might have a fever. His chest was damp with sweat.

She maneuvered him gently around, a light touch forcing him to lean against the edge of the vanity. "First things first," she said. "Let me help you with this. Then you can tell me all about it."

Chapter Ten:
Saturday, December 12, 2015

"HEY, RJ? WHAT DO YOU MAKE OF THIS?"

Rick Jameson swiveled in his chair, turning away from the computer terminal. John Zuchoruv stood at his side, lost in concentration as he studied the blueprint in his hand.

Rick struggled to keep the frustration from his voice as he answered. "What is it?"

"I just can't make sense of this sectional view. What do you think?"

By shoving his mouse pad aside, Rick was able to clear enough space for John to set the drawing down on the computer desk. Rick spent less than thirty seconds looking things over before arriving at the conclusion there was nothing difficult about the detail in question.

The revelation failed to surprise him.

He had come to expect the frequent interruptions in his work routine as an everyday occurrence. If two hours went by without such a disturbance, Rick found himself wondering if something had happened to John.

John seemed like an intelligent enough person, a recent graduate of the local technical school. His grades had been excellent, placing him near the top of his class. And he had come highly recommended by the Mechanical Drawing instructor at the school.

But something seemed to have happened after he entered

the real world. Maybe he wasn't used to having any responsibility, or it could have been that he just lacked confidence in himself. Whatever the reason, he hesitated over the simplest details, pondering techniques that, even for a beginner, should have been second nature. He was drawn to Rick whenever he had any questions.

ADVANCED ENGINEERING was a small design shop, employing less than a dozen people, and though Rick was only twenty-six, he had a grasp of machining practices and 3-D techniques that went far beyond his years. It just came easily to him, with each new software program the company purchased rapidly mastered. He often felt all the challenge had gone out of his life. Things just came *too* easy.

"So what do you think, RJ?"

John's question dragged Rick from his reverie. "Listen, it's simple, really," Rick told him, his attention immediately returned to the problem at hand. "Let me show you."

Rick re-positioned his chair to align himself with the monitor of his computer. His fingers became a blur of motion, his right hand manipulating the mouse while his left struck a multitude of keys that sent the screen through a changing series of commands and configurations. In seconds, an isometric view was revealed, detailing a portion of a part very similar to the one on the drawing.

Using the cursor on the screen, Rick selected certain areas. "What you're seeing there isn't a true section," Rick explained. "They just highlighted this portion to detail the notch on the inboard surface, which normally wouldn't be visible in a sectional view. Make sense now?"

"Yeah. I suppose so." The words came slowly, John obviously not convinced.

Rick manipulated the mouse further. On the screen, the wire frame image of the picture changed, a textured shading replacing the stark outline of a few seconds earlier. As the mouse slowly rotated, guided by a light touch from Rick, the video rendering also moved, revealing a nearly picture-perfect image of the part in question. Details stood out with the stark realism prevalent in computer imaging.

"Does that make any more sense?"

John rubbed his neck. His head moved back and forth as he looked first at the video image, then at the view on the blueprint, and again at the picture on the monitor. "I think I'm beginning to see it."

Rick glanced at the clock above his desk. It was nearly 11:30. "Listen, I'm meeting my brother this afternoon. If you really don't get it, I'll try to help you some more on Monday. But I need to get going. All right?"

"Sure. That would be fine."

John left the room, still shaking his head in wonder, and Rick exited the program and shut down the system, taking care to save the files he was working on before closing down. Grabbing his coat from the closet on the way out, he punched the clock and made for his car.

He considered taking Central Avenue out to the Expressway, avoiding the worst of the Toledo traffic, then decided against it. It just seemed too far out of the way. Besides, how bad could things be on a Saturday afternoon?

Sitting in his Bronco, watching the traffic light at Monroe and Secor change to red for the third time, Rick found himself thinking about his brother. Twelve years separated them in age, but sometimes it seemed like a generation or two. Everything about Daniel was old-fashioned. Conservative in his tastes, he chose to go with the flow, content with the *status quo*. New ideas scared him. Rick had to badger his older brother for a year and-a-half before Daniel finally gave in and purchased a computer for his home. No doubt Daniel never even used it himself, but Rick was certain Becky and the kids did. He was also convinced the only way his brother would ever enter the modern world would be by being dragged into it, fighting the change tooth and nail.

Even Daniel's job seemed like an anachronism. It was

hard to believe places like CONSOLIDATED CASTINGS could still stay in business. With new techniques in manufacturing and design appearing on the market on a nearly daily basis, it was only a matter of time before those ancient foundry techniques became completely obsolete. And where would Daniel be then?

The accident three days earlier was just another case in point. What kind of outdated safety features did the shop have, anyway, that would permit such a tragedy? Rick hadn't spoken with his brother since it happened, but Becky had told him all about it.

It had been Becky's idea for the two of them to get together today. With his car finally in motion once more, the line of cars crawling steadily northward toward the state line, Rick's mind flashed back on the telephone conversation the night before.

Concern was obvious in his sister-in-law's tone. "I tell you, RJ, this thing has really spooked your brother."

"Why do you say that?"

"You should see him. He just seems so quiet. So withdrawn."

"How can you tell?"

She failed to join in with his laughter. "I'm serious here."

"I know. I'm sorry, Beck."

"He's talking like he's never going back to work. Like he never wants to see the place again. Do you think he means it?"

"I wouldn't worry about it. You know how Dan gets sometimes. He always was one to blow things all out of proportion."

"I know you're right. And yet...."

A silence lingered on the line. Rick felt she had more to say. It seemed like the best thing to do was to wait her out, give her the opportunity to clear things in her head.

"I just don't know what to do, RJ. Do you think you could talk to him?"

"What good will that do? Let's face it. Since when has he ever listened to his kid brother?"

"But this is different. He needs to talk to someone."

"What's wrong with his wife?"

"I don't know. It's almost like I'm talking to a stranger anymore." Her voice was beginning to change, ever so slightly. Was that the beginning of tears?

Rick felt suddenly uncomfortable. He cut her off before things could get any worse. "Listen, Beck. I have to work tomorrow."

"On Saturday?"

"You know how it goes."

He stopped, feeling he'd said enough to effectively avoid the issue. When she made no reply, however, he realized she was still expecting something from him.

"Look," he began anew, "I can probably get out by noon or so. How about if I stop over then?"

"That would be great. Maybe the two of you could go out to lunch together? To get his mind off things."

"Yeah. I guess we could."

"I'm sure it will do Dan some good."

"I'll see you then."

"All right. And RJ.... Thanks. I owe you one."

Bedford, just north of Toledo and across the Ohio line into Michigan, had grown by leaps and bounds in the last few years. When Daniel and Becky moved to the suburbs thirteen years earlier, right after Lisa was born, their house had been one of only a few in a secluded section between Jackman Road and Lewis Avenue. Now, with the recent spurt of new homes in the vicinity, the neighborhood seemed almost as crowded as the places down in Toledo. From the looks of things, the building boom showed no signs of collapsing in the near future.

Rick slowed down through the sub-division, keeping a sharp lookout for the occasional youngster braving the cold to build a snowman or haul a sled along the edge of the road. It was rare to have this much snow so early in the year, and the neighborhood children seemed determined not to miss it.

At last he came to Daniel's place.

The sidewalk needed shoveling. Rick noticed that right off the bat and felt immediate concern. Daniel was one of those strange birds that was out there if it even looked like it was going to snow. Personally, Rick couldn't understand that type of thing. His philosophy was, if you wait long enough the stuff's going to melt, anyway. So why bother? But the fact that his brother had yet to do anything with the snow was significant. It just wasn't in Daniel's nature to let such a task go undone.

Rick plodded to the front door, where Becky greeted him. Stepping inside, he slipped off his boots while she helped to peel the winter coat off him.

"How's he doing?"

Concern etched her face. "About the same. All he does is sit in the family room and stare at the TV. Most times, he doesn't even bother turning it on."

"Where are the kids?"

"Visiting with friends."

"I thought it seemed awful quiet in here."

"I'm just so worried...."

"Maybe you're over-reacting," Rick interrupted, hoping to head-off an approaching incident. "It's only been a couple days. He probably just needs some time to sort things out in his head."

"I don't know. It's like he doesn't seem to care anymore. It was all I could do to get him to shave and put on clean clothes today."

Rick, still standing in the front doorway, hesitated. His brother had always intimidated him to some degree. Rick was only nine when Daniel moved out of the house. They had been almost strangers then, the difference in age precluding them from having much in common. By the time Rick had graduated and entered the work force, Daniel had a wife, two kids, and a house in the suburbs. A world of difference *still* separated them. Now that they were both working adults things were a bit easier, but it was hard to erase a lifetime of conditioning.

Rick followed Becky into the family room. Daniel sat

slouched in the recliner, staring into space.

"Your brother's here," Becky began.

Daniel grunted something in reply.

Before Becky could say more Rick cut her off. "So, Dan. Anything new or exciting?"

Daniel faced him, a numb expression on his face, but said nothing.

Rick could feel the tension in the room, a palpable aura that stood between Daniel and Becky. Though he had no idea how to handle the matter, he figured the best way to start was by getting his brother someplace where he couldn't just sit and mope.

"Listen, why don't we get out of here for a while? Grab a bite to eat, just you and me. What do you say?"

For a long thirty seconds no one said a word. Finally Daniel pushed himself to a standing position. "I suppose I may as well. Not much sense sitting around here, is there?"

Becky accompanied them as they headed to the front hallway. Without a word Daniel donned coat and boots. He made no attempt to bid his wife goodbye. She started to reach for him as he passed through the doorway, but Rick stopped the motion with a hand on her shoulder.

"Don't torture yourself, Beck. He's just in one of his moods. Don't worry."

He flashed a smile, which she attempted to return, and then they were gone.

Chapter Eleven:

"SO WHAT DO YOU THINK OF THOSE lowlife boyfriends of ours', takin' off to go skiing and leavin' us to fend for ourselves this weekend? Is that a bitch, or what?"

Though Jackie Somerset wouldn't have used those exact words to describe how she felt, there was no denying Rachel Keller's meaning. Jackie considered the point as the two women walked through the near-empty corridors of Devon Mall.

The matter had dominated her thinking since Brad brought it up on Wednesday. At first she had been upset with his decision to take off without her. It showed how used to getting his own way he was, and how easy it was for him to take her for granted. He hadn't even stopped to think what the decision would mean to her.

She just wished Brad would consider her feelings, at least once in a while. Wasn't that what a relationship was all about?

On the other hand, she wasn't much of a skier, and even if he had invited her along she probably would have declined. Was it fair, then, to deny him something he wanted to do? Maybe she was just being selfish, after all.

Besides, the day hadn't been too bad so far. Rachel had picked her up about ten, and they had spent most of the morning shopping. Or, more correctly, looking, for neither of them had purchased anything.

Rachel continued. "Serve them right if we just find ourselves a couple of young studs for the evening."

Feeling the statement didn't justify a response, Jackie said nothing.

Rachel came to a stop beside her. "You're awful quiet today, Jackie. What gives?"

"Oh, I don't know. Just thinking."

"'Bout what?"

"Nothing in particular, really. Just that lately, I guess I've been sort of...." Jackie searched her mind for the appropriate word. "Bored, I guess."

"Yeah. I know what you mean." By this time they had reached an empty bench, and both women sat down. Rachel crossed her legs, working the Bass sandal from her right foot and letting it dangle off her toes as she rocked back and forth. The maneuver seemed to relax her.

Jackie shook her head at sight of Rachel's footwear. "I don't know how you do it."

"Do what?"

"Wear sandals this time of year. Don't your feet freeze?"

Rachel shrugged. "You get used to it."

"Not me. I've got two pair of socks on, and my toes are *still* cold."

"That's the difference between you and me. You're too tense all the time. You need to lighten up. Go with the flow. You can't let the weather get you down. You got to do somethin' to show your defiance, otherwise you get like.... Well, like *you*. Bored."

"What's the weather got to do with it?"

"Everything. I mean, let's face it, Jackie. What the hell can you do in this type of weather, anyway? Neither one of us skis. We don't know no one who's got a snowmobile. 'Bout all we can do is shop, and even that gets to be a drag after a while. And if that don't convince you, take a look at how deserted this place is. People don't even like to leave the house in this type of weather. They stay home and watch TV or who knows what. No wonder you're bored, Jackie. Hell, everyone's bored."

Then, as an afterthought, Rachel added: "Everyone but Jeff and Brad, anyway."

Jackie considered Rachel's observations for a few moments, choosing finally to reject the logic behind them. "No. This isn't just a case of cabin fever. I think there's more to it than that. You ever think about your future?"

"Ew!" Rachel wrinkled her nose in disgust. "You mean dyin' and all?"

"Don't be morbid. I'm not talking about anything as disgusting as that. I mean your future with Jeff."

"Oh." Rachel hesitated. "I guess I think about it. I don't know. What difference does it make?"

"I wonder about me and Brad sometimes. Where's it all going? Somehow, I just can't see him settling down. With a family and all."

"Is that what you want?"

"Someday. Not right away. But someday. How about you?"

"I don't know. Guess I never gave it much thought. Tell you what I could use, though."

"What's that?"

"A cigarette. Think I'll light one up."

"Not here, you won't." Jackie pointed to the NO SMOKING sign fastened to a nearby garbage can.

"Shit." Rachel sprang to her feet. "Guess that means it's time to get movin'. You hungry?"

"Getting there," Jackie admitted. "What do you have in mind?"

"Applebee's is right across the street. Want to try it?"

"Might as well. We've pretty much exhausted everything there is to see at the mall, anyway."

Though Jackie had rejected most of Rachel's theory, she did agree with her friend on one point, attributing the scant crowds at the shopping center to the lousy weather. The snow was keeping everyone at home. Obviously, no one wanted to go anywhere on such a cold day.

The restaurant across the street disproved the theory. The

place was packed.

"Where'd everybody come from?" she asked, as they stepped through the double doors and into the foyer.

They were greeted by a young woman with a quick smile. "Table for two?"

"That's right."

The hostess glanced at a chart beside her, then did a hasty survey of the crowded establishment. "I'm guessing about a twenty minute wait. Is that okay?"

Jackie answered for them. "Yeah. I guess so."

The two women backed away, taking up a position at the side of the doorway.

"Is it worth waiting for?" Rachel asked.

Jackie shrugged. "By the time we drive somewhere else, and wait for a table *there*, it will probably take us even longer. Might as well hang in here."

As it was, they had less of a wait than they anticipated. Within three minutes of their arrival they were approached by a man in his mid-twenties. He dressed casual, and walked with an air of self-assurance.

"I couldn't help noticing that you two were waiting for a table. My brother and I just sat down. Haven't even ordered yet. There's room if you'd care to join us."

"Thanks, but I don't think...."

Jackie got no further before receiving a gentle jab in the side from her companion. Rachel flashed a "hush-up" look and took over. "Yeah. That would be super."

"Great. I'll let the hostess know there'll be two joining us."

Jackie waited until he was out of earshot to accost her friend. "You can't be serious?"

"Why not? The boys are out of town. No sense us being alone, now is there? Besides...." Rachel leaned closer and winked. "What did I tell you? Two young studs."

There was a smile on her face as she walked away. Jackie sighed and followed her to the table.

*****

"I'm Rick," he began, once they were all seated. "But call me RJ. All my friends do. This here's my brother Dan."

His brother was obviously the older of the two. His hair sported a touch of gray. No more than a hint, really. Jackie suspected it was premature. It gave him a distinguished, almost thoughtful, look, lending dignity to his appearance.

Or maybe it wasn't the hair. It might have been something else. Like his attitude. As the conversation progressed he remained silent, content to let the others do the talking. RJ dominated their end of the dialogue, speaking for both of them.

Though, to be honest, Rachel did most of Jackie's talking, as well. Rachel had always been the confident one of the pair, the one that got them into places.

Like their present circumstance.

Jackie always felt uncomfortable around strangers. It took her a long time to warm up to people. Not so with Rachel. You could plop her down in the middle of a crowded room and she'd feel at ease. It was one of the things Jackie envied about her friend.

Content to sit and watch the others, Jackie took time to consider their new companions. Rick was handsome enough, in a rugged sort of way, and he carried himself with an air of self-confidence. It was obvious Rachel was attracted to him. She hadn't taken her eyes off him since they sat down, and he seemed equally interested in her.

Something about his brother, though, fascinated Jackie. There seemed a deep integrity behind Daniel's eyes. It was the type of face you trusted on the instant, though she couldn't say why.

Further observation revealed something else. An intense pain - a hidden sorrow - seemed to lurk beneath the surface. Once, during an inadvertent moment of eye contact, a peculiar sensation came over her. It was like he was pleading with her, begging for help, yet at the same time remaining unaware of his own need.

A chill passed over her, wondering what could bring such a sensation into a person's life.

At last, during a gap in the talk, Jackie spoke up. Her eyes remained locked on Daniel, gauging his reaction. "He doesn't say much, does he?"

"Who, him?" Rick laughed as he took a sip from his drink. "Oh, he's not always like this. Just had a bad week. Right, bro?"

Daniel's eyes met Jackie's. He immediately bowed his head, as though afraid to face her. "That's putting it mildly," he muttered.

"Oh, we all get those days," Rachel put in, oblivious to the interplay. "You'll get over it. Everyone does."

He said nothing further, and Rachel and Rick resumed their conversation.

Jackie found herself wishing - not for the first time - that the meal would get there in a hurry. She could think of nothing better than to eat and get out of there. The only comfort in the whole experience was the realization that she would never see Daniel Jameson again.

Chapter Twelve: Sunday, December 13, 2015

THE POUNDING ON THE DOOR STARTLES Jackie. As she rises from the couch she punches the remote control, switching off the television. Walking to the front window she glances out, looking up and down the deserted street, careful not to show herself through the curtains. It's dark outside, the winter sun having disappeared already, and from her vantage point she fails to make out who is at the door.

The pounding repeats itself.

"Just a minute," she yells. Jackie lives in an upstairs flat, a small one-bedroom place that stays perpetually neat and tidy. Pictures on the wall are of the K-Mart Special variety, crudely rendered landscapes mounted in cheap frames. The passage of time - and a succession of previous renters - has worn the carpeting, the nap beaten into a trail through each room, while the dingy white of the walls cries out for a coat of paint.

It takes nine steps to reach the door at the top of the stairs. She opens it, clicks on the light switch, and walks down to the entrance way. Brushing aside the curtain, she sees Brad outside. A smile crosses her face.

The deadbolt is thrown back and she opens the door to let him in. He brushes past her and up the stairs before she has the opportunity to say anything.

"Got anything to drink?" he begins. "I'm parched."

She closes the door, shutting out the cold night air.

"There's beer in the fridge."

He takes the steps three at a time. She follows at a more sedate pace. By the time she reaches the tiny kitchen Brad is leaning back in a chair, his feet propped up on the table, a Budweiser in his hand. He hasn't bothered to take off his coat, though it is now unzipped.

Jackie sits down across from him. For a few minutes no one speaks, as Brad works at lowering the level in his bottle.

At last Jackie breaks the silence. "How was your trip?"

"Shitty." He takes another gulp of beer. "The snow just wasn't right. Too dry. We spent most of the weekend indoors."

He puts his drink on the table and springs to his feet. He seems filled with nervous energy as he paces the room, Jackie following him with her eyes.

"That's too bad."

"What the hell. We'll just have to go again later." He walks behind her, placing his hands on her shoulders to start a gentle massaging action with his fingers. He doesn't look at her, his eyes focused instead on the opposite wall. "So what did you do while I was gone?"

"Went shopping."

"By yourself?"

"Of course not. Rachel came along."

"Was that all?"

"Just about. Why?"

"Just curious." His hands continue their motion, rubbing her shoulders and upper arms. "So you didn't do anything else all weekend?"

"No." She twists her neck to attempt to see him better. "What are you getting at?"

"I thought maybe you might have gone out to lunch or something."

She hesitates. The words come slow in reply. "Well, sure. After shopping we stopped at Applebee's, and...."

With a quick motion Brad pulls her toward him, the sudden motion cutting off her words and eliciting a yelp of surprise. Off balance, with the chair tilted on its back legs, Jackie's arms flail in the air until grabbing the edge of the table for support.

Brad's knuckles whiten as his fingers press into her shoulders.

A startled expression crosses Jackie's face. "Brad! What are you doing?"

He bends over, his face inches from hers. His gray eyes are emotionless, his voice a monotone. "I know about you and those other guys."

She seems confused - uncertain how to react to the accusation. The words come in a stumbled flow. "I don't understand. What are you talking about?"

"You were seen. You and Rachel. With those two guys at the restaurant."

"That was nothing. Believe me." An edge of panic begins to rise in her voice. "The place was crowded and they offered us a seat. That's all."

"Then why didn't you mention it sooner?"

"I forgot. I didn't think it was that important."

He continues to squeeze her shoulders.

"Brad. You're hurting me. Stop it."

He says nothing. The pressure continues.

"Brad! Please stop it. Please."

Tears are in her eyes now, and her hands clench tightly to the edge of the table. She bites her lower lip, a tiny trickle of blood dripping onto her chin.

For several moments they are locked in silence, his face towering menacingly above hers. Finally he lets go, the suddenness of the move causing her to nearly tip over.

She catches herself in time, rising from her chair to stand facing him, her back against the wall. A trace of fear remains in her eyes.

Brad steps closer. He raises a finger, tapping it against her chest. "It better not have been anything. Understand?"

She nods her head.

He spins around, walking away from her. "I'll call you later."

He doesn't bother to look at her as he leaves. His steps sound heavy as he plods down the stairs, and the door slams behind him.

Jackie walks around the table, holding the edge for support, and plops down on one of the chairs. Only then does she take a deep breath.

Chapter Thirteen: Tuesday, December 22, 2015

THE F-14 FIGHTER PLANE WAS, FOR THE most part, intact, though there were a few glaring discrepancies. The left wing was completely unattached, and rested beside the fuselage. The forward landing gear had snapped off, and the cockpit was missing. The pilot, wearing a drab gray flight suit, could just be seen beneath the right wing, its shadow concealing the top portion of his body.

Jeff Jameson picked up the errant wing from the table as his mother walked by. "What do you think, Mom?"

"Very nice," Becky answered. "You're really getting good at those models."

"Yeah. I think it's my best one yet."

"But you know what I think?"

"What?"

"I think it's time for you to start wrapping things up and get ready for bed."

"Do I have to?"

"You still have school tomorrow, you know."

"It's only half a day. And then I'm done for the rest of the year."

Lisa, sitting on the floor in the living room with her face buried in a math book, didn't even bother to look up as she commented. "It's only eleven days."

"I don't care," Jeff replied. "It's still time away from

school. And then two more days and it's Christmas!"

"Don't remind me," Becky Jameson put in. "I still have some last minute shopping to do. Now come on, let's get moving. Both of you."

"Yes, Mom," the two children answered in unison.

Jeff carefully placed the remaining pieces of his model - as well as the glue, some toothpicks, paintbrushes, and several small glass jars of paint - in the cardboard box, then headed for his room in the back of the house. Lisa closed her school book and gathered her papers and pencils together. She stood up and walked toward the recliner in the center of the room.

Daniel Jameson failed to acknowledge her presence as she bent down to kiss him on the cheek. "Good night, Dad."

He said nothing.

Lisa placed her hand on his shoulder. "Dad?"

He turned to face her. "What's that?"

"Good night."

"Yeah. Good night."

She smiled, the expression making her look more like her mother than ever, and walked away. He watched her disappear down the hallway, marveling at how much she had grown lately. It seemed everything was changing, at a faster pace than he could adjust to.

He could hear them now, in the back of the house, getting ready for bed. Jeff, always the talkative one, babbled on to his mother. "I'm glad we only have half a day at school tomorrow. I don't think I could stand a whole day."

"You never were one to sit still for long, were you?"

"I can't help it, Mom. I just get excited. Weren't you excited when you were little?"

"I'm *still* excited. But for different reasons. I just enjoy seeing you guys having such a good time."

"So what time can we get up on Christmas?"

"Why don't we talk about that later, okay?"

"I guess."

"Now get to sleep."

"All right. Good night, Mom."

The sound of footsteps drifted out to Daniel in the living room, as his wife moved around in the back of the house, and a few moments later her voice continued. "And how about you, Princess?"

"Mom!" Exasperation was evident in Lisa's voice. "I thought you weren't going to call me that anymore?"

"I never do when your friends are around, do I?"

"No. But I still don't like it."

"I'll try to remember."

Lisa's voice acquired a conspiratorial edge, the words barely reaching to the other part of the house. "Mom? Is Dad going to be okay?"

"What do you mean?"

"He just seems so quiet. So moody, I guess. Is he all right?"

It took several seconds for Becky to answer. "I'm sure he'll be fine. Just give him time. Okay?"

"Okay."

Jeff called from his room. "Dad?! Are you gonna come say good night?"

"In a little while," Daniel answered, though he made no attempt to move. He sat staring at the blank television. The Christmas tree behind him reflected off the screen in blinking diamonds of red, blue, and green. A soft whirring sound reached him from an animated ornament dangling from one of the branches, the sound unusually loud now that Lisa and Jeff were absent from the room.

He considered getting up and going back, to say good night to the children, but he found he lacked the energy to respond to his intentions.

It had been nearly two weeks since the accident at the shop. In that time, something had changed in him. He was aware of the change, conscious that he wasn't acting normal in his behavior, but unable to alter his attitude. His perception of life and everything around him had twisted in a way he couldn't begin to comprehend. He found it difficult to be enthusiastic about anything. What he used to consider important seemed now to be mere trivialities.

And what did it all matter, in the scheme of things?

The sound of movement subsided from the back of the house as the children settled down and Becky came out to join him. Daniel exhibited no reaction when his wife entered the room, dressed now in her night clothes. She gravitated to her favorite position on the couch, snuggled into the corner, legs tucked under her, throw pillow clutched against her stomach.

Out of the corner of his eye he watched her, taking in the curves of her body visible even through the old nightshirt she wore. Her hair hung limp at her side. Her face portrayed a raggedness, an edge of exhaustion normally concealed from the world. It was only when she was alone, and caught off-guard, that she could allow the weariness to show through. But he knew it was there. If not from her appearance, then from her actions.

Ninety seconds of silence was all Becky Jameson could manage. "You coming to bed?"

Daniel faced her, registering neither surprise nor acceptance with her presence, and said nothing.

She leaned forward, drawing closer. "What's going on, Dan? Why won't you talk to me about it?"

"There's nothing to say." His voice came as a low mumble, from deep in his throat.

"Yes there is. You're just not the same anymore. You've been this way ever since the accident. It scares me." Her voice trembled with the next words as she fought to control her anxiety. "You've got to snap out of it."

He had been telling himself the same thing. He knew it wasn't rational, the mood he was going through, and that he should just get on with his life, but as much as he thought these thoughts, he couldn't find it in his spirit to respond to them. It was like all the energy had been siphoned from him, leaving an empty shell where there had once been a vibrant person. He knew it was wrong - knew it was irrational behavior - but there was nothing he could do to change.

He didn't expect her to understand it. How could she, when he didn't understand it himself? But she could at least sympathize with him.

Becky snuggled back into the couch, breathing a heavy sigh. "So when are you going back to work?"

"I don't know. I don't know if I *can* go back there."

"Now that's just plain ridiculous. Listen to yourself. The chances of something like that happening again are.... I don't know, it will probably never happen again. There's nothing to be afraid of."

He bolted out of his seat, turning his back on her. A moment later he spun around. He could feel the anger rising in him. Anger, not at her, but at himself.

"Is that what you think? You think I'm afraid to go back to work?"

She stared at him a moment, her confusion obvious. "What is it, then?"

"God, I thought you knew me better than that. If you could have seen Mike, lying on that stretcher in the ambulance. He looked worse than a dead man. And all I could think was, it was all my fault. My fault."

"That's ridiculous." She was beside him now, her fingers resting lightly upon his arm, the touch of her skin failing to convey to him the compassion she felt for him. "You did everything you could have done. Everything anyone could have done. I'm sure Mike realizes that."

Daniel shook his head violently back-and-forth, interrupting her. "You don't understand." Further words halted in his throat, as Becky continued to stare at him.

He pulled away, turning to face the other direction. Somehow, it was easier to speak without looking at her. "I was talking to Mike, right before it happened. He was at his work station, and I asked him to find something out for me. That meant he had to cross the shop."

He took a deep breath. Images flashed through his head, scenes he would have liked to ignore. He tried to forget them, but they refused to cooperate, returning frequently to him - especially at night.

"All I could do was stand there, helplessly watching, as the molten metal reached him. Everything was just so incredibly horrible. His screaming. And the smell." He shook his head, which did nothing to clear the memory. "I'll never forget the smell."

"But you didn't just stand there. You ran over to him, didn't you? You saved his life."

"But if I hadn't been there, he wouldn't have been in danger in the first place." Daniel returned to his chair, slumping back into its comfortable confines. "The whole thing was all my fault."

Becky knelt down on the floor beside him, her hands finding his, though he failed to respond to the attention. "You can't do this to yourself, Dan. None of this was your fault. No one is blaming you for anything. If you were thinking clearly you'd realize that. It doesn't do you any good, and it doesn't do Michael any good, to torture yourself this way. It's got to stop."

"I can't help it."

Becky hesitated, choosing her next words with care. "Maybe you should see someone."

The look he gave her displayed his obvious distaste with the notion, but Becky - committed to what she had to say - continued anyway. "Connie at work was having some problems a few years ago and went to a therapist. Dr. Antonio Bargalony. He works out of Riverfront Rehab down in Toledo. She said it really helped her a lot."

Daniel made no reply.

For a moment they stared at one another, until Becky - apparently resigned - stood up. Her voice expressed her frustration. "You're impossible. I just don't know what to do for you. How to make it better."

"I don't think you can." He had already accepted that fact. This was something he had to work out on his own.

He heard her moving, toward the Christmas tree, and a moment later the colored reflections disappeared from the television screen.

"I'm going to bed," she told him. "You do whatever it is you want to do. Apparently, I don't have a say in things, anyway."

Chapter Fourteen: Wednesday, December 23, 2015

IT WAS AFTER MIDNIGHT BY THE TIME Daniel switched off the light in the living room and trudged down the hallway toward the bedroom. A swath of light from the front window illuminated the carpeting, the outside lamp providing glow enough for Daniel to discern objects in the rooms he passed.

Jeff lay on his back, his arm dangling over the side of the bed as he slumbered. An assortment of plastic models - military planes dominated the display - covered the top of his dresser, as well as the shelf over the foot of the bed. Daniel wasn't sure he could fall asleep with all that armament directed toward him, but it didn't seem to disturb his son any.

Lisa's door was closed. It was a habit she had begun on her last birthday, declaring she was older now and needed her privacy. Daniel paused, catching the gentle sound of her breathing through the panel, and moved on to his room at the end of the hallway.

Closing the door behind him, being careful not to make a sound as the latch engaged, he undressed in darkness. A whispered voice caught his attention.

"Don't forget to leave the door open."

He grunted something noncommittal in reply.

"What time is it?"

"'Bout one o'clock," he answered.

"One o'clock!" Becky sat up against the headboard, rubbing her eyes. He could just make out her features, her hair dangling over her shoulders in late-night disarray.

"Go back to sleep," he suggested, as he crawled in on his side of the bed, turning his back to her.

A moment later he felt the soft touch of her fingers against his arm. Her warmth enveloped him as she moved closer, her breathing caressing him with its rhythmic motion.

The sensation disturbed him. Lately - even before the accident at the foundry - he had felt uncomfortable with their lovemaking. Recent events had accelerated the condition, causing him to question every move she made and every reaction she exhibited. He found himself avoiding intimacy with Becky. He lay still, making no response, and eventually she rolled over to her side of the bed. It felt empty, and colder, with her no longer against him. Yet, strangely, it felt more comfortable, more acceptable for the time being.

He quickly fell asleep in his self-imposed isolation.

Chapter Fifteen:

TWENTY-SOME YEARS OF GETTING UP AT six o'clock in the morning had developed into a habit Daniel Jameson had learned to live with. Even now, with no intention of leaving for work, he still found himself up before the rest of the family. He sat in front of the television, barely watching the John Wayne movie on the cable station, as the house came to life, exhibiting its customary degree of pandemonium.

A flurry of activity usually accompanied the morning rituals, as clothes for everyone were procured, breakfast prepared, and lunches packed. With the children only having a half day of school things seemed to go a little more smoothly than normal - the noise level in the kitchen managed to stay several decibels below the accustomed amount - but there were the usual distractions. From the usual source.

"Mom!" Jeff wailed. "I can't find my geography book."

"Did you look on your bookcase?"

"Yeah."

"Are you sure?"

His voice resumed several moments later. "Here it is!"

"Where was it?"

His answer came in a much quieter tone than his previous words. "On the bookcase."

"What do you need your book for, anyway?" Lisa asked. "It's not like you'll be doing any work today."

"I just don't want to lose it. Okay?"

"I guess. I just don't understand...."

Becky cut her off. "Don't worry about it. Just worry about yourself. All right?"

"Yes, Mother."

Daniel managed to avoid the family, walking out to the mailbox to retrieve *The Toledo Blade*, and while they continued their morning activities he examined the newspaper. He had long been in the habit of reading the journal in its entirety. He found himself following his normal routine, though for the most part he gleamed no comprehension from the articles. It was more of a mindless activity, something to occupy him for a length of time, rather than a learning experience.

It also allowed him to avoid any interaction with the rest of his family.

He was reading of the President's latest *faux pas* when Becky called from the front of the house. "I'm leaving now! We have to get there early with the snacks for Jeff's Christmas party."

"All right," Daniel answered. He didn't even notice that she hadn't kissed him goodbye.

Jeff yelled out a moment later. "Bye, Dad!"

The door slammed shut behind them, and silence invaded the house.

No.

Not silence.

Approaching footsteps sounded.

When Daniel pulled the paper from his eyes Lisa stood before him.

"Aren't you going to miss your bus?"

"No," she replied. "It doesn't come for another twenty minutes."

"I see. So why didn't you let your mother drop you off while she was taking your brother over?"

"And spend extra time at school?" She said it as though it was the most ridiculous idea in the world. "Get real, Dad."

He returned to his reading, aware somehow even through the page that she continued to stare at him. Attempting to ignore her did no good. Resigning himself, he placed the paper on the floor beside him. "What is it?"

"Something's wrong. Isn't it?"

"Why do you say that?"

"You're just so quiet anymore. You hardly even notice us."

He hesitated, wondering what to say. How could he explain things to her when he couldn't even explain things to himself?

"Sometimes things happen that affect people," he began, stumbling with the words. "Things beyond their control. And it changes them."

"You mean, like the accident at the shop?"

"Yeah. Like that."

"But I don't understand. You're okay, aren't you? I know you got stitches and all, but isn't everything better now?"

As if of their own accord, the fingers of Daniel's right hand found the scab on his left arm, a jagged line that glared at him with its whiteness. It served as an ever-present reminder of an experience he would just as soon forget. He scratched at the spot, as though he could remove the defect, and stopped only after noticing Lisa intently watching the movement.

"Physically," he began, "I'm all right. But mentally, I don't know. I just don't know."

Lisa sat down on the coffee table, leaning closer. "What's going to happen? To you and Mom?" Then - as an afterthought - "To all of us?"

"I don't know, Princess. I wish I did. I suppose we'll get through it all somehow."

"What if we don't?"

He had no reply.

The same question had occurred to him, usually late at night when he felt the most insecure. Possibilities floated through his head - of what life would be like on his own, without Becky and the kids. It was a scenario he dreaded.

For a moment Lisa stared at him, as though uncertain what to make of his indecision. A drop of moisture appeared at the corner of her eye. "Oh, Dad...."

She flung herself against him, wrapping her arms tightly around his neck. "I don't want to see anything happen to you. I want you to get better."

"So do I, Lisa." He ran his fingers through her hair, feeling the gentle softness, smelling the pleasant aroma of the shampoo she had used that morning. It reminded him of when Lisa was little, and Becky and he would bathe her in the miniature plastic bathtub, and she would squirm and giggle and splash in joy. Half the time they ended up more wet from the experience than the little one.

She was growing up so fast, and he had hardly noticed it. Had he really been that preoccupied with his job? How much of life had he missed lately?

Lisa pulled back, urging her tears away with repeated snifflings. "I want this to be a happy Christmas. Not a sad one. Okay, Dad?"

"I'll try my best. That's all I can do. But I can't promise you anything."

"Jeff's worried, too, you know."

"Is he?"

She nodded her head. "He doesn't say much, but I can tell."

"I thought the only thing your brother was worried about was what he's getting for Christmas?"

"The little squirt *is* pretty greedy, isn't he?" She smiled, and Daniel found himself returning the gesture.

"See, Dad? That wasn't so hard!" She hugged him again, though this time her breathing was more relaxed - more comfortable. "I love you, Dad."

"And I love you."

"Well, I better get ready or I'll miss my bus." Lisa pulled away again. "See you after school."

"Count on it."

"Remember," she added, failing to conceal the excitement in her voice, "we only have half a day today." Her words trailed away as the door closed behind her.

The house took on a new personality after Lisa's departure. Shadows lurked everywhere, threatening Daniel with their oppressiveness. He considered switching on more lights, to dispel the gloom, but he knew it wouldn't change things. The somber character of the surroundings would remain.

He switched off the television. His first few days at home he had resorted to its artificial warmth, to remove the boredom and keep his mind occupied. But after a while it served only to recall to him the things he wished to forget. All it took was a face that looked anything at all like Michael Blake's, or a casual reference - the soaps seemed filled with them - of someone in a hospital, and the disturbing visions returned. It was better to be bored than to be reminded.

He wandered the house, plodding from room to room. On occasion he would pause, as his eyes took in a sight and his mind reflected on its significance; the cabinet tucked away into a corner of the family room, the first piece of furniture Becky and he had purchased as a married couple - the dirty scrap of plaster scribbled with names, resting on a shelf in Jeff's room, a reminder of the baseball game when Jeff had broken his ankle sliding into home plate - Lisa's framed certificate for taking second place in the regional art competition, displayed beside her winning charcoal sketch. Every article had a past, a history, a story to tell of a life shared as a family. Each article made him more aware of what he had built up over the years, and what he stood to lose if he continued on his present course of inactivity.

He knew he had to get over the depression gripping him. His family was depending on it. He was depending on it.

He just wished he knew how to accomplish the feat.

Chapter Sixteen:

AS THE MORNING DRAGGED ON DANIEL came to the realization he had to get out of the house. With no particular destination in mind he took off in the car because, at that moment, in his mind, anywhere was better than the loneliness of the empty building he called home.

He drove as though on automatic pilot, paying little attention to the sights around him, oblivious to the world outside his car windows. On one occasion a furious motorist, cut off at a stop sign, shook an angry fist at him and voiced some words that were extremely uncomplimentary. Twice horns blared to reprimand his inattention. But each of the occasions went unnoticed as he continued on his way.

When finally he came to a stop it was in front of an all too familiar structure. Getting out of the car, pausing only long enough to deposit some quarters in the parking meter, he approached the hospital slowly. His eyes scanned the windows of the fifth floor, as though he could peer within and avoid having to enter the building.

He forced himself to trudge forward. A cold wind blew off the Maumee River, sending gusts of powdery snow off the piles of white the plows had left banked on the sides of the road. The particles bit into his face. It was like standing in a sand-blasting booth. Lowering his head, he shoved his hands ever deeper into his coat pockets.

The doors slid open of their own accord as he reached the entrance. There was no need to stop at the receptionist's desk.

He knew where he was going. Though, if someone had asked, he couldn't have explained why.

Falling in line behind a trio of elderly ladies he entered an elevator that smelled of antiseptic. The odor was nauseating in the cramped confines, though he seemed to be the only one that took notice of the fact. The cage lifted him upward to the desired floor, where he waited for the others before forcing himself into motion.

His steps slowed the closer he drew to his destination. Though he would have liked to turn around and leave, something seemed to be propelling him forward, urging his body on against his will.

Daniel hated hospitals. For a place of recuperation, they always seemed extremely depressing to him. Perhaps it was the reminder of man's tenuous grip on his mortality that disturbed him so, the notion that all of us were doomed someday to enter the spic-and-span environment of the medical community, never to return to the world outside.

The last place he had seen his father alive was in a hospital. A shrunken, shriveled body that he barely recognized, unconscious on a bed with tubes protruding from his arms, it certainly wasn't the man he recalled from his childhood years. It was an image that had lingered for years, and on days like today re-surfaced to haunt him anew.

He ignored his broodings as best he could and prepared himself for the coming encounter.

Michael Blake lay on his back, labored breathing coming from the sleeping form. His face looked pale, the cheeks sunken in as though from malnutrition. Already the strength seemed to be evaporating from his body. The skin of his arms was wrinkled, like old pieces of leather, with pale blue lines snaking beneath revealing the path of his life's blood. He seemed fragile, helpless, like some delicate creature. Not at all like the robust individual Daniel had been joking with just two weeks earlier.

Plastic tubes connected him with hanging IV bottles,

while electrical lines monitored his vital signs. It all seemed so artificial - so UN-lifelike.

Daniel's eyes wondered away from the face, down the torso, to examine the folds and creases of the hospital linen that, while concealing much, revealed plenty concerning the body beneath. He could make out the shape of Michael's left arm, beneath the covers, and his chest heaving in and out. The mound that was his body tapered some at his waist, then spread out again at the hips.

Partially down the length of the bed the bumps ended abruptly, much sooner than they should have, the sheets smoothing out as they flattened against the mattress. The bed seemed to stretch on an unusual length beyond that, totally out of proportion with the size of its inhabitant.

"He looks better, don't you think?"

Daniel took a deep breath as he turned toward the sound of Amy Blake's voice.

"It's nice of you to come visit him, Dan."

He managed a weak nod in reply.

Amy pointed past him, at the basket of flowers on the window sill. "Those came yesterday. From Mr. Baker, at CONSOLIDATED. Everyone's been so nice...."

"It's the least he could do," Daniel interrupted.

"No. Don't say that."

"But it's true. After what happened...."

"No." She shook her head back and forth several times, worrying her lower lip while doing so. "I can't let myself be bitter. I was at first. Angry with the shop about what happened to Mike. And at the doctors for not doing more for him." She paused a moment in reflection. "And at myself, for not being there when he needed me."

She sighed, her voice moderately stronger as she continued. "But it doesn't do any good. It doesn't change anything, does it?"

She seemed to expect an answer, and he forced himself to oblige. "No. It doesn't."

"Exactly. All I can do now...." She paused to place a hand carefully against her bulge of a belly, a slight smile lighting her face as she did so. "All *we* can do now, is hope for the best."

She made a motion toward the bed. "Here. Let me wake him up."

"No."

She directed a questioning look his way.

"Let him sleep," Daniel continued. "He probably needs the rest."

"I'm sure he'd want to see you."

"Just tell him I was here. Okay?"

"Sure. If that's the way you want it."

He turned then, to get away from the shattered form on the hospital cot. Amy's words sounded faintly from behind him as he walked down the hallway. "Thanks again for coming, Dan."

The elevator was empty, the cramped little space ominously quiet. By the time it reached the ground floor Daniel had made a decision.

"I need a drink."

He hardly noticed the cold blasting against his face on the way out to the car. But for the distant look in his eyes he could have been a statue, or more correctly some animatronic creation, as he walked along the sidewalk, unaffected by the elements, intent on his purpose.

The only problem was he had no purpose. No reason. No thought, other than to run away.

Reaching the car, Daniel slipped behind the wheel. For several minutes he sat there, motionless, as frozen as the world outside. Spying the GPS on the car's dash a recklessness took over. Turning the device on, he pushed the appropriate buttons to search for a location. He entered the letters slowly. P. A. P. A. SPACE J. O. E. '. S.

After a few seconds a mechanical-sounding female voice sounded. "Searching for location."

The image faded back, revealing a route marked in purple

on the miniature map displayed on the screen. Estimated time to arrival showed 12 minutes.

Daniel started the car, shifted to reverse, and backed out of the parking space. Before shifting into drive he reached for the GPS.

"What the hell," he muttered.

Switching the device off, he headed in the familiar direction of home.

Chapter Seventeen:

GUNFIRE EXPLODES AROUND HIM, sporadic shots from either side. Protective gear covers his ears, a necessity in the deafening environment. Involuntary spasmodic twitches wrack his body with each report. His face is taut, his arms stiff in front of him, as he stands at the railing. His eyes narrow, focusing along the length of the automatic's barrel.

The black silhouette of a standing bear lurks across the massive room, a red circle approximating the animal's heart. He could have chosen the deer or the fox, which are actually more difficult targets, but he chose the bear. He always chooses the bear.

Gun smoke muddles the air, the dirty vapor obscuring the view. The target becomes less defined. It takes only a modicum of imagination to forget the cutout is a bear, the image becoming almost man-like in appearance.

A smile wrinkles the corner of his mouth as his finger tightens on the trigger. His back stiffens in anticipation of the coming recoil. His breathing halts.

In an instant it happens.

The bullet erupts from the barrel, echoes of the explosion reverberating around him. He stands still for a moment, poised in his shooting stance. As the last lingering remnant of the shot dies away he lowers his arms. There are now five holes in the chest of the inanimate beast, where seconds earlier there had been only four.

Brad Wilkens turns around. Jeff Black, standing on the other side of the protective barrier, flashes a thumb's up. Brad is all smiles as he heads for the exit.

"Nice shootin', bud," Jeff begins. "You look like a pro in there."

"Shit. This is getting too easy."

"So what say we head over to *Papa Joe's* and down a few cold ones?"

"Can't. I was supposed to be at Jackie's an hour ago."

"Let her wait."

His smile is a lecherous grin. "It's not her I'm thinking about." He considers a moment longer. "Oh, what the hell. Can't have her thinking she's in control, now can I? Sure. Let me put my gear away and we'll grab a few."

Chapter Eighteen:

JACKIE DREADED THE COMING EVENING. Apprehension overwhelmed her, and had for most of the day, when she considered what the night would bring. A queasy sensation gripped her in the stomach.

A week and-a-half ago the situation would have seemed inconceivable.

One of the things that first attracted Jackie to Brad was his easy-going, cavalier attitude. It often seemed he didn't know how to be serious - that life was a joke to him, and he alone knew the punchline. He was easy to talk to and fun to be with. Always the center of attention, Brad dominated any group he was part of. Just being next to him made Jackie feel more important somehow.

They had first met seven months earlier - at *Papa Joe's*, of course - a casual meeting with a group of friends. Jackie hadn't spoken much, as usual, finding it easier to blend with the others, and it had surprised her when Brad called to ask her out. Reluctant to accept, she was too shy to turn him down. They began meeting on a regular basis, their relationship developing at a rapid pace.

Too rapid, Rachel warned.

Rachel saw something in Brad, an element hidden to Jackie, and attempted, over time, to warn her friend.

But, of course, Jackie would see none of it.

Until now.

The events a week and-a-half ago were still fresh in Jackie's mind. Brad had seemed so relaxed on his arrival at her apartment that evening. So casual about his ski trip. She had never expected him to turn on her the way he had. She realized he had a temper - she had seen it displayed before - but it had never been directed at her before.

Or had it?

Had she just been too blind to notice? Or too stupid? The off-handed remarks he frequently threw her direction, even his lack of concern regarding her feelings, were all clues to something deeper. They epitomized an inner lack of respect, not only toward Jackie, but toward everyone.

The realization had profoundly affected their relationship. She felt suddenly trapped, in a situation with no chance of escape, where even something as casual as an innocent encounter at a crowded restaurant could be blown out of proportion and used against her.

Jackie had managed to avoid him for a few days after the incident in her kitchen, coming up with a string of excuses why they couldn't get together, but Brad had pushed the issue. They had met several times since then, always in what Jackie felt to be a safe environment - crowded rooms with no chance of being alone with him.

It was anything but enjoyable. She found herself on edge, watchful of her every move. Her words were analyzed before speaking them, in fear they'd be misconstrued and used against her. She watched his face constantly, attuned to his mood swings, prepared to change topics on the instant should he react adversely to something she said.

They were going out again tonight, and Brad had made it clear that he wanted some time alone with her. She couldn't put him off any longer on the point. Two weeks earlier she would have welcomed the opportunity. But now...?

And yet, with all her trepidation, she refused to believe there was anything actually bad about Brad. More like misguided. Brad never was much for talking about the past. From the few things he had told her she knew his childhood had been an unpleasant one, with an abusive father that left Brad alone with his mother when he was only twelve. She died soon after he left high school, killed in an auto accident. Brad had been on his own ever since.

It was no wonder he had grown up with an utter disrespect for anyone in authority, and the conviction that it was him against the world. She had often thought his defense mechanism, his way to avoid the anguish in his life, was his reckless attitude. He fought back however he could because, in his mind, he had to. It was the only way to survive. How could he not help being abusive and inconsiderate at times?

Jackie had to believe last week's incident was an abnormality, a rare occurrence that would not repeat itself. It was only a question of giving herself time to overcome her apprehensions. It was her problem now, one she would have to deal with.

And one she would have to deal with alone.

She wanted more than anything to talk to Rachel about it, but she realized she couldn't. Even though the two of them had been friends for a long time, there were certain subjects they couldn't discuss. Brad was definitely one of them.

Jackie glanced once more at the clock. Brad was nearly two hours late. The fact failed to surprise her. It was just his way of doing things. She had gotten used to it, over time. It hardly bothered her anymore. Besides, it gave her that much longer to prepare for the coming encounter.

Chapter Nineteen:

"I HAD A NICE TIME TONIGHT, BRAD." A slight quiver - a trace of hesitation - punctuates her words. He doesn't seem to notice. "Thanks for dinner."

The sapphire blue Camaro pulls up in front of her apartment. A light snow is beginning to fall, a fine mist that causes the streetlights to shimmer in and out of view. Several houses have their Christmas decorations turned on. The lights fail to portray any warmth, instead projecting a somber coldness to the surroundings.

Jackie slips her gloves on and buttons the top of her coat, in anticipation of stepping out into the cold.

Brad turns the engine off, depositing the key in his coat pocket.

She halts her activities. The words come slowly, enunciated with care. "What are you doing?"

"I thought I'd come in for a little while."

"It's kind of late."

"I don't have to stay long." His hand strays to her side of the car, the fingers rubbing against the material of her pants. He leans toward her, to plant a kiss on her lips, at the same time slipping his hand between her thighs.

"No." She shakes her head as she pushes his advance aside, then reaches for the door handle. "Not tonight."

"Wait a minute." He grabs her arm, twisting her around so they face each other. "Are you mad at me?"

"No. I'm not mad."

"Yes, you are. I can tell."

"No. Really. I'm okay. Just a little tired, that's all."

For a moment they stare at one another, their breaths making vapory trails in the cold air of the car. Brad's hand remains on her arm, the fingers tightening. Their eyes lock.

"You're hurting me."

He says nothing.

"Brad. You're hurting me."

Slowly, as though through a great effort, his fingers release their hold. She pulls away, steps out of the car, then hesitates, reluctant to close the door and end the night on such a sour note. She stands, confused, as flakes of white swirl around her.

"Listen, if you want to come in for a few minutes, I guess that would be okay."

Not bothering to wait for a reply, she closes the door and begins walking up the sidewalk toward the front door. Patches of ice litter the walkway, which forces her to step carefully. The beckoning doorway is dark, and by the time she manages to find the lock and open the door Brad is at her side.

In silence they tramp up the stairs to the second floor, entering through the small dining room and into the equally small living room. Jackie slips off her boots, leaving them next to the stack of newspapers in the corner.

"Just throw your coat anywhere," she suggests, reaching into the closet for a hanger. "Do you want a cup of coffee or something?"

"No. That's okay."

She turns around. Brad's coat is off. He removes his shirt, discarding it carelessly on the floor.

"What are you doing? I thought I made it clear to you that I wasn't in the mood?"

"Moods change, baby."

Two steps bring him next to her. His arms gravitate toward her shirt, the right hand reaching beneath the material.

"No!" She makes a motion to stop him, but the movement

is halted as he pushes her against the wall. His body presses forward as he bends to kiss her neck. She attempts to squirm away, but he has left her no maneuvering room.

"Please, Brad...."

She breaks away, slipping beneath his arms and then around him. The suddenness of the movement causes him to fall forward. His nose flattens against the wall with the impact. Jackie flinches at the sight, a look of concern on her face.

Brad reaches for his face. When his fingers withdraw they are tinted in blood, a red flow trickling across his upper lip. He stares at his fingers for a moment, as though in disbelief.

Jackie's hand flies to her mouth. "I'm sorry." The words are a whisper. "Brad. I'm sorry."

He still stares at his fingers. "Goddamn it!"

"I didn't mean to...." She starts to back away, her steps unsteady.

He spins around, a bestial fierceness overcoming his features. His eyes glisten in the indirect light coming from the next room, imparting a vacant, faraway look to his expression. Shadow obscures his lower face.

Jackie continues to back away on wobbly legs, coming up hard against the couch and nearly falling over. Her chest heaves in the beginning throes of panic. "I'm sorry, Brad." The words come in a rush.

He advances toward her. "Why, you...."

The next moment Jackie is sprawled on the couch, with Brad's body pushing heavily upon her. In one swift motion he lifts her shirt, at the same time pushing up on her bra and exposing the breasts. His hands squeeze tightly, ruthlessly, against the flesh.

His head descends. The smell of beer and cigarettes waft over her, and she struggles to turn away. It is to no avail. His lips find hers in a kiss that is neither sensual nor enticing.

A moment later the smell is gone, as his mouth departs for other regions. He pulls against her pants, manhandling the material past her hips. The tearing of the fabric sounds plainly.

With one hand still holding her down, Brad manages to loosen his own pants.

Jackie closes her eyes as the couch begins moving to the rhythm of his exertions.

Jackie, fully clothed, sits on the floor beside the toilet, staring at the closed door in front of her. Her hand holds shredded pieces of toilet paper, which she wipes continuously against her by-now-red eyes. A pile of discarded tissue lays in a heap on the floor beside her.

From the other side of the door footsteps can be heard, and occasionally the slamming of cupboard doors. Brad's voice reaches in to her, his irritation obvious. "God, don't you have anything to eat around here?"

She bends over, holding her hands against her ears to block out the worst of the racket, but there is no escaping it.

Again the sound of footsteps, and once more Brad's voice. "There's not even any beer in the fridge."

The footsteps grow louder, approaching closer. His next words sound from directly outside the door. "So are you coming out, or what?"

She says nothing.

"Listen, I'm sorry 'bout what happened. I don't know what got into me. All right? Is that what you wanna hear? I made a mistake and I'm sorry." His speech comes out in a jumbled flow, as though he feels the urge to say something but lacks the skill to locate the appropriate words.

Jackie looks toward the door. Indecision runs rampant across her face. She starts to get up, reaching for the doorknob, when a loud slam against the panel causes her to jerk away. Brad hits the door a second time, the intensity of his blow forcing her back to the floor.

His footsteps resume, this time walking away. "Jesus Christ, I don't know what you expect from me. I said I was sorry, didn't I?"

His words grow more faint as further distance separates

them. "I'm outta here."

His heavy footfalls sound as he descends the stairs, followed by the slamming of the door at the bottom landing. The only sound remaining is the stifled whimpering from the young woman sitting on the worn floor in the bathroom.

Chapter Twenty: Thursday, December 24, 2015

THE FIRST THING SHE HEARD IN THE morning was Paul McCartney's voice, bemoaning the lack of songs of a silly nature. It was enough to make her get out of bed and turn the radio off, rather than hitting the snooze button as she normally did.

The carpet felt cold against her feet, and she had to stifle the urge to crawl back under the covers. A draft infiltrated the room, sneaking through a crack at the edge of the window, then slipping past the curtains to wander across the room and find her. It brushed against her legs, raising a row of goosebumps.

She scurried to the bathroom, which always seemed to be the warmest place in the apartment, and slammed the door behind her as she reached in to turn on the shower. Soon a hot flow was gushing from the nozzle, raising a cloud of steam that brought added warmth to the tiny room.

She caught her reflection in the mirror as she straightened up.

"God, Jackie, aren't you a sight?"

Her eyes were swollen, her cheeks puffy and red. She hadn't bothered to remove her make-up the night before, and a dark smudge of mascara dribbled past her left eye. Her hair looked atrocious. But, then again, she never did like the looks of it in the morning. And it was such a shitty color. It always reminded her of dirty dishwater.

Grabbing the hem of her nightshirt, she lifted the garment over her head. The maneuver made her aware of a dull ache in her chest. Dropping the clothes, she leaned closer toward the mirror. A vivid red mark blemished the underside of her right breast, standing in marked contrast to the paleness of the rest of her skin. She poked at the spot, delicately, and was startled by how tender it was.

"Damn it, Brad."

She stretched her arms and legs - tentatively, at first - in search of additional aches and pains. She felt stiff, but not really sore. That was a relief. The way she'd been thrown around, she had expected to be in worse shape.

She grabbed a towel, then sat down on the edge of the tub to test the water.

For a moment she paused, reflecting on the events of the previous evening. She had been intimate with Brad enough times to realize he became totally self-involved when it came to sex - oblivious to her needs and desires as he concentrated on his own urgings - but even so, his actions had taken her completely by surprise. It was like being with another man the night before. As though a stranger had invaded her apartment.

Maybe he *wasn't* any good for her. Rachel had seen it a long time ago, but look what it had taken to convince her of it. Maybe it was time to reassess the way she felt about things. After all, it wasn't like they were totally committed to one another. She was young enough to find someone else.

The hell with Brad, anyway.

As she stepped into the shower the tears began anew, a nagging question returning to her. Why didn't he call to apologize? Everything would be so much better if he'd only apologize. Couldn't he have at least done that much?

Chapter Twenty-One:

"CAN YOU PASS ME THE HAM, UNCLE Rick?"

"Sure thing, Jeff."

Rick Jameson reached across the table for the platter of meat, handing it over to his nephew.

"Thanks. I sure love ham."

"You must," Lisa said, a look of disgust on her face. "What is that, your sixth piece?"

"Nope. It's only my fourth." The words came out garbled, between chews.

"What a pig."

"That would make me a cannibal, wouldn't it? Get it?"

"That's not what I meant. How dense can you be?"

Jeff stuffed another piece of meat into his mouth, then leaned closer to Lisa. He managed an "Oink, oink," between chews, which he further exaggerated by leaving his mouth open.

"Oh, gross." She turned aside to avoid the scene.

Becky, saying nothing, presented her son a look of reproach, and he turned away from Lisa.

The dinner lapsed once again into silence.

Returning to his meal, Rick considered the evening so far. Daniel had yet to speak since sitting down at the table, while Becky couldn't have said more than a half-dozen words since he had gotten there. She failed even to admonish Lisa and Jeff to eat more vegetables.

There was no denying the fact that something was

bothering both of them. The children felt the tension as well. Obviously uncomfortable with the atmosphere, they spoke only when necessary, and then in short clips and phrases. Jeff's recent comedic outburst concerning the meal was the first sign of animation the entire evening.

Rick glanced once again at his watch, urging the hands forward in their seemingly immeasurable circuit. In many ways he would have liked to stay home today, but he knew the family was counting on him to be there. And he hated to disappoint the kids.

The Christmas Eve get-togethers had been a family tradition for longer than he could remember. Rick's earliest recollection of the event was when he was in first grade. There had been aunts and uncles and cousins and who-knew-who, all crammed in their parents' little place. Extra tables and chairs had been scavenged from somewhere, resulting in wall-to-wall confusion. The racket had been unbelievable and, to an excitable six-year old, a dream come true.

Presents were everywhere. Rick would never forget the scale-model aircraft-carrier he received that year, or the hours he spent shooting planes and missiles and anything else he could get his hands on across the room. He could remember wishing it would never end.

Things had changed over the years, with people losing contact with one another and families drifting apart. Wasn't that the way life was supposed to be? Changes, whether for the good or bad, were unavoidable. Now it seemed the only time they saw their cousins was at weddings and funerals.

The notion reminded Rick of their parents' death. It had been almost six years since their father passed away, closer to seven for their mother. Rick, away at College both times, had reacted with a coldness he still didn't understand. Young and independent, he refused to let their deaths interfere with his future, denying to himself the loss. Wrapped up in his classes, he took time out for a whirlwind trip back - just long enough to attend the services - then returned to school.

Looking back on it now, he wondered how he could have been so uncaring.

Doreen had moved out to California the year Rick came back to Toledo. They didn't see much of her anymore, though she left a standing invitation for them to visit. Chances were they'd never take her up on the offer. She was a stranger. Sometimes, Rick even forgot he had a sister.

All that was left now was Daniel's family. And even that small group gave indications of collapsing. Rick had sensed the friction between his brother and Becky for a while, regarding it as one of the normal pratfalls of marriage. They had fought in the past, but had always managed to weather through it.

Lately, though, the dissension between the two seemed to have grown. The recent accident at CONSOLIDATED - and Daniel's subsequent moodiness - had only served to accelerate the deterioration.

At last the meal was over, and everyone moved into the family room to gather around the tree. Rick retrieved Lisa's and Jeff's presents from the Bronco. Jeff displayed an initial bout of disappointment at his package, which was noticeably smaller than his sister's.

"Don't let the size fool you," Rick told him in a whisper. "I spent every bit as much for yours as I did Lisa's."

That seemed to appease him, and the package was unwrapped in record time. Jeff held up the box and read from the cover, which depicted armed warriors and mythical beasts. "*Explore mystical realms and magical kingdoms in QUEST OF THE DRAGON. Match your wits against the awesome secrets of the ancients*. Cool! A computer game!"

"Not *any* computer game," Rick corrected. "It's the latest DVD title. It's a lot better than those wimpy X-Box games you play. There's even an expansion disk with it, so you can build alternate worlds and have new adventures. I think you'll have fun with it."

"I *know* I will. Can I go try it out, Mom?"

"Aren't you forgetting something?"

Jeff walked over to Rick, throwing his arms around him in a hug. "Thanks, Uncle Rick. I think it's great."

"I'm glad you like it."

Jeff ran from the room with undisguised exuberance.

Lisa, who managed to restrain her enthusiasm easier than her brother, was just finishing unwrapping her present. She held it up for all to see. "Look what RJ gave me."

It was an acrylic art kit, with a rainbow of colors in individual tubes. Included with the paint was a palette and an assortment of brushes.

"I know how much you like to draw," Rick commented, "so when I saw this I thought of you. Do you like it?"

"I sure do. Thanks a lot." She approached him, bending over to give him a quick kiss on the check, then turned toward her mother. "All right if I go to my room?"

"Go ahead," Becky replied.

The room quieted once the children were gone, but things failed to relax. If anything, the atmosphere was worse than it had been at the kitchen table.

Rick shifted in his seat, which did nothing to make his position more comfortable. "You mind if I grab a Pepsi?" he said at last, looking for any excuse to relieve the tension.

Becky rose to her feet. "Don't be silly. I'll get it for you." She was to the doorway before he could stop her. "You two just sit right here."

Rick waited until he heard the clatter of glass and ice cubes from the kitchen, then leaned closer toward his brother. He kept his voice to a whisper. "What the hell's the matter with you?"

"What do you mean?"

"You know damn well what I mean. How long are you going to keep this up?"

Daniel nearly said something, then hesitated. For a moment neither of them spoke, and at last Daniel replied. "You don't understand what I've been through."

"You're right. I *don't* understand what you've been through. Probably never will. But I *can* tell you what you're heading for if you don't straighten up. How long do you think Becky's going to put up with this?"

"This is none of your business, Rick. Why don't you just stay out of it?"

"And watch you screw up your life? Becky's life? The kids' lives?"

"I told you it was none of your business."

Their voices had risen by now. Rick, fighting back the anger, jumped to his feet. Two steps took him directly in front of Daniel. "When are you going to wake up and see what you're doing?"

"It's my life...."

"Bullshit! It's not just your life you're screwing with. Becky deserves better than this."

Daniel made no reply.

For a full minute Rick stood there, reluctant to leave but uncertain what to say if he stayed. "Hell," he managed at last. "I don't know why I'm even standing here talking to you."

Rick walked out of the room. A moment later he hesitated, debating whether to return, deciding at last against it. Sometimes Daniel was just too bull-headed to reason with.

Rick stormed into the kitchen, his pace slowing at sight of his sister-in-law. Becky leaned against the closed door of the refrigerator, her forehead pressed against it while her arms hung limply at her side. She seemed lost. Deserted.

Feeling incompetent, uncertain for how to respond, Rick stood frozen in the doorway. "I'm sorry, Beck. I didn't mean to lose my temper in there."

For an awkward moment he remained where he was, silence enveloping the room. Becky made no reply, not even looking his way. He wondered if she was even aware of his presence.

"I'll see myself out the door," he said at last. "Tell Lisa and Jeff I hope they have a Merry Christmas."

To himself, he added - "Though it will be a miracle if they do."

Chapter Twenty-Two:

RACHEL KELLER STARED AT THE SMALL package on the table, taking in the red poinsettia paper done up with a sparkling silver bow. It hadn't been there a moment earlier, when she stepped into the kitchen to get Jeff another cup of coffee. She was certain of that. He must have put it there while she was out of the room.

Though she couldn't quite understand why, she found herself hesitating, making no move to pick it up. "What's this?" she asked at last, wondering if her voice sounded as surprised to him as it did to her.

Jeff Black, sitting across the table from her, smiled his most captivating smile. "Why don't you open it?"

She picked up the box, giving it a tentative examination. Her eyes remained locked on him, awaiting a signal. "It's not very heavy."

He smiled once more, not saying a thing.

She felt confused. What did he expect from her? How was she supposed to react? The entire thing was so unexpected. For one of the few times in her life she felt at a loss for words. It was a situation she wasn't comfortable with.

Her hands felt clumsy, and she dropped the box in spite of herself.

"Is something wrong?" Concern was obvious in his voice.

"No. Of course not." She attempted to mask her nervousness. "It's just that...."

"What?"

"This is all so unexpected, that's all."

"It's Christmas, isn't it? What's so unexpected about presents at Christmas?"

She continued to stare at the package. It was obviously jewelry. What else would fit in that size of a box? But what? Surely not a ring? After all, they had never even discussed anything like this before.

"Open it," he prompted.

With shaking hands, Rachel carefully undid the silver bow and ribbon. The paper slipped off, and in her hands was a velvet-coated case. She squinted as she pried it open.

Something reflected light from inside, a bright star that immediately caught her eye. Her motions accelerated. She held the ring up, the diamond in the mounting casting miniature dazzling rays of white and yellow, each facet glistening as though imbued with a light of its own.

Rachel's breathing stopped. "I don't believe this." The words came slowly. "I just don't believe this."

"Believe it." Jeff was beside her now, his hand on her arm. He bent down beside her, their faces inches apart. "You like it?"

"Like it? I love it!" It slipped easily over her knuckle, and she held her hand up to examine the look of it in the light. No matter which direction she held it, it still looked stunning. "Perfect fit. How'd you know?"

"I borrowed one of your old rings a while ago and took it to the jeweler's. I hope you don't mind?"

"How could I possibly mind? It's beautiful, Jeff. Thank you." She flung her arms around his neck, and their lips met. He felt warm against her, imparting a feeling of security. At that moment she could think of nothing else but being in his arms.

With time the moment ended. Rachel fell back to her seat and examined the ring once again. It seemed impossible to pull her eyes away from it. It was more beautiful than she could have ever imagined. "I just don't know what to say."

"Say you will."

"Will what?"

"Marry me."

She faced him, probing his features.

"Not right away," Jeff quickly added. "Whenever you're ready. What do you say?"

Rachel's vision was blurring, the tears in her eyes a definite distraction.

But she didn't mind. "Of course I'll marry you."

She jumped from her seat to pace the room, her eyes ever on the ring adorning her finger. "I still can't believe this. Wait 'till Jackie hears about it."

The thought struck her like a revelation. "Jackie! I've got to call her right away. Let her know...."

Her hand reached for her purse, her intention to grab the cellphone within. Jeff blocked the movement. He placed the purse on the floor, out of her reach, and turned her gently around to face him. "Why don't you wait?"

His lips found hers, and she agreed on the instant. Jackie could wait until later.

Chapter Twenty-Three:

AMY BLAKE LEANED AGAINST THE SINK and splashed cold water on her face, hoping it would help her regain some strength. It worked, to a small degree, but the sick feeling in her stomach refused to go away. Not that she really expected it to. It had been with her now for the past two months, on an apparent cycle where every third day was the worst. Today just happened to be one of those days.

She stared at her reflection in the mirror, twisting a bit to take in the unfamiliar appearance of her belly. She forced a smile. "If the pregnancy is this bad, what's the labor like?"

She shuffled out of the bathroom and made her way to the chair beside her husband's bed. The room was dark, save for the backlash from the lights in the hall and a modicum of illumination from the half-parted curtains on the window. For a moment the view through the glass distracted her. The night seemed to glow, the nearby rooftops dazzling with reflected light. She could make out The Maumee River a block away, a ribbon of black flowing peacefully along. Ice was just starting to form at the edges, white chunks along both banks.

She paused, mesmerized. It all seemed so peaceful. So serene. Even the gusts of snow, swirls of sparkling white, seemed somehow comforting. How could anything bad ever occur in such a beautiful world?

The thoughts vanished as she turned toward Michael. Toward reality.

As Amy took her seat the nurse poked her head into the room. She was a large black woman, with arms the size of a normal person's thighs. Her physique failed to match her disposition. Laughter shone in her eyes and lit her features, while her voice betrayed a sing-song lilt. "You okay, Mrs. Blake?"

"I'm fine, Terry. Just a little morning sickness."

Terry glanced at her watch. "You mean ev'nin' sickness, don't you?" she laughed.

"Yeah. I guess you're right."

"Land sakes, child. You do look pretty ragged. Maybe you should be headin' home? You've been here all day."

"No." Amy reached out, her hand clasping Michael's arm. Just knowing he was there made everything more bearable. At least they were together. "No. I'd like to stay a little longer, if that's all right. I sort of hate to leave him."

"Of course. That's just fine. Is there anythin' I can get you?"

"No. Thank you. I'm okay."

"Well, just holler if you change your mind. I'm right down the hall."

"Thank you."

Terry started to turn, then caught herself. "Oh. Mrs. Blake?"

"Yes?"

"Merry Christmas."

"Thank you. Merry Christmas to you."

Amy no longer noticed the electronic hum of the medical instruments in the room. Anymore the rhythm was just another part of her day-to-day experience. At least Michael's breathing was no longer labored, his condition having improved steadily every day for the past week. It almost made her feel like the worst was over.

Somewhere down the hall a television came to life. Voices she failed to recognize - a man and a woman - blended in a duet.

"Please Come Home for Christmas."

Amy listened for several moments, then buried her face in the pillow that cradled her husband's head. The tears were not long in coming.

Chapter Twenty-Four: Saturday, December 26, 2015

"BECKY THREW ME OUT."

"What?" Rick Jameson blinked twice against the early morning glare and stared out at his brother, who stood on the front step. Daniel held a suitcase at his side, the bag stuffed to the bulging point. His coat was unzipped and he wore no hat. The wind blew his hair back from his face, leaving the impression he had an unusually broad forehead.

"Becky threw me out," Daniel repeated. Rick said nothing - for a moment could think of no reply - and Daniel continued, his voice calmly unemotional. "Can I come in?"

"Sure. Sure."

Rick stepped aside, closing the door behind his brother after he passed through, then led the way into the living room, which resembled nothing less than a miniature disaster area. Newspapers were strewn about the carpeting. A stack of books on an end-table had collapsed, some of the volumes landing on the sofa but most spilling onto the floor. Two cans of beer accompanied an empty bag of Bar-B-Q chips, all perched atop the thirty-two inch television in the corner of the room. Rick cleared two places to sit on the couch, dumping an accumulation of debris in a pile. "The maid will clean it up later," he commented with a dry chuckle. "You know how bachelor living can be."

"I guess I'm going to find out."

Rick paused. He studied Daniel's face, trying to read the blank mask staring back at him. It was impossible to determine his brother's state of mind. He seemed devoid of emotion, as though all feeling had been drained from him. Anger he could understand. Or sadness. But this total lack of expression seemed unnatural.

"She really threw you out?"

A trace of exasperation tinted Daniel's reply. "Would I be here now if she hadn't?"

"Damn." Rick plopped down on the couch and threw his legs on the ottoman. "Damn." He shook his head. "So what are you going to do?"

"I don't know. I'll need to live somewhere...."

"Don't even worry about that. You're welcome to stay here. Really."

"Thanks, Rick. I appreciate it. I just don't know...." Daniel stumbled with the words. "It just doesn't make sense to me. Everything going on, and all."

"You're telling me." Rick leaned closer. They had talked some at lunch several weeks ago, the afternoon they had spent together, but not enough to explain to Rick what was happening. Never one to say much about himself, Daniel had been more tight-lipped than usual that day. Now seemed a good time to press the point further. "What *is* going on here, anyway? This can't all be because of the accident at CONSOLIDATED?"

Daniel answered with no hesitation. "Of course not. But it took the accident at the shop to make me see it."

"See what?"

"Remember when Dad died?"

The change of topic startled Rick. Images flashed for an instant through his head - his father standing in the front doorway, shaking his fist and yelling, as Rick drove away in his '95 Mustang. It was the last time he had ever seen his father alive.

Rick fought to suppress the visions before they became more vivid to him. "Of course I remember when Dad died. Just because I was away at college at the time...."

Daniel shook his head, cutting his brother off. "This isn't about your relationship with Dad. You can't do anything about that now, anyway."

Daniel stood to begin pacing the room, as though the movement assisted his thinking. "Hell," Daniel continued, "Dad was only sixty-six when he died. Worked his entire life. Raised a family. Struggled all those years. And for what?"

"What are you getting at?"

"Don't you see? I mean, what's the point of it all? What did he get out of it? What do *any* of us get out of it? We make all these big plans. Have all these dreams for the future. But what if that future never happens? What then? I could have been killed two weeks ago."

"But you *weren't* killed."

"I could have been."

"Damn it, Daniel, we can argue this point back and forth all day and not get anywhere. You could walk out the front door right now and get hit by a car. Just because it *might* happen doesn't mean it *will*. Or even that the chances of it happening are remotely possible. You can't live your life looking over your shoulder all the time. You can't just lock yourself away in a box somewhere, afraid to do anything or go anywhere. That's not life."

Daniel made no comment.

"And what about Becky and the kids?" Rick added. "Is any of this fair to them?"

"I know. I've been awful to them. You don't have to tell me that."

"Then do something about it. Think of them for a change, and not just yourself."

"I am thinking of them."

"Yeah. Right." Rick chuckled with a sarcastic little laugh. "The selfless husband and devoted father."

Daniel turned away a moment, as though embarrassed to continue. When he did start anew his voice was subdued - barely above a whisper. "I can understand how this must look to you, but there's more to it than you know. This whole thing started long before the accident."

Apparently tired of pacing, Daniel sat again. Rick shifted in his seat, watching his brother intently. It was obvious Daniel had some things to work out. Maybe it was best to just let him talk his way though it.

"It hasn't been too good between Becky and me lately," Daniel began after a lengthy pause. "I don't know. Maybe it was the demands of her job. Or the demands of mine. Or maybe we've just changed with age. We hardly ever talk anymore. It's like we inhabit the same house, but we live separate lives, isolated from one another. We don't seem to have anything in common anymore."

"What about Lisa and Jeff?"

"That's part of the problem. They seem to be aware of what's going on. Especially Lisa. It's like they're withdrawing. Pulling away from me. I can feel it. You know, we don't do anything as a family anymore. We used to go to the zoo. Or even just eating out somewhere. But anymore...." His voice trailed away to nothing.

"They're growing older, Daniel. Lisa's a teenager, for goodness' sakes. Hell, when I was her age the last thing I wanted was to spend time with my parents. You know that. What they're going through is a normal part of growing up. Accept it. Then get on with your life."

"It just doesn't seem that easy anymore."

"So what are you going to do about it?"

"I wish I knew. I think I just need more time. To sort things out in my head and all."

Rick considered his options. On one hand, he didn't want to be an enabler. The longer Daniel stayed in this crazy mood of his, the harder it would be for him to recover. He needed something to snap him out of it. *Someone* to snap him out of it. Maybe it would be better not to sympathize with him. If his life was difficult enough without Becky and the kids, maybe he would start to realize how lucky he was.

Then again, if Rick turned him away now, who knows what might happen? Where would he go? What would he do? No matter what their differences over the years, they were still brothers. That had to mean something.

There was just no easy answer.

Rick swallowed hard before speaking. "You're welcome to stay here as long as you like. You'll have to sleep on the couch...."

"That would be great. Really."

Rick continued as though there had been no interruption. "Just keep this in mind."

He stood and walked to a position in front of Daniel before continuing. "I hope you realize how lucky you are. Becky's a good person, Dan, and those two kids of yours are great. If you screw this up now, you're liable to regret it. Now, and for the rest of your life."

Rick turned and left the room, not bothering to gauge his brother's reaction. After all, Daniel was a big boy. Let him face up to reality.

Chapter Twenty-Five:

SITTING IN THE CAR, STARING AT THE building across the parking lot, Daniel felt isolated somehow. The insulated cocoon of the car's interior shielded him from the worst of the traffic noises around him, stranding him in the private world of his own thoughts. In the silence his mind screamed at him, pleading, as he wondered again just what he was doing here.

No answer came to him.

The logical part of his brain told him what he was doing made no sense. There was no reasonable explanation for why he was here. No good could come of this. Yet here he was just the same. As though some inner urging, some animal instinct he could no longer control, was guiding his actions, and he was an unwelcome participant being manipulated against his every desire.

He continued his perusal. The building's appearance was drab, the illuminated beer signs in the windows failing to bestow anything in the way of either light or warmth. The dirty white paint of the exterior walls had blistered and peeled with age; the wood of the front door was worn smooth by the multitudes passing through the portal. His eyes lighted on the garish neon sign above the doorway, announcing the establishment: *PAPA JOE'S.*

Daniel glanced at his watch. In the ten minutes he had sat there only six people had entered the bar, while one couple had departed. Not much business for a Saturday, though it was early evening. Maybe things didn't pick up until after dark.

He shifted in his seat, uncomfortable, yet hesitant to step from the car. He tried to remember what Jackie looked like. It had been two weeks since he'd seen her, sitting across the table from him at the restaurant. He recalled the cut of her chin, and the soft curves of her cheekbones, and the way her short blond hair was cropped neatly above the collar. There was no denying her attractiveness. The T-shirt she had worn, though doing little to enhance her figure, had failed in the least to conceal it.

She had seemed the quiet type, withdrawn, adding little to the conversation, as though she preferred to keep her thoughts to herself. Her attitude imparted an aura of mystery that compelled Daniel to find out more. In the past two weeks her image kept returning to his mind, drawing him forward with a recklessness he never before realized he possessed. It brought out a part of him he couldn't begin to understand.

The air in the car was beginning to cool. Daniel pulled his coat tighter, blew on his bare hands, and considered removing the keys from his coat pocket. It would be so easy. Just start the car and drive away from this place, and forget everything about it.

Forget everything about Jackie Somerset.

The easiest thing in the world to do - the best thing in the world to do - was to go back to Becky, tell her what a fool he had been, and beg her to forgive him, so they could get their world back together again. It was the sensible course, and Daniel couldn't think of a single reason why he shouldn't follow through on the idea.

"What the hell."

He stepped from the car, the crunch of hard snow beneath his boots sounding distinct and clear in the sub-freezing air, and headed for the entrance to the bar.

Jackie sat immobile, aware that Rachel's eyes were upon her. She knew Rachel would say something. It was just a matter of time. For three minutes they sat in silence, the car's engine purring on, as though in anticipation of making a speedy getaway. Occasionally Rachel would turn away, glancing over at the building in front of them, her face taking on a reddish tinge from the neon glare.

"So you gonna sit there all night?" Rachel asked at last.

"I don't want to go in there."

Rachel took a quick look around. "I don't see Brad's car anywhere."

"What if he shows up?"

"I thought you said he was working late today?"

"What if I'm wrong?"

Rachel reached out, touching Jackie on the sleeve. "I don't know what's goin' on here, but you're starting to scare me. Just what happened between you and Brad, anyway?"

Jackie swallowed hard, holding back the words. "I can't tell you."

Rachel made to protest, but Jackie continued before anything could be said. "It's just something me and Brad have to work out on our own. All right?"

For a moment their eyes met. Jackie wanted more than anything else to tell Rachel all about it, and Rachel was obviously willing to hear her out. But it just didn't seem fair to Brad. After all, Rachel had such bad feelings about him to begin with. What would she think if Jackie told her what had been going on?

And then there was Rachel's attitude - that holier-than-thou way she had of pointing out a person's mistakes. Jackie didn't feel she could put up with that. Not now. Not after everything else.

She tried to make light of the situation, aware that her voice failed to conceal her anxiety. "I appreciate your concern, Rachel. I really do. But it's not that big of a deal. So let's just leave it alone. Okay?"

"If that's what you want." Indecision painted Rachel's features, as her gaze wavered between Jackie and *Papa Joe's*. "But I really would like to stop in." Rachel lifted her hand, examining the sparkle from the ring adorning her finger. "I just want to.... You know.... Show off a bit to some of the regulars."

Jackie managed a smile. "Of course you do. Who can blame you?"

"Then you'll come in with me?"

"Sure." Jackie swallowed hard. "What are friends for, anyway?"

"Great." Rachel switched off the engine. "I promise we'll be in and out before you know it. What could possibly go wrong?"

"Another beer, Mac?"

Daniel looked up from his drink as the bartender approached. In the hour he had sat there he'd gone through four beers and who knew how many bowls of popcorn. Never much of a drinker, Daniel realized he would pay in the morning for tonight's indiscretion. His head was beginning to feel a bit woozy already, but that only made it easier to sit there and waste the night away. What did he have to go home to, anyway?

"Sure," Daniel slurred. "I'll have 'nother."

The bartender departed, returning with another glass of brew. "You waiting for someone, buddy?"

Daniel waved the question aside. "No. No one." He took a sip from the new drink, mumbling into the foam. "No one at all."

Vaguely aware of movement beside him, Daniel failed to register the person who wandered over to sit down on the stool next to him. His eyes remained as focused as possible on the rows of bottles behind the bar, the labels blending into a blur of colors, everything around him disappearing in a misty haze of uncertainty. He was finding it harder to concentrate.

"What are you doing here, Dan?"

He almost missed the words, the quiet tone of the delivery barely intruding on his thoughts, but the voice sounded familiar. Straightening up, he swiveled to face Jackie Somerset.

She was every bit as attractive as he had remembered, and

Daniel smiled at the sight. He felt better just having her next to him.

Her feelings were obviously different than his. Her look was intense, a cross between anger and pity. She spoke again, not allowing him time to answer. "You shouldn't have come here."

A hundred words floated through his mind. He selected a sentence at random, barely aware of what he was saying. "I wanted to see you again."

"Damn." She turned away for a moment, not allowing him to see the anger melting from her face. In spite of herself she smiled. It was a nice change of pace to have someone show an interest in her.

Taking a moment to rummage through her purse, Jackie removed a pack of cigarettes and a worn book of matches. She lit up, took a deep breath, and expelled slowly the blue wisps of smoke. It helped to strengthen her, fortifying her will for the task ahead. She faced Daniel again.

"You have to leave," she told him.

"Why?"

"Because I want you to."

"Really?"

"Yes," Jackie lied.

For a long moment nothing was said. Daniel stared into the deep blue of her eyes, searching for a meaning behind the words, but came up with no solution.

Jackie turned away, embarrassed with his open admiration of her. She felt her hand begin to tremble, and deposited her cigarette in the ashtray on the bar. She didn't look at him - afraid to meet his gaze - though her voice became more sympathetic. "Listen, Dan. I'm flattered that you wanted to see me. I really am. But I don't want to get in trouble."

She took a quick look around, to see whether anyone had noticed them. Rachel sat at a table in the corner, surrounded by a half-dozen or so people fawning over her engagement ring. Across the room, Marge was fiddling with the jukebox, scanning the list of titles. The others in the room were occupied as well, lost in their own concerns. No one took any interest in Jackie or the man sitting at the bar next to her.

Even so, she couldn't help feeling apprehensive. Everything just felt wrong. "It's not a good idea for us to be seen together. Okay?"

Something clicked in the back of his mind, and, in imitation of her, Daniel took a moment to survey the surroundings. He caught sight of nothing out of the ordinary, and returned his attention to her.

"Boyfriend?"

She nodded.

"But that's not why I'm here. I mean...." His thoughts running in a confused jumble, he did his best to concentrate. The alcohol in his system made the task a trying one. He needed to explain to Jackie why he was there. Why it was so important that he see her and talk to her. But before he could do that, he needed to understand the urge himself.

He finally settled for a weak explanation. "I just wanted to see you, that's all."

"Why?" A trace of her initial anger returned. "Why did you want to see me?"

The question frightened him, and he turned away a moment to hide his indecision. "I just wanted to talk to someone. That's all. I thought you might be a good person to talk to."

Jackie reached out, her fingers landing softly against his left hand. His wedding band glowed dull in the room's dim light, but it caught her eye nonetheless. She rotated the ring. The action focused Daniel's attention, and she stopped, her point made.

"Go home to your wife, Dan. That's the best thing for both of us."

"Yeah. I guess you're right."

His legs a bit wobbly, Daniel stood from the stool. "I'm sorry if I caused you any trouble. I didn't mean to." He felt he should say more, but the words eluded him. "Oh, what the hell."

Jackie made no reply. Embarrassed with the situation, she turned away, the sound of footsteps dying off as he shuffled away.

Chapter Twenty-Six:

PAUSING IN THE DOORWAY, HIS FACE devoid of emotion, Brad Wilkens surveys the room, his eyes the cold gray of dead winter. He sees Rachel first, sitting at a table in the corner, but shows no interest in the activity surrounding her. His head turns, continuing his visual circuit, and comes to rest facing the row of worn stools at the bar.

It takes a moment only to locate Jackie, who leans close to the man beside her, touching his hand. They face away from Brad, making it impossible to detect their expressions. They speak in whispers, the words failing to carry to the doorway. The man gets up to leave as Brad steps forward.

Halting, Brad waits as the stranger passes, heading for the door and out into the darkening evening. Brad hesitates, taking a step to follow, then changes his mind. He makes instead for the bar and sits next to Jackie in the recently vacated stool, reaching out for her hand.

The action startles her. She turns, a smile on her face.

The expression evaporates at sight of Brad.

He makes no attempt to keep his voice down. "What the hell's going on here?"

Jackie hesitates, uncertainty clouding her features. She worries her lower lip but remains silent.

Brad stands. "I asked you what's going on?"

Her figure seems to collapse, shrinking away from him. "Nothing. Nothing's going on."

"Who was he?"

"I don't know. Just some guy...."

He steps forward, grabbing her upper arm and pulling her so she sits precariously balanced on the edge of the stool. Jackie tries to resist, but Brad might as well be made of stone for what little affect she has on him.

"Don't be giving me none of that shit. Who was he?"

"I don't know. Just some guy I met once before. It's not important."

"Goddamn." Brad turns away for a moment, glancing at the door, then returns his attention to Jackie. "He's the one you met at the restaurant. When I was out of town."

Jackie says nothing, the look in her eyes betraying the answer. A hushed silence grips the smoky room, all eyes by now attracted to the scene.

Jackie squirms, but Brad only increases his hold. "It wasn't anything, Brad," she manages. "Really."

Rachel approaches. "Leave her alone, Brad."

Brad's eyes remain locked on Jackie. "Stay the fuck out of this, Rachel. It's none of your business." He hesitates a moment, then releases Jackie in a shove that pushes her against the bar. "I'll deal with you later."

Six long strides take him to the doorway. He passes through, the panel slamming shut behind him. A moment later the tension breaks, the crowd reacting as one as they follow Jackie to the door.

The alcohol has done its work. Daniel walks in a slow, leisurely fashion, his movements uncertain. He takes a deep breath as he reaches his car. He stops to look around, taking in the surroundings.

A slamming door catches his attention, and he turns back toward *Papa Joe's*.

A man in his mid-twenties approaches, heading purposely forward. For several seconds Daniel shows no reaction, but then it becomes clear the stranger is coming for him. Daniel backs away from the car, his hands lifting in a gesture of confusion.

"What's going on...?"

Brad is in striking distance by now. "You son-of-a-bitch!"

The fist lashes out, catching Daniel across the chin. His head jerks back, the unexpectedness of the blow sending him to the pavement as blood trickles from the gash in his lower lip. On hands and knees beside his car, his fingers numb from the snow and ice, Daniel shakes his head, attempting to clear his senses. The next moment two hands grab his coat collar and yank him to his feet.

Brad slams Daniel against the car, the mirror catching him in the side. Daniel barely has time to grimace in pain before something hard and metallic jabs into his stomach.

His eyes open wide at sight of the .45 automatic. The blue steel of the handgun looks colder than the ice on the nearby cars. Brad maintains a grip on Daniel's collar with his left hand while his right pushes the automatic's barrel deeper into the folds of Daniel's coat. The expression on Brad's face is one of bestial rage. His voice is coarse. "What's the idea of screwing around with Jackie?"

"I wasn't...." Fear animates Daniel's eyes, his voice cracking. "I mean...."

"Save it, asshole. I don't want to hear none of it."

The gun shifts, coming to rest beneath Daniel's chin, forcing his head backwards. Daniel closes his eyes against the pain.

Brad leans closer. "I can't think of one reason why I shouldn't blow your fucking brains out right now. Can you?"

It's obvious Daniel wants to reply, but finds it difficult to do so with the barrel jammed against his jaw. For a moment they stand in silence, locked in their embrace.

"Brad."

Jackie steps closer and raises her voice.

"Brad!"

His gun hand remaining immobile, Brad faces this newest distraction. "You stay the fuck out of this!"

She takes another step, her motion hesitant with fear.

"Let's think about this for a moment, Brad. You don't want to do anything you'll regret later, now do you?"

Brad's eyes shift. Behind Jackie a small crowd has gathered, spilling out from the bar, expectation high on their faces. For a moment nothing is said. No movement transpires.

At last Brad pulls the gun away. Daniel breathes again, his figure relaxing. Brad smiles, a half-leer of insincerity, while holding his hands out in mock apology. "Hey. No hard feelings, right?"

Quick to agree, Daniel nods.

A snarl crosses Brad's face as he continues. "Like hell, man."

Brad swings his arm in a short arc, the barrel of the gun catching Daniel across the cheek. Daniel's head slams against the car going down, a moan of pain escaping his lips. He lands hard against the ice and makes no further movement.

As though he hasn't a care in the world Brad walks over to Jackie. The automatic disappears into an inside pocket of his coat. "Let's get out of here."

He takes two more steps before realizing Jackie hasn't moved.

"What the hell are you waiting for? I said we're getting out of here."

She says nothing, defiantly glaring at him, though it's obvious from her stiff posture that her strength is a momentary thing. Her legs appear wobbly, her body shakes from something more than cold.

A single step brings him within striking distance. He raises his hand, as if to slap her, but at the last minute decides instead to grab her arm. "Come on."

"No!" She struggles against him, leaning back with her full body weight in resistance. "I'm not going anywhere with you, Brad. Not now. Not ever."

"You stupid bitch. I ought to...."

His sentence is left incomplete, the unexpected blow to his back forcing air out of his lungs like a drowning man gasping for breath. He has no option but to release his grip on Jackie as he lurches forward. Managing to grab the handle of a nearby car for support, he prevents himself from hitting the ground. In a second he is composed. He whirls about to meet his assailant.

Daniel stands beside Jackie, arms stiff before him, fists held tight together. His legs are spread, providing a firm stance for support. Blood runs from a gash in his cheek, the bright red liquid forming miniature rosettes as it splashes to the dirty snow at his feet.

His eyes glare as he speaks through clenched teeth. "I don't think the young lady wants to go with you."

Brad makes no answer, pondering his next move. He looks toward the crowd, as though seeking support. No sympathy can be found in the faces staring at him. Jackie shuffles sideways, to a position just to the right and slightly behind her defender.

Daniel remains motionless, poised for action.

For a long minute no sound is heard, the stalemate undecided.

"Fuck it." Brad kicks at the ice, dislodging a few pebbles, and turns away.

Jackie approaches Daniel, resting her arm lightly against his shoulder. He makes no response as he watches Brad get in his car and drive off. By then the two of them are alone in the parking lot, the other patrons having abandoned the cold for the warmth and security of the barroom.

Chapter Twenty-Seven:

SHE FELT ABANDONED. DESERTED. SHE knew it was crazy. Watching Brad drive off in his car should have brought a sense of relief to her. A sense of freedom.

Instead she felt alone.

Jackie had never realized how much she relied on Brad's strength. How comforting it was to know he was there for her. Now, with him gone, it was like a part of her life had been torn away. An impulse swept over her, to go running after the Camaro before Brad could get too far away, but she managed to squash the urge. She knew it was the wrong thing to do.

Besides, there were other matters that needed attending to.

Jackie turned toward Daniel. He stood staring into space, seemingly oblivious to what he had just been through. The gash across his cheek had stopped bleeding by now. The blood had frozen into a ragged black line that ran from the bridge of his nose to the middle of his chin. The skin around the tear was turning a dark red - nearly purple. It was an ugly feature, reminding her of those grotesque decorations people apply to themselves at Halloween time. Only this wasn't theatrical paste and cosmetic paint. This was real.

Jackie didn't want to look at it, but she made herself do so. She forced a smile, as though all was right in the world and there wasn't a thing to worry about.

Retrieving a tissue from her coat pocket, she leaned against him to dab at his cheek.

Daniel flinched in pain.

"Sorry." She withdrew her hand, feeling like she had done something wrong. "Are you all right?"

"Yeah. Just great." A weariness had settled upon him. Now that the crisis was ended his body relaxed with fatigue.

Short, unsteady steps brought him to the side of his car, which he rested against for the support it offered. Everything around him seemed to be spinning. An obscene light from the back of his head was forcing itself forward, further muddling things, confusing the already murky picture in his mind of what had just occurred.

Too much to drink. Shake it off, Daniel.

It felt better to look at Jackie. To see the concern on her face. Though something about her seemed different now. She looked for all the world like one of those waifs charities picture in an attempt to loosen the old purse strings, lost and alone in a cruel, uncaring world. Like she had just been abandoned by her best friend.

"How about you?" he finally asked. "Are you hurt?"

"No. I'm okay, I guess. I just feel so bad about.... Well, you know."

"Yeah. I know." He shook his head, which failed to clear his senses in the least, and regretted even that small movement. "That's quite a boyfriend you've got there."

"Brad's something, all right. Has a lot of energy. Though he does tend to over-react."

"That's putting it mildly." Daniel reached for his cheek, tenderly placing his fingers against the flesh. It felt numb, but whether from pain or cold he couldn't say. A dollop of dried blood came away on his fingertips. "I'd hate to see him if we had really done anything."

Jackie smiled, but the expression quickly passed, replaced with a look of concern. "That's quite a gash you've got there. Maybe you better have it looked at."

He attempted to smile through the pain. "I'm sure I'll be okay once I get it washed off. I don't think it's as bad as it looks."

"Well, it looks pretty bad." She hesitated, uncertain what was expected of her. Daniel remained slumped against the car, as though grateful for the support it offered. "You think you can make it home all right?"

"I don't know. I feel sort of woozy."

"I'd offer to drive you, but.... You know.... It might look sort of funny."

"What do you mean?"

"It's just that...." She nearly bit her lip, to stop the flow of words, but his expression prompted her to continue. "What will your wife say?"

He hesitated.

Jackie thought he hadn't heard her at first, and was about to repeat her query, when he reluctantly responded.

"I doubt if she'd notice," Daniel finally answered. "I'm not staying at my house right now."

"Oh?"

It was obvious she was curious, but the last thing Daniel wanted to talk about was his problems. "It's not important." He opened the car door and plopped down behind the steering wheel, pausing for a moment to watch the speckles of light flashing before his eyes. They dissipated after a few seconds, though the dizziness remained, and he found himself grabbing at the wheel to stop the world from spinning. "I'll be okay," he mumbled.

Then, more to himself than to her: "At least, I think I will be."

Jackie felt obligated to do something for him. She owed it to him. She just wished she didn't feel so damn uncomfortable about the whole thing. The guy was practically old enough to be her father!

And then there was Brad to consider.

"Wait here," she said at last, with a sinking sense of resignation.

"Why?"

"Just give me a minute to let Rachel know I'm leaving. I'll

be right back."

"What do you mean?"

She sighed in exasperation. "I mean, I can't let you leave like this. Not in this condition. It wouldn't be safe. You can come to my place. Just for tonight, you understand."

Jackie gave him a few seconds to protest, in the hopes that she wouldn't have to follow through on her offer, but he said nothing. Committed to the task, she would just have to make the best of it.

He watched her head back to the bar. With an effort Daniel removed his key ring, inserted the key in the ignition, and slid over to the passenger's seat. It felt good to lean back against the headrest and close his eyes. Just for a minute, anyway. Long enough for Jackie to get back to the car.

Jackie had to wake him when they got to her apartment. Daniel was exhausted. His face felt on fire, a searing line crossing his cheek, tracing the path the gun barrel had carved on his flesh. He seemed to be having trouble navigating, like he was no longer in control of his faculties. He was certain he wouldn't be able to function on his own.

By leaning against Jackie he managed to make it up the stairs to her flat.

By the time she brought a pillow and blanket out to him he was asleep on the couch. Fetching a washrag damp with warm water, she carefully cleansed his cheek, touching the damaged flesh with short little dabs. From time to time he would flinch, but she managed the procedure without waking him.

He looked much better afterwards. The skin had only punctured in one small area, most of the wound consisting of a vivid red bruise. It almost seemed to accent his features, highlighting the masculine aspects of his face, bringing out a rugged handsomeness Jackie hadn't noticed before.

A smile graced her face as she took a final look at him before shutting off the overhead light.

Chapter Twenty-Eight: Sunday, December 27, 2015

DANIEL AWOKE TO THE SMELL OF steaming coffee and the sound of sizzling bacon. He could hear movement from the other room, the rattle of dishes and silverware being shuffled about. It all seemed familiar to him. Just a typical Sunday morning.

The feeling of normalcy disappeared when he opened his eyes. Daniel blinked twice, taking in the cheap prints on the walls and the worn carpeting on the floor. He sat up, flinging off the blanket, and felt a jolt run through his head. The sensation brought to mind in vivid detail the night before.

"Oh, God," he mumbled, the words slurring from his lips. He grabbed the sides of his head, hoping the pain would abate some, but the headache refused to cooperate. He was with it for the duration.

Footsteps approached and Jackie entered the room. With her frayed jeans and T-shirt she looked barely older than his daughter. The tail of the shirt was tied in a knot above her waistline, exposing a few inches of midriff, at the same time pulling the material tightly against her breasts.

Daniel felt suddenly uncomfortable and turned his head away.

"How'd you sleep?" she began, her tone cheery.

"Great," he mumbled to the floor. "Just great."

Walking up to him, Jackie cupped his chin in her hand and

twisted his head ever-so-slightly, exposing the side of his face to the light. "Don't look half bad today."

Daniel said nothing. Her touch was gentle, a delicate caress that comforted him.

The feeling disappeared as she drew away. "There's some aspirin in the bathroom. If your head's feeling sort of...." She made a winding motion with her finger. "You know."

"Yeah. I think I could use some."

"Breakfast will be in about fifteen minutes. If you want to take a shower or anything...."

"Thanks. I think I will."

The water felt refreshing running down his chest. He kept the stream cool, closing his eyes and burying his face beneath the flow so the cleansing liquid ran through his hair and down his back. It stung against his cheek, but he didn't care. The shower revived him, bringing a sensation of normalcy.

His clothes felt soiled putting them on. They smelled of beer and cigarettes - souvenirs of *Papa Joe's* - but he had no choice in the matter but to wear them. By the time he was fully dressed he felt like he could use another shower.

The scrambled eggs were just right, not too runny, with just a touch of brown around the edges. Jackie scraped them from the frying pan into a large bowl. Daniel entered the room as she set the bowl on the table.

"You look a lot better now," she confided.

"Thanks. I feel better." He stood a moment, as though uncertain what to do next.

Jackie, noting his confusion, pushed a plate toward him. "Have a seat. Coffee's almost ready. How do you like it?"

"Milk and sugar."

She fixed two cups then sat down beside him.

Daniel waited for her to start eating before saying anything. "You didn't have to go to all this trouble for me."

"What trouble?"

"All this." His waving hand indicated the breakfast she had prepared. "And letting me stay here. You didn't have to do this, you know."

"Sure I did. If you hadn't been there last night, to stop Brad...." She halted in mid-sentence, biting her lip. Had she said too much already?

"What do you suppose he would have done?"

"I don't know." Her voice quieted, her gaze lowering. "I thought I knew him, but lately...." She considered a moment longer. "It's hard to tell."

"Why do you put up with it?"

She struggled to hold back the tears. "What am I supposed to do? Fight back? You saw what Brad's like."

"There must be something you can do about it. File a restraining order...."

Jackie stood, moving to the stove, turning away so she wouldn't have to look at him. "Yeah. Like Brad's going to obey a restraining order." She took a deep breath, satisfied the tears would not make an appearance after all, and faced Daniel once more. "Listen. I appreciate your concern. But it's my problem. I'll figure out some way to work things out."

She turned back toward the stove.

"Anyway," she continued, with a trace of irritation in her voice, "it's your fault Brad was so pissed off."

"My fault?"

"Yeah. If you hadn't shown up at the bar last night, Brad wouldn't have been in such a bad mood. What were you doing there, anyway?"

Daniel's mind flashed back. Surely it was more than twelve hours since he'd been sitting on the bar stool next to Jackie? It seemed like a lifetime ago.

Somebody else's lifetime.

It had seemed like the right thing to do at the time. Later, when that crazy boyfriend of hers had him pushed up against the car with a gun shoved into his chin, Daniel had plenty of opportunity to reconsider his actions.

Jackie was still waiting for an answer. Daniel collected his thoughts, attempting to put them into words. "Life's been kind of mixed-up lately. At home. At work."

"That's not a reason. Sounds more like an excuse to me."

"Maybe it is. Maybe I've just been feeling sorry for myself lately. Things go wrong and you can't shake the feeling that it's all your fault. If only you had done something differently"

Jackie shook her head. "Doesn't work that way. You think I asked for this? You think I want Brad to be beating me up? It's like they say. Life's a bitch. What you gonna do about it?"

The words effectively ended the chance of further conversation. Breakfast lapsed into comparative silence, the only sound the subdued sound of two people eating.

Daniel found himself hurrying, anxious to be done and out of there. After all, Jackie was only being polite to him. He had done her a favor last night, and she was returning one this morning. They were even now, the score one to one, and the best thing to do was to clear out of her life. It had been stupid of him to look her up at the bar. He should have known better than to stick his nose where it didn't belong. He was lucky to even *have* a nose anymore to stick anywhere, considering Brad's behavior.

The coffee had cooled considerably by now, and Daniel downed a deep gulp. No sense dragging things out further.

"I really should be going." He pushed himself away from the table. "Thanks for everything."

She jumped to her feet. "Any time."

Jackie brushed against him as they left the room. She made her way to a closet, where she retrieved his coat. "Here's your things."

Daniel scratched his head. "I must have really been out of it last night. I don't even remember taking my coat off."

"You didn't. I came out after you fell asleep. You looked sort of hot. I hope you don't mind."

"No. I appreciate it." His mind wandered a moment, picturing Jackie bent over him in the middle of the night. What had she been wearing? What would have happened had he waken up then?

Daniel forced the image aside. He dressed in silence, feeling more should be said, but without a clue as to what it could be. He had expected something from her, some sort of revelation or explanation or who-the-hell knew what, and it hadn't come. Daniel realized it wasn't her fault. His expectations had gotten the best of him, pushing him into a situation where he didn't belong.

He just wished everything didn't have to be so awkward.

"Goodbye, Dan."

He grunted something in reply and began trudging down the stairs to the front entrance. His hand was on the knob when Jackie felt the urge to say something. She nearly ignored the idea, deliberating over the usefulness of it, but her impulse got the better of her.

"Dan!" She had to raise her voice, to be certain he heard.

"Yes?" Expectation showed on his face.

Jackie smiled. "I was just wondering.... Do you have any plans for Thursday night?"

"Thursday night?"

"Yeah. You know. New Year's Eve?" Daniel remained silent. *God, he wasn't making this any easier.* She continued, the words gushing forth. "You're welcome to stop in. That is, if you're not doing anything."

"Really?"

"Really."

"Thanks. I'd like that."

Daniel stepped into the cold, the door closing softly behind him, and Jackie slumped back against the wall. A smile graced her face. *So would I.*

Chapter Twenty-Nine:

THE CAMARO IS PARKED AT THE CURB. Brad slouches behind the steering wheel, scrutinizing the lights from Jackie's apartment across the street. He has been there for hours, the car's engine extinguished the entire time. He seems oblivious to the cold, unaware of the passing of time, an intentness of purpose driving him as he endures his silent vigil.

The door opens across the street and Daniel steps out, pulling the collar of his coat tighter against the cold. He looks neither right nor left. Ducking his head, he rushes to his car, jumps in, and the motor springs to life. The car idles for two or three minutes while Daniel scrapes ice from the windshield.

Brad's hand reaches over to the passenger's seat, the fingers entwining around the grip of the Smith & Wesson .45 sitting on the leather. His gaze doesn't waver as he pulls the automatic closer. With a steady motion he lifts the handgun. He sights along the barrel. His eyes squint against the glare of snow outside. Breathing pauses.

"You son-of-a-bitch." The words are harsh, with deadly intent.

For thirty seconds he is motionless. Then he replaces the .45 on the seat beside him.

Daniel is in his car by now. Brad watches him pull away, but makes no attempt to follow.

His head turns, looking up at the front window of Jackie's apartment. He hesitates. Deliberating.

Finally he starts the engine and pulls away from the curb.

Chapter Thirty:

"I'M HUNGRY, MOM. WHEN ARE WE GONNA eat?"

Becky looked up from her book. It must have been at least the fifteenth interruption of the morning, but she managed to keep a smile on her face, trying her best to disguise the irritation she felt. "How can you be hungry? You just had breakfast an hour ago."

Jeff considered for a moment before shrugging his shoulders. "I don't know. But I'm still hungry."

"Well, you'll just have to wait."

Jeff slumped away, his disappointment obvious. He passed his sister in the hallway. Usually they exchanged comments, or at least the scathing looks siblings routinely save for one another, but nothing passed between them. It had been that way since yesterday morning.

When Daniel left.

Lisa entered and plopped down on the couch beside her mother.

Becky set her book down. "I suppose you're hungry, too?"

Lisa shook her head and forced a weak smile. "I'm not the one with the bottomless pit for a stomach. Remember?"

"He does manage to put the food away, doesn't he?"

"You think Dad will call today?"

The change of topic caught Becky by surprise. "Why do you ask?"

"He said he would yesterday, and he didn't. Do you think

something happened to him?"

"Of course not. I'm sure he's all right."

"Then why didn't he call?"

"He probably just got busy, that's all."

"Will he be coming back? To live with us?"

Becky pondered the question before answering. It had been the hardest thing in the world to do, telling Daniel to leave. It seemed so unfair to him. And to the kids.

And to herself.

She realized he was going through a difficult time. The accident at the foundry had affected him in ways she couldn't begin to understand, increasing the widening rift between them. She had tried to be understanding, and sympathetic, and everything a good wife should be, but it didn't change things. There was nothing she could do to help him. He seemed determined to face it alone.

Becky couldn't afford to be so self-centered. It wasn't fair of Daniel to drag her and the kids down with him. She hoped he would get over it, and come to his senses, before the situation deteriorated to the point where there was no fixing it. Until then, since he insisted on doing things on his own, that was the way it would have to be.

Would she welcome him back at that point?

"I don't know," Becky replied, to answer Lisa's spoken question and her own private thoughts. "Your father needs time right now. To be by himself." She smiled, but Lisa failed to reciprocate. "Everything will be okay, Princess."

Lisa made no reply, not even to remind her mother not to call her Princess.

The chiming of the front doorbell intruded. "I'll get it!" Jeff called.

A minute later he was back in the room. "Mom? There's some lady at the door. Wants to talk to Dad."

"I'll take care of it," she told him.

Becky opened the front door and was greeted by an

attractive blonde standing on the front steps. Her clothes were perfection, and she wore them as though they'd been tailored for her.

"Becky?"

"That's right." The woman looked vaguely familiar. "Do I know you?"

"Teri Stone." No recognition. "From CONSOLIDATED?"

The light went off in Becky's head. "Of course! I'm sorry, Teri. Guess it's been so long I didn't recognize you. Won't you come in?"

Teri entered the hallway, Becky closing the door against the coldness sneaking in behind them. "We can go in the other room if you'd like."

"I can't really stay long," Teri replied. "And I apologize for dropping in unannounced. Especially on a Sunday."

"That's okay. We weren't doing anything special."

"Is Daniel home?"

"He's...." Becky hesitated, debating just how much she should say. "He's out right now. Over at his brother's. Is there something you needed to see him about?"

"I just wanted to let him know how Michael Blake's doing. He's coming home from the hospital today."

"That's great! Oh, I'm so glad. Daniel will be pleased to hear." Maybe it would even bring him to his senses. "Michael must be doing better, then?"

"A bit. He's still a long way from back to normal. The hospital wanted to send him to Lake Park, at Flower Hospital, for rehab and physical therapy, but Amy insisted he come home. Said she didn't want to start the new year with him in the hospital."

"I hope she can handle things all right by herself."

"From what I hear, she's getting a lot of help through the church they attend. They even managed to scrounge up some in-home nursing care for Michael."

"Even so, it still must be pretty hard on her."

Teri nodded in agreement but said nothing. An awkward silence intruded. Becky had the distinct impression there was more Teri wanted to say, but it was as though she felt too uncomfortable to bring it up.

"Was there something else?" Becky prompted.

"I was just wondering. How's Daniel doing? We haven't heard from him since.... You know, since it happened. We all figured he'd let us know by now what was going on."

"We've been pretty busy here, with Christmas and all."

"But Daniel's okay?"

"Oh, sure," she lied. "Couldn't be better."

The sound of Teri Stone's car pulling away from the house had barely faded when Becky retrieved her cellphone from her purse. Accessing the contact information, she skimmed down the list of names. Her finger wavered over the miniature image of her husband smiling at her. She hesitated, as if seeing the picture for the first time. She noticed the cut of his hair. And the stern look in his eyes, even though he attempted to smile.

It still felt too soon. She wasn't ready for this. She scrolled further down the list, stopping at her brother-in-laws' number.

Rick answered on the first ring.

"Hello?"

"Hi, Rick." Becky thought she detected some apprehension in his voice, but she could have been wrong. Maybe she had just caught him at a bad time. "I was wondering how Daniel was doing."

"Then why call me?"

"I don't know. It just seemed...." She paused, searching for the appropriate word. "Safer. To talk to you first, I mean."

"You really need to talk to him, Beck. This is between the two of you."

"I know. I know."

An awkward silence lingered as she struggled with what to say. "Can you put him on for a minute?"

Rick was slow in answering. Or maybe she was just imagining things. "Sorry, Beck," his voice came at last. "He's not here right now."

"Oh?"

"Yeah. He just stepped out. I think he said he was going to get some donuts or something. Was there something you wanted to tell him?"

"Just let him know Michael Blake's coming home from the hospital today."

"Will do. Anything else?"

"No. I guess that's it."

"So how are you doing, Beck."

"Fine. Okay, I guess. Listen, I really have to be going. Just tell Daniel I called. Okay?"

"Will do."

The line went dead as he hung up.

For a moment Becky failed to react. Then a feeling washed over her; a feeling that she was all alone in the world. She felt an intense desire to be with her children. Replacing the receiver, she headed back to Lisa and Jeff's rooms.

Chapter Thirty-One:

AS SOON AS HE HUNG UP THE PHONE RICK began pacing the room. He hated to lie to Becky, but he hated even more to tell her the truth - that he had no idea where Daniel was. She had enough on her mind as it was.

It hadn't worried him to come home last night and find Daniel's car gone. Daniel had fidgeted all day, roaming from room to room as though in a trance. The restlessness had grown as the day progressed. Rick left in the afternoon, to catch up on some shopping, and he suspected Daniel hadn't bothered sticking around for long after his departure.

It wasn't until this morning, when there was still no sign of his brother, that Rick became concerned. There was no denying Daniel wasn't in the proper frame of mind lately. Who knew what stupid things he was capable of doing?

Rick was still contemplating the possibilities forty-five minutes later when his brother walked in the house.

"Well, well. Look what the cat dragged in."

Daniel made no reply as he shucked off his boots and hung up his coat. Taking care to avert his face, he passed Rick in the hallway. Daniel headed for the kitchen, where he took a mug from the cupboard and poured himself some coffee. He was sitting at the table, drink raised to his lips, by the time Rick joined him.

Rick stood in the doorway, glaring disapproval. "So aren't you going to say anything?"

"About what?" Daniel asked, his tone the picture of

innocence.

"Let's not be playing twenty questions, all right? I'm not a kid anymore, Dan."

"You're not my keeper, either."

"Don't you think I have a right to know what you're up to?"

"Why? Because I'm staying at your house?"

"That's one reason."

"I can leave anytime you like."

"Damn it, Daniel. Cut the crap."

"No, Rick. You cut the crap." Daniel's tone, in contrast to his words, was calm and cool. They could have been discussing the weather for all the feeling Daniel displayed. He seemed isolated from the conversation, as though his mind was preoccupied elsewhere. "You're not my personal nursemaid, Rick. I appreciate you letting me stay here. I really do. But that doesn't give you the right to get involved with my problems."

"I get it now. You're pulling the big brother shtick here. No sense talking to Rick. What does he know? He's just a kid. Is that it?"

Daniel made no reply as he sipped from his mug.

Rick plopped into a chair, shaking his head. His voice, which had started to rise in anger, was more subdued by now. He could have been talking to himself. "I just don't understand how someone as smart as you can be so stupid."

"Meaning...?"

"Meaning.... Whatever is bothering you, Dan, you don't have to face it alone. I know I haven't always been there for you. Most of the time it feels like we live in two different worlds. But if I can be any help, just say so."

"You wouldn't understand."

"Try me."

Daniel hesitated, pondering his next words. He took time to sip at his coffee, collecting his thoughts, while Rick hovered on the other side of the table.

"I stayed at a friend's house last night," Daniel admitted,

the words slow in coming.

"Anyone I know?"

"You met her once before."

"HER!" Rick was on his feet. "You spent the night at a woman's house?"

"It's not what you think."

"I don't believe this." Rick turned away, words momentarily evading him. Daniel had always been the sensible one. The reliable one. The type of person who never took chances, and did just what was expected of him.

And now?

"What are you using for brain's these days?" Rick continued, making no attempt to conceal his opinion of the matter. "Or are you doing all your thinking with your pants?"

Now it was Daniel's turn to stand up. Setting his cup on the table, he moved in closer to Rick, anger evident on his face. Rick stepped forward, ready for anything, but his expression changed as he caught a good look at his brother. Rick's hands sought the table surface, to steady himself, as he stared at the raised welt crossing Daniel's cheek. "God, Daniel! What happened to you?"

Daniel's anger evaporated as he turned away, his fingers unconsciously moving to cover the mark. "I ran into a little trouble last night, that's all."

"A *little* trouble? I'd hate to see what you call a *lot* of trouble. You should have someone look at that."

"No. It's okay. Really. Listen, I just had a bad night last night, that's all. I really don't want to talk about it. All right?"

"Yeah. Sure. I understand." Rick nodded his head in sympathy, though his tone lacked any conviction.

Feeling there was nothing more to say, Rick turned to leave. He took three steps down the hallway before changing his mind and facing the kitchen once again. "Oh. By the way. Becky called me earlier."

"What did she have to say?"

"Not much. Just that Michael Blake was coming home

from the hospital today. She thought you might want to know."

Rick took a step away, then added: "Hey. Maybe you should stop over and see how he's doing? That is, if you can drag yourself away from your girlfriend."

Rick left without waiting for his brother's reaction. By then he was beyond caring what Daniel thought about anything.

Chapter Thirty-Two: Thursday, December 31, 2015

"HOW MANY MORE OF THOSE YOU GOT left to run?"

Jeff Black looked up from the drill press as Kenny Jergenson walked up. Kenny was the machine shop's group leader. It fell to him to see that everyone stayed on task. Most of the time he was a decent guy to work with, but some days he was a real pain in the ass.

Today was one of those days.

To Jeff's left was a cardboard box of machined parts. They had been shipped out a week ago but had failed to pass the customer's inspection, so now they were in to be re-worked. Two of the holes were undersized, which meant they had to be set-up in a drilling fixture and reamed to the proper dimension. Jeff had been hard at work all morning on it.

He took a quick guess at how many were left, then looked at the clock. "I'd say I should be done in another half hour."

"Well, let me know as soon as they're done. We want to get them out of here today."

"Speaking of getting out of here.... I was hoping to take off when I'm done."

Kenny gave his best why-are-you-doing-this-to-me look. "I don't know...?"

"Come on, Kenny. It's New Year's Eve. I was hoping to be home by now."

Kenny's eyes lit up, as though he had been let in on a secret. Leaning closer, his voice took on a conspiratorial edge. "Big date tonight, huh? You and Rachel?"

"Yeah. Me and Rachel."

"I still don't see why you had to go and give her that ring. Shit, why buy the cow when you can get the milk for free? Know what I mean?"

As though he had just come up with the most clever line imaginable, Kenny broke into laughter. Jeff forced himself to chuckle along.

"Besides," Jeff continued, after what he assumed was a reasonable interval, "Brad was gonna stop over to my place this afternoon. We figured we might start celebrating a little early."

Kenny still made no sign of committing to an answer. Jeff never could understand why Kenny made such a big deal out of everything. It was like he expected the whole world would fall apart if these parts didn't get out by this afternoon. Jeff suspected what it really got down to was a power thing. Kenny had the authority to boss the other guys around, and he took advantage of it whenever he could.

"So how about it?" Jeff prompted. "Can I take off early?"

"I suppose. Just don't let the boss see you."

"How's he gonna see me? He's not even in today."

"Yeah. Well, sometimes he sneaks in, to see if everyone's working or not. And if he sees you're gone, it will be my ass in a sling, not yours."

"You know what, Kenny? You worry too much."

Kenny moved down the line to the next work station while Jeff stole a quick glance at the clock over the office door. With luck, he'd be out of there by 11:30. He knew Brad was planning on being over by lunch, so that didn't give him much time.

Jeff considered increasing the feed on the drill press, but no sense rushing things and taking a chance on the holes being oversize. Slow and steady was the only way to do it. Jeff would just have to stay at work until the parts were all done.

Chapter Thirty-Three:

THE CAMARO IS SITTING IN FRONT OF Jeff's house when he drives up. Jeff pulls in the driveway, behind his parents' Buick Le Sabre, and Brad steps out of his car. They meet at the steps leading to the wide front porch.

"You kept me waiting long enough," Brad begins. "About time you showed up." It's impossible to tell whether he's angry or just being sarcastic.

Jeff shrugs. "Nothing I could do about it. Had a bunch of parts that needed to be done today."

He unlocks the front door and Brad follows him in. The house has a cold, almost vacant, feel to it. Most of the curtains are closed, the shades pulled down. No lights are turned on.

Brad walks along the hallway, entering the living room off to the left, where he plops onto a sofa. He seems at ease in the surroundings, as though he's spent a lot of time there. "So when are your folks due back from Florida?"

"Two weeks yet. Every year it's the same thing. They leave the week after Thanksgiving and come back the second week of January."

"Must be nice to have this place all to yourself that long. Hell, you and Rachel can do whatever you want."

Jeff shrugs the observation off. "Listen, there's some beer in the fridge. Help yourself. I'm just gonna hop in for a quick shower."

"It better be a quick one. I waited around long enough already today."

*****

Jeff returns to the room twenty minutes later, coming to an abrupt stop as he enters. Brad sits on the sofa, a can of beer on the end table beside him. He holds his .45 automatic, caressing the metal lovingly, as though it was the most important thing in his life. Captivated with the handgun, he fails to detect the new presence in the room.

"I hope that thing's not loaded," Jeff remarks, entering and sitting in a wooden rocking chair across from his friend.

A smile lights Brad's face as he looks up. "Damn right, it's loaded."

"What gives? If you're trying to be funny, I think this is a bit much."

"Nothing funny about it." He sets the gun down on the cushion beside him. His hand continues to fondle the weapon, his fingers running over the grip. "I just want to be ready when I get that bastard alone. I'll teach him not to be screwin' around with Jackie."

"Not this again." Jeff gets up, his frustration obvious, and leaves the room. He returns within a minute, can of beer in hand, and sits once more in the rocker. "So you think this is gonna impress Jackie? Win her back for you?"

"It might."

"God, how stupid can you get."

Brad pulls his attention away from the gun to focus in on Jeff. "What's that supposed to mean?"

"Jackie's bound to come in contact with other guys once in a while. What are you gonna do? Shoot them all?"

"Damn right. If that's what it takes to keep her."

"Keep her?" Jeff, finding humor in the comment, laughs out loud. "Wake up, Brad. Jackie isn't some sort of possession. Like a car or.... Shit, I don't know what. It doesn't work that way. She's a human being."

"Don't hand me that morality crap. Jackie's mine. That's

all there is to it."

"Well, at least one of you thinks that, anyway. You ever consider asking Jackie how she feels about it?"

Jeff pauses to take a swig from his beer. Brad stands, his face tense, his eyes ablaze with fury. "You're being awful fucking bold with your comments. What are you trying to say? That Jackie's not my girl anymore?"

Jeff begins once more to laugh, but the sound stops abruptly as Brad steps toward him. Brad grabs the collar of Jeff's shirt, pulling him closer. "Cut the shit, Jeff. You got something to say about Jackie, you say it."

Bolting from the rocking chair, Jeff brushes Brad aside, taking a step away from him. Where before his expression was one of amusement, it has been replaced now by a look of intense concern. "God, Brad, what's come over you?"

No comment comes as the two glare at one another.

Jeff shakes his head. "I guess this shouldn't surprise me none. Not after that stunt you pulled the other day at *Papa Joe's*."

"Where'd you hear about that?"

"Hell, I lost track of how many people told me what happened. I'm amazed you didn't get your ass thrown in jail, from the way you behaved."

"That bastard had no right screwing around with Jackie."

"God, Brad. Listen to yourself. No right? I just don't understand you sometimes."

"What's to understand?" In an instant, the anger in Brad's tone has evaporated, replaced by a calm, matter-of-fact presence. His entire body appears now to be under control. "A man's got to do what a man's got to do."

"What's that supposed to mean?"

"It means I'm not putting up with this shit anymore. Jackie's got herself a lesson comin'. So does that bastard that's been sniffin' around her."

Jeff shakes his head. "It's over, Brad."

"No."

"Yes it is. Jackie doesn't want anything to do with you anymore. Ask anybody at the bar. They'll tell you. Let it go."

"No!" Brad reaches for the automatic, which still sits on the couch cushion where he left it. "I'll get that bastard." A look of pleasure crosses his face as he picks up the handgun.

He holds it before his face, gazing with open admiration. For a moment, he seems to be addressing the cold metal, and not his friend on the other side of the room. "You just wait and see. We'll show them all."

Brad moves for the doorway. Jeff moves faster, blocking the exit. "You're not gonna shoot anyone, Brad. Give me the gun."

Brad stands motionless, his eyes shifting between the gun in his hand and Jeff, standing not five feet in front of him.

"Give me the gun, Brad."

Brad hesitates, a look of understanding entering his eyes. "You don't think I can do it. You don't think I have the balls to kill someone."

"It's not a question of balls. I just don't think you're stupid enough to screw up the rest of your life over a woman. It's not worth it, Brad."

"I could do it, you know. It's easy."

"Give me the gun."

"All you have to do is aim."

The gun raises.

Jeff takes a step back, fumbling against the door jamb as he makes his way from the living room into the hallway. Any trace of humor is absent now from his face. Comprehension envelopes him, but by then it's too late.

The automatic explodes, a single report, the blast echoing through the house.

Brad takes a step forward, casually looking at the shuddering form on the floor at his feet. Jeff's hands grip his stomach, striving in vain to staunch the flow of blood painting red the carpet beneath him. Pain-etched lines cross his face.

Blood splatters from his mouth as he tries to speak. "You son-of-a-bitch." A dull luster enters Jeff's eyes. "You son-of-a-bitch."

Brad bends down, bringing his mouth to within inches of Jeff's ear, and whispers. "I told you it was easy."

The automatic moves, the barrel coming up against Jeff's temple. The second shot is much quieter, the report muffled by flesh and bone and gray matter.

Chapter Thirty-Four:

OF THE TWO SETS OF EYES, IT IS debatable which is the most lifeless. Jeff Black would never again view the world, a pale fogginess having enveloped his orbs. Brad Wilkens, sitting relaxed in the living room, stares at his friend with equally lifeless eyes. He gazes, unemotional, in silent contemplation.

The beer cans have been removed from the scene, eliminating the evidence of his visit. Removing his cellphone he calmly selects a number, then listens for the dial tone.

Across the room a chirping sounds from the body on the floor, the phone in Jeff's pocket announcing the new call. The tone halts as a familiar voice answers the phone in the killer's hand. "You've reached Jeff. Leave a message at the beep."

Brad speaks, his voice portraying no emotion. "Hey, guy! Where you at? I'm down at *Papa Joe's*. What say you get your ass down here and we'll do some celebrating?"

Brad disconnects, stands up, and calmly heads for the door. He pauses a moment, contemplating the lifeless form on the floor, before leaving the house.

Chapter Thirty-Five:

FOR THE THIRD TIME THE DOORBELL rang, the melodic chiming carrying clearly through the front door. The noise evaporated once outside, as though absorbed by the brisk wintry air. Rubbing her hands together for warmth, then stamping her feet against the porch floor, Rachel attempted to peek through the curtains at the side of the entrance way. It was wasted motion. All was dark within the silent house.

"That's strange."

Rachel rang the bell once more, tapping her foot as her patience wore thin. "Come on, Jeff. I'm freezing my ass off out here."

After a minute's wait, with still no response, she tried the knob. It turned, and with a shove she pushed the door open. "Jeff?!"

No answer came.

"Jeff? Are you here?"

Rachel stepped in, pulling the door shut behind her, and clicked on the hallway light. A peculiar odor assaulted her. It wasn't strong, just a hint unusual, but it caused Rachel to pause. Something just didn't seem right.

Taking a single step further, she caught sight of a pale-colored something on the floor, in the doorway leading off to the living room. She couldn't make out at first what it was, but she found herself slowing in her motions. Another step, and she was certain what she was looking at was a human hand, the rest of the form hidden from view by the hallway wall.

"Jeff?"

The body came into sight as she approached. Jeff's face was barely recognizable, the gun blast obliterating much of the detail. Blood was everywhere. It soaked the carpeting. A splotch of red on the wall behind the body had dripped onto the baseboard. Even the furniture revealed specks of blood on the fabric.

For a moment Rachel froze. *This can't be real. I must be imagining things.* She bent at the knees, reaching out, ever so slowly, to touch the form. Her fingers came in contact with the left forearm. It felt cold. Hard. Like a frozen piece of meat.

It was only then that she screamed. Jumping back, coming up against the door of the front closet, she shielded her eyes as the screams pealed from her throat. For a minute she continued, lost in panic, until the wailings were replaced by the muffled sound of sobbing.

She forced one more look then ran for the kitchen, seeking solace away from the cold figure on the floor.

It took four attempts stabbing at the buttons on her cellphone to reach 911. The efficient voice on the other end had barely answered when Rachel began.

"He's dead! Dear God, he's dead!" She gulped a deep breath of air, which had no effect in composing her, then forced herself to continue. "Please do something. Please!"

"Calm down, ma'am." The man's voice was businesslike, with a reassuring quality. "We're here to help. But you have to calm down and tell me exactly what's going on."

"He's dead. I.... I walked in. And found him.... He's so cold. So cold."

It took three minutes for the operator to gather the necessary information, but to Rachel it felt like an eternity. It was impossible to concentrate. She found her mind wandering as the voice continued. "And you're sure there's nobody else in the house?"

"I don't know. I don't think so...." Her words trailed off, a jumble of thoughts confusing her speech.

"Please don't stay in the house, ma'am," the voice on the phone prompted. "It may not be safe. Can you go to the neighbors? Or do you have a car?"

She nodded her head twice, then realized finally she had to say something. "Yes. It's parked out front. My car, that is. Right out front."

"Then stay in your car. And lock the doors. Don't touch a thing in the house. Someone is on the way right now."

"Thank you." The words were barely a whisper. Chances were the person on the other end of the line didn't even hear them.

Without even realizing what she was doing Rachel removed the phone from her ear. The operator's voice continued with instructions, the words fading away as Rachel, moving in a daze, dropped the phone onto the floor.

A feeling of exhaustion overcame her. She leaned against the wall, grateful for the support, deliberating what should be done. She didn't want to look at Jeff again. Not the way he was now. But she needed to. She had to know for certain.

On a certain level she realized it might not be safe to stay in the house, but she couldn't force herself to leave. She made it as far as the front hallway before collapsing on the floor, legs tucked beneath her. Reaching out, she could just touch Jeff's hand. The fingers were stiff, and she initially drew away from the contact. But then, with an effort, she tried again.

It all seemed so unreal. She needed more. She desired more than anything the reassuring feel of Jeff's warmth, the closeness that came when he wrapped his arms around her. But the feelings were denied her. For now and forever.

A glint of light drew her eyes, the ring on her finger sparkling. It all seemed so unfair, as though the jewel was mocking her.

She slipped the ring off, cupping it in her hand. With a sudden motion her arm lifted, drawing back for a throw.

At the last minute she changed her mind and returned the

ring to its rightful place. Her eyes grew weary as she stared at the jewelry, until eventually she could stand it no longer.

She was still sitting there, crying, five minutes later, when the first of the police officers arrived.

Chapter Thirty-Six:

AT 4:25 PM HOMICIDE DETECTIVE Benjamin Tuppelo sat in the Toledo Police Department squad room at The Central Station. His desk looked relatively neat, having spent most of the day catching up on paperwork. It was a rare occurrence to see Tuppelo's desk neat. He wasn't much for doing paperwork. Hardly a day went by when he couldn't be heard commenting on what a waste of valuable manpower it was to be sitting at a desk when there was real work to be done elsewhere. Just hearing him say it made those who didn't mind doing the paperwork flinch with a twinge of guilt, as though they were involved in something that was beneath them.

Tuppelo was leaning over to deposit a folder in his bottom desk drawer when the sound of footsteps approached.

"Hey, Benji. What you got going?"

Tuppelo closed the drawer with an exaggerated amount of force, hoping to drown out Garry Benson's words. Maybe then he would go away.

But when he looked up Benson was still there.

Tuppelo made no attempt to hide his displeasure. Benson was one of those guys that never seemed to show up unless something bad was brewing. Around the office he was routinely referred to as "The Angel Of Death," a title Benson seemed to accept with a marked degree of pride.

Tuppelo leaned back in his chair, the ancient springs squealing in protest. He didn't know what Benson was leading up to, but he was fairly certain he didn't want any part of it. "I'm pretty busy, Garry." Opening the bottom drawer of his desk, he removed the folder he had just deposited, throwing it on the desk top. "Got a ton of paperwork to catch up on."

"Well, Captain says you're not busy enough. A call just came in he wants you to take."

That changed things. The folder was forgotten. Without hesitation Tuppelo sprang from his seat and grabbed his coat from the back of the chair. Anything to get out of the office. "What have you got?"

"Homicide." Benson consulted a slip of paper in his hand. "Young man in his mid-twenties. Name's Jeff Black. Captain wants you to get right on it. A cruiser's there already."

"Anyone call Newt?" Edgar Newton was the Lucas County Coroner, and as such would be routinely summoned on the case.

"He's out of town for a few days. Clark's on call. Remember?"

"That's right." Tuppelo waited several seconds, with Benson failing to comment further. "Well?"

"Well, what?"

"So was Clark called?"

"Yeah. Sure. Why wouldn't he be? He should be there by the time you arrive."

Benson dropped the paper onto the desk. The note listed an address in the north part of the city. Tuppelo recognized it as a fairly well-to-do neighborhood just off Alexis road, nearly in Sylvania. Not the type of area he would have expected to encounter a homicide, but he was experienced enough to realize violent death could rear its ugly head anywhere.

Benson remained standing, his gaze shifting between the detective and the desk.

"Now what?" Tuppelo asked. "You expecting a tip or something?"

"Just wondered what you thought of it."

"Hell, I don't think anything of it. Give me a chance to get a few more of the facts first. All right?"

"Ten will get you one, there's booze involved."

"What makes you say that?"

"Hey, it's bound to be. New Year's Eve and all. Chances are, someone started celebrating early, and things just got out of hand. You'll probably spend ten minutes there and wrap it all up."

"Thanks a lot, Garry. Coming from you, that means I won't get home until next year for sure."

As Tuppelo headed for the exit he was met by Harrison Fielding. The Department had two kinds of Detectives - those handling property crimes, such as burglaries, and those handling personal claims. Such as murder. Fielding was another of the Homicide Detectives. Fielding fell in step beside Tuppelo, joining him stride-for-stride. They could have been twins, each towering over six feet tall, though Tuppelo had a weight advantage of perhaps fifteen pounds. Tuppelo was also the older of the two detectives, having served twenty-three years in the force to Fielding's eleven.

Tuppelo stopped at the squad room door, his arm blocking further progress. "Where are you going?"

"I'm supposed to tag along," Fielding answered, buttoning his overcoat. "Make sure you don't stop at a bar on the way over."

"Sounds more like your style."

"Well, if you insist."

As they hit the sidewalk Fielding pulled a crumpled fedora from his coat pocket, taking care to shape it carefully before placing it on his head. He adjusted the hat as they weaved their way among parked cars, stopping twice to check how it looked in side-view mirrors they passed.

Tuppelo shook his head. "That is one UGLY hat, you know that?"

Fielding paused to spread his arms, mocking a modeling stance. "You got to admit, it looks good on me."

"I'll admit no such thing."

By then they had reached the car. Tuppelo slid in behind the steering wheel, Fielding riding shotgun, and they pulled into traffic, headed north. The car came to an immediate stop at the first red light.

"Why don't you go through it?"

"What's your hurry?"

"We're on a case, aren't we?"

"The guy's dead already. Getting there a minute sooner isn't going to change things."

The light switched to green, and motion started once more.

"You know," Fielding began, "Indy's not such a bad name."

Tuppelo turned toward his partner. "What are you going on about?"

"I think I'll change my name to Indiana. You know. Like in the movies."

"Not this again." Tuppelo signaled for a right-hand turn, merging into the next lane to enter the expressway, headed north. "For the last time, you do *not* look like Harrison Ford. You have *never* looked like Harrison Ford. And you never *will* look like Harrison Ford. Do I make myself clear?"

For thirty seconds all was silent. Tuppelo took his eyes off the traffic long enough to gauge the reaction to his comments.

Fielding had the sun-visor pulled down, examining himself in the mirror as he toyed with his fedora. "Indy. Yeah. I like that."

Tuppelo shook his head and turned his attention back to driving.

There was no mistaking the house in question. An ambulance perched out front, warning lights flashing. Two patrol cars, painted a simple white with a blue streak running down the side, were at the scene. One was pulled halfway onto the lawn, its headlights illuminating the front porch, while the other parked at the end of the block. A crowd of perhaps a dozen people had gathered, kept in check by a single uniformed policeman wielding a flashlight. Tuppelo recognized the officer.

"Everything under control, Matheson?"

"Yeah, yeah. Everything's just dandy."

Fielding, walking over from the other side of the car, delivered a stern glance. "What's *your* beef?"

"It's too friggin' cold to be standing out here all night doing crowd control. Why do these things have to happen in winter?"

Fielding shook his head as he walked toward the house. "You're right, Matheson. Damn inconsiderate of this joker to be killed on your shift, if you ask me."

"Up yours, Fielding."

Picking up the pace, Fielding caught up to Tuppelo at the front door. "Do you believe that guy?"

"Drop it, Harrison."

There was no ignoring the tone of Tuppelo's voice. The matter was dropped. Fielding had learned early on that Tuppelo was a good guy to joke around with, but when it came time to do a job, he was all business. They had work to do now, which meant there wasn't any room for shenanigans.

A uniformed officer ushered them into the front room. "Got a bad one here."

Tuppelo's first reaction at sight of the corpse was to turn away for a moment. He had seen enough of death to know the gritty reality of the situation, but it still caught him by surprise every time he saw a new body. It bothered him to think this lifeless shape in front of him had once been a living, breathing, caring, human being. He wondered if he would ever get over that momentary shortness of breath that always came to him on such occasions.

Clark Czemicki was kneeling on the floor, bent over the body, probing with a wooden stick, scraping body tissue into a little plastic bag. He seemed totally captivated with the activity, as though it was the most interesting thing in the world to be doing.

Tuppelo grunted a greeting. "What's it look like?"

"Well.... He's dead, I can tell you that."

Fielding shook his head. "This from the expert. How much they pay you for these brilliant observations, Czemicki?"

The Assistant Coroner didn't bother to look up. "More than you're worth, Fielding."

Stepping over the still form, Tuppelo pointed at the dead man's stomach and head. "Looks like he was shot twice."

Czemicki nodded. "That's all I've found so far. The bullet to the stomach was probably first."

"How do you figure that?"

"Look at his head! Christ. Would you bother shooting someone a second time after you'd done that to him?"

Tuppelo turned to the officer who had met them at the door. "Who found the body?"

"The dead man's fiance. Rachel Keller. She's in the kitchen."

Fielding shifted position, affording him a better view of the corpse. "Positive identification? I mean.... Hell, the guy's in pretty bad shape. Know what I mean?"

"She says it's him. No doubt in her mind about it. Want to talk to her?"

The two detectives swapped glances. "Your turn," Fielding pointed out, as he stooped beside Czemicki to examine the body in more detail.

It was dark in the kitchen, the only illumination a 40-watt bulb on the hood of the stove. The impression hit Tuppelo that he was walking into a cave. It even seemed colder than the front of the house. Without giving it another thought, he reached for the light switch.

"Please don't turn it on," a feminine voice requested from the darkness.

"Pardon?"

"It hurts my eyes. The light. Guess I've been crying too much."

He adopted his most compassionate tone. "Of course. I'm not much for bright lights, myself."

In silence he entered the room. For such a big man, it was amazing how quietly he moved. He pulled out a chair, lifting it off the floor so it wouldn't scrape against the linoleum, and sat down across from her.

He was in no hurry. The last thing she needed at a time like this was to have a bunch of cops jumping down her neck. There were detectives down at the station that operated like that, giving no regard to what the victim was going through, but Tuppelo refused to subscribe to that policy. She would have plenty of time to answer questions later.

As it turned out, she began before he was seated. "I just can't believe this is happening. Why would anyone kill Jeff? Why?"

"That's what I'm here to try to find out."

Rachel lifted her head to look at him. Light reflected from the moisture in her eyes.

He extended his hand in greeting. She showed no sign of responding, so he withdrew the offer. "Homicide Detective Benjamin Tuppelo." He presented his ID, realizing she wouldn't bother to look at it. They never did. He replaced the wallet, then drew out a notebook and pencil from an inner pocket of his coat. No sense putting things off any longer.

"I'd like to ask you some questions. If you're up to it."

"Why not? What better way to celebrate the New Year?"

Tuppelo didn't roll his eyes, but he did come close to it. It was going to be a long evening.

Chapter Thirty-Seven:

"SO WHEN ARE YOU GOING BACK TO work?"

"I don't know." He paused, considering the question. "I'm not even sure I can."

"That's a pretty defeatist attitude, don't you think?"

"I suppose." Daniel stopped to take a swig from the can of Pepsi in front of him, using the action to delay the conversation. He really wasn't in the mood to talk about his problems.

It was nearly nine o'clock. Daniel had arrived at Jackie's apartment at six, taking her out to dinner at a steak place she recommended. It wasn't the type of place he would have chosen, barely one step above a bar, with a ubiquitous barrage of country music in the background, but the steaks were good, and Jackie looked terrific, and he couldn't imagine a more enjoyable way to usher in the New Year. He felt young, carefree, and for a few hours he had forgotten all about the foundry accident and the subsequent complications in his life.

His only complaint of the evening was the crowds. He never had felt comfortable when a lot of people were around, and of late it had been even more difficult to be around others. He always found it easier to deal with people on a one-to-one basis.

Though even that had its downfalls.

Arriving back at Jackie's place the conversation had shifted to weightier topics. Topics Daniel would just as soon have left undiscussed. He resisted at first, refusing to comment on the situation, but eventually Jackie's insistence on the point had over-ridden his reluctance.

He ended up telling her everything; about the accident, and his subsequent depression, and even touching on his problems with Becky. She was a good listener, saying little, commenting only when she was uncertain on a detail, content to allow him the time he required to clear things in his own mind. It occurred to Daniel that she was accustomed to not having much input in a conversation.

"I just don't know what I'm doing anymore," Daniel concluded, surprising himself with his own candor.

Jackie, arms on the table, folded in front of her, leaned closer. "Is it worth ruining your marriage over?"

Daniel stood up, turning away from her. "That's it. Give me something else to worry about."

"Hey, I was just asking!"

Jackie felt suddenly on the defensive. It had been like that, off and on, the entire evening. Daniel seemed prone to sudden mood shifts. He was never violent, like Brad. More like he was angry with himself, and disappointed with his own behavior. The spell would last a few minutes, his voice lowering as he became more introspective, then he would turn back to something more pleasant, and his eyes would light up with renewed enthusiasm. He seemed younger then. More fun to be with.

"How old are you?" Daniel asked.

The abruptness of the question startled her. "What?"

He sat down, sliding his chair closer. "I asked you how old you are."

"Twenty-five. Why?"

Leaning back, a look of triumph crossed Daniel's face. "Next August, I'll have twenty-four years in at CONSOLIDATED."

She failed to see the connection. "So?"

"I've been working at that place for nearly as long as you've been alive. Think of it. I wasted an entire lifetime there."

"It couldn't have all been a waste?"

"It might as well have been. I still get up every morning, and go through the same mindless routines. I still pay the same bills, month after month after month. Just once, I'd like to do something different. Something exciting."

For a full minute neither spoke. "Is that why you came to *Papa Joe's*?" Jackie asked at last, hesitant to voice her concern for fear what his answer would be. "Was I to be your 'something different?' Your little bit of excitement, before you scurried back to your wife and family?"

"You make it sound so dirty."

She leaned over, grasping his hands. They were good hands, steady and firm. The hands of a worker. Jackie smiled. "I didn't mean it to sound that way."

"Really?"

"Really. I'm glad you came to the bar. I'm glad I met you, Daniel Jameson."

She leaned closer. Daniel could smell her now, a delicate fragrance that was either perfume or shampoo. He was uncertain which. Either way, it fit her. He moved forward. Jackie's eyes closed as their lips met.

The kiss lasted three seconds before Daniel pulled away.

Jackie's eyes opened with his abrupt withdrawal, her confusion obvious. For a moment they just looked at one another, until Daniel beat a hasty retreat to the living room.

Jackie followed him. He sat on the couch, staring across the room. He failed to acknowledge her presence as she drew closer.

"What was that all about?" Jackie asked, making no attempt to hide her irritation. She stood with her hands on her hips, glaring at him.

Daniel made no comment. A whirlwind of emotions flashed through his head, his thoughts a confusing jumble. Things were happening too fast. He hadn't intended this to happen. Now that it had, what should he do next? What would

Jackie do next?

She gave him a full minute to answer, but he failed to take advantage of the lull.

"I don't believe this." Jackie did an abrupt about-face, took two steps away, then reversed her motion, ending up in front of Daniel once more. "Tell me this, then. Why did you come here tonight? What were you expecting to happen?"

"I don't know," Daniel admitted.

Jackie could feel her frustration growing. "Look. It's obvious you're having problems. You have a lot of things to sort out. Maybe it would be better for both of us if you just left."

"I don't want to."

She sat down next to him, taking his hand. Her mind struggled for what to say. Unable to find the right words, she began anyway. "Maybe this is all my fault. There's no denying Brad and I had a lousy relationship. For the longest time I couldn't admit that. Even to myself. But, considering what's been going on lately...."

She forced aside the image of Brad's last visit to her apartment.

"But I felt trapped, Daniel. Helpless. Until you came along. At last there was somebody in my life that would treat me with respect. Listen to what I had to say. Do what I wanted to do for a change."

She took a deep breath. It felt good to unburden herself to someone. Just talking about her problems made her feel less alone.

It also made her examine her motives more than she ever had in the past. "Maybe what I'm feeling for you is only gratitude," she continued.

Daniel turned to face her. "Does it have to be that way?"

"Not necessarily."

Jackie stood to walk away from him. It was easier to be firm when they weren't so close.

"I won't be used again, Daniel. If nothing else, I learned that from my time with Brad. If you want to make this relationship work, then I'm willing to try. But if I'm just some sort of fling. Just a good time while you're waiting to get back to your wife. Then forget it. I won't let you do that to me."

It was Jackie's turn now to retreat, while she still felt strong, before the approaching tears got the better of her. She made it as far as the kitchen, where she slumped against the refrigerator.

She didn't hear Daniel approach. His arms wrapped around her, drawing her closer. She turned and fell against him, burying her face in his chest to hide the tears.

Chapter Thirty-Eight:

A RAPPING SOUNDED AT THE FRONT DOOR. Daniel stepped back from the refrigerator, his hold on Jackie relaxing. She pulled away, grabbing a napkin from the table and wiping her eyes as she spoke. "Now who could that be?"

"Are you expecting anyone?"

"No."

Jackie descended the stairs, pulling the curtain aside to look out. The man standing on the top step was big. Even through his coat she could detect the bulk of his physique. She latched the safety chain and opened the door enough to peek out. "Yes?"

"Jackie Somerset?" Even the voice was large.

She deliberated slamming the door and running back upstairs. "That's right."

"Benjamin Tuppelo. Toledo Police Department." He held up a wallet, revealing the badge within. "This is my partner, Detective Harrison Fielding." He motioned behind him. It was only then that she noticed the other man, standing on the sidewalk, surveying the area. "May we talk to you for a few minutes?"

Panic hit her, wondering what two police officers were doing at her front door this time of night. It was an unsettling feeling to be approached so unexpectedly. She felt a slight tremor in her fingers and hoped they didn't notice.

"Please. Come in." She closed the door, unhooked the chain, and opened the door to its fullest. They followed her up the stairs.

"What's going on?" Daniel asked, as she walked in.

She shrugged. "I don't know."

Tuppelo and Fielding joined them, and introductions were exchanged. The apartment seemed smaller than ever with the detectives present. They were an intimidating presence in the room.

"We just have a few questions," Tuppelo began, addressing Jackie. "Do you know Jeff Black?"

"Sure I do," she answered. "He's my best friend's boyfriend. That's Rachel Keller. Jeff and her just got engaged a week ago."

As she watched the lackluster expression on the detectives' faces a hollow feeling overcame her.

"Why do you ask?" she managed, knowing something was wrong and dreading what it could be. "Has something happened?"

"Mr. Black is dead, Miss Somerset."

"Dead?" The word stuck in her throat.

"It appears to have happened sometime this afternoon, though we won't know for certain until we have the full medical report."

"Dead?" Jackie was having trouble with the concept. Her legs felt suddenly unsteady. She would have collapsed had Daniel not moved over to wrap his arm around her, offering support.

His voice brought additional strength. "What happened?"

"He was shot with a handgun, most probably a .45 caliber automatic."

"Where...?" Jackie stumbled with the word. "Where was this? I mean.... How...?"

"There's a lot of things we haven't determined yet. Mr. Black was home at the time. His body was found in the front of the house. There's no signs of forced entry, and nothing seems to be missing, though we haven't ruled out the possibility that it may have been an armed robber."

"Does Rachel know?"

"I'm afraid so. Miss Keller discovered the body."

"Poor Rachel! Is she okay?"

"She's at her parents' house now."

"I should go see her. If that's all right?"

"Of course, Miss Somerset. It would probably be the best thing for her. And while we don't want to keep you from your friend, if we could just have a few more minutes of your time first...."

Jackie barely heard the words, her attention wandering as she contemplated what Rachel was going through. It all seemed so unbelievable. This sort of thing just didn't happen to people like them. What could she possibly say to Rachel to make things all right? Not that anything she said could ever make things all right.

"Miss Somerset?"

Tuppelo's interruption refocused her attention. "I'm sorry. What were you saying?"

"Do you know anything concerning Mr. Black's activities today? If he was meeting anyone, or doing anything out of the ordinary?"

"I really couldn't say. Rachel said something about he had to work this morning, so I suppose he was at the shop for a while."

"Yes. She told us about that. Is there anything else?"

"Not that I can think of. I'm sorry. I'm not being much help to you, am I?"

Tuppelo smiled. The expression looked foreign on him, like he was unaccustomed to it, but it helped to set Jackie's mind at ease.

"There is another thing," the detective continued. "We still haven't recovered the murder weapon. Do you know if Mr. Black had a handgun?"

"I wouldn't know about that."

"Do you know if he has any acquaintances that have a gun? Somebody from work, maybe?"

"Not that I know of."

Daniel leaned closer, whispering into her ear. "How about Brad?"

She turned toward him, a look of shock on her face.

Fielding spoke for the first time. "What was that, Mr. Jameson?"

Daniel's voice was cold. Unemotional. "Brad Wilkens has a gun."

"Brad Wilkens." Fielding turned toward Tuppelo. "Where have we heard that name before?"

Jackie supplied the answer. "Jeff and Brad are... That is, Jeff and Brad *were* best friends."

Tuppelo nodded in comprehension. "I remember now. Miss Keller mentioned Wilkens. He was supposed to meet Black at some bar today."

"That would be *Papa Joe's*. They hang out down there a lot."

Fielding approached Daniel. "And you claim Wilkens has a gun?"

"That's right."

"And how would you know that, Mr. Jameson?"

Daniel could feel Jackie's eyes on him, pleading with him not to say more, but there was no turning back now. "We had a misunderstanding the other night."

The two detectives exchanged a quick look of dawning comprehension.

"Did Wilkens threaten you with his gun, Mr. Jameson?"

Jackie's heart was racing. Words rushed forth. "Brad didn't mean anything by it. Honest. He just likes to show off. You know. Sort of a macho thing."

Jackie continued, anxiety rushing her words. "Listen. It's just ridiculous to think Brad had anything to do with this. Brad and Jeff are best friends."

Tuppelo wandered how many best friends he had arrested during his time on the force, but he left these thoughts to himself. The young woman was obviously upset. No sense stirring things up if it was unwarranted. Though he did make a mental note to question Daniel Jameson further about this, when Jackie Somerset wasn't present, at the first available opportunity.

"Thank you, Miss Somerset," Tuppelo said at last. "We're sorry to have taken up your time. You will let us know if you hear anything that might help us in our investigation?"

"Of course."

They said their good-nights, and Jackie walked them to the top of the stairs. She watched in silence as they left.

Jackie whirled on Daniel the minute the detectives were gone. "What was the idea of dragging Brad into this?"

"You're getting awful defensive all of a sudden."

"Why shouldn't I be? You as much as accused Brad of shooting Jeff."

"I wouldn't put it past him."

"Brad may be a lot of things, but he's no killer."

"You could have fooled me the other night. Or did you forget how he had his gun jammed into my throat?"

Jackie turned away, hesitated a second, then faced Daniel again. "Listen, I don't want to talk about it. All I want to do is go see how Rachel's doing. The poor thing. She must feel awful right now."

"You want me to drop you off at her place?" he offered.

"No. I think I'll just drive over myself." Then, as an afterthought: "Maybe you should just head home."

"Home?"

"Well, you know what I mean."

"Yeah. Right."

"Anyway, I got to go."

"You mind if I call you later?"

"I don't know. I guess it would be okay." She had her coat on by now, and was rummaging through her purse for her keys. "Listen, I'm just not thinking straight right now. Let's talk about it later. Okay?"

"Sure."

They headed down the stairs together. At the sidewalk they paused. It was an awkward moment, with neither knowing what was expected of them, each waiting for a sign from the other which never arrived. Without another word between them they went their separate ways.

Chapter Thirty-Nine:

NEITHER MAN SPOKE UNTIL THE CAR WAS in motion.

"What do you think?" Fielding asked.

Tuppelo, never one to rush into things, considered before making his reply. "About what?" he asked at last.

"About this Wilkens character. You think he's the killer?"

"Based on what?"

"Well, you heard what Jameson said. Wilkens threatened him earlier...."

Tuppelo interrupted. "He never said that."

"Well, sure. Not in so many words. But he didn't have to. You saw the expression on his face."

"So you're ready to accuse somebody because of the expression on that guy's face?"

"No." Fielding paused to rethink his strategy. "But if Wilkens has a violent streak, don't you think he'd be capable of shooting someone?"

"Possibly."

"Damn right he would. I think we should bring him in for questioning."

"What good would that do?"

"Give us an idea what type of character he is. Find out what he's been up to. Hell, maybe even scare him into revealing something."

"That might work," Tuppelo admitted.

Fielding smiled, pleased that his suggestion was being

taken under consideration.

"On the other hand," Tuppelo continued with barely a pause, "if he is the killer, bringing him in too soon would tip him off that we know something. Even though we don't. The minute he gets home he ditches the gun, and we're sunk." Tuppelo turned toward his partner. "Then what?"

"Yeah. I see what you mean." He considered further as the car took a turn. "So what do we do?"

"What else? Leg work. We'll begin by investigating Wilkens' whereabouts at the time of the murder. Then a background check. See what we can find out about this 'misunderstanding' he had with Daniel Jameson. Maybe we'll be lucky and something will turn up."

Tuppelo glanced at his watch. "Anyway, it's too late now to be checking into things. Let's call it a day. I'm looking forward to getting home. Melissa was sending the kids over to her mother's, so for a change we'll have a nice, quiet evening. Just the two of us."

"You're not serious?"

"Course I'm serious. Why wouldn't I be?"

"Because it's New Year's Eve. Time to do some heavy duty celebrating."

They had reached the station by now. Tuppelo pulled into an empty parking space and shut off the motor. He turned toward Fielding, a grin on his face. "Tell you what, Indy. Why don't you go ahead and do my celebrating for me."

"All right." Fielding adjusted his fedora, leaning over as he did so to glance in the rear-view mirror. "It's your lost."

"Just be sure to tell me in the morning whether I had a good time or not. Okay?"

Chapter Forty:

THERE WAS A TIME - NOT VERY LONG AGO, actually - when Jackie Somerset as much as lived at Rachel Keller's house. Many were the days they would go home after school together; hanging out on the back porch when weather permitted, or, when forced to do so, retreating to the secret confines of the rec room in the basement. She and Rachel would listen to CDs here - that ancient medium that was so prevalent before the advent of digital downloads - and talk about guys and dating and football games, and share more happy times than she could ever remember.

More often than not Rachel's mother would invite Jackie to stay for supper. She was always quick to accept the invitation.

The quality of the food had nothing to do with her acceptance. Jackie always appreciated the relaxed atmosphere of the place, where nothing was expected from her, and she could just be herself.

It had been so different at home. No matter what Jackie did, no matter how hard she worked at school, it was never enough for her mother. The woman expected wonders from her, wonders Jackie was unable to fulfill. With time their relationship deteriorated into a series of arguments - shouting matches - with neither one claiming victory.

In many respects they had both lost.

It was even worse when her father was home. He was abusive toward his wife, indifferent to Jackie and her older brother, and unconcerned with day to day activities such as paying bills and providing for his family. It had been a bittersweet day when Jackie packed up her belongings to move out on her own.

Once in an apartment Jackie found herself visiting less and less at Rachel's. Anything reminding her of childhood was avoided as much as possible. She couldn't even remember the last time she had spoken to Rachel's folks.

It felt strange, now, to be standing at their front door. She only wished something more pleasant had been the impetus for her visit.

Mrs. Keller answered the knock. She was a study in gray, sallow complexioned, with frizzled hair that had lost most of its original blond. A drab sweater was clenched around her shoulders. She was a short woman, reaching barely to Jackie's chin, her limbs frail and slender.

Her eyes were puffy and red. "Oh, Jackie. I'm so glad you could come." She stood on tiptoes to deliver a light kiss on the cheek.

Jackie gave her a quick hug. She felt awkward doing so, but it was something Rachel's mother always expected. She certainly couldn't let her down. Especially today, of all days.

They pulled away from each other, Jackie forcing a light touch to her words. "Why wouldn't I come?"

The old woman seemed confused. Uncertain how to react. "Well, don't just stand there," she finally managed. "Come on in."

Jackie entered the front room, Mrs. Keller quietly closing the door behind her.

"How's Rachel doing?" Jackie asked.

"Shh!" Rachel's mother held a warning finger to her lips, then motioned upstairs with her eyes. "'Bout as good as to be expected. She's sleeping now, poor thing."

"Then maybe I should leave? Come back later...?"

"Of course not. Do come in."

Jackie was ushered into the living room. Rachel's father

perched in his favorite chair. He made no attempt to look at the two women as they entered. The lights were turned low in the room. The TV was off.

"Frank. Look who's here. It's Jackie."

He turned, acknowledging her presence with a grunt.

Jackie stammered for the right words to say, realizing there weren't any right words in such a situation. "Maybe I should just come back later."

"No, no." Mrs. Keller steered her into the room. "We won't hear of it. Come sit with us a bit."

"But you probably have plans. New Year's Eve and all...."

"No, dear. Nothing. And even if we did, how could we? Now? I mean, after all...." Her voice faltered, the words trailing away.

Mr. Keller broke the silence, his voice shaken with fury. "When they catch the son-of-a-bitch that done this. I hope they blow his goddamn brains from here to kingdom come."

"Now, Dear. Is that any way to talk in front of Jackie?"

"I can talk any goddamn way I want to. Hell, this is my house, ain't it? Wasn't it my future son-in-law some son-of-a-bitch murdered? I'll say whatever I want."

Jackie offered reassurances. "It's okay, Mrs. Keller. I can understand how upset you both must be."

"Mom!" The voice filtered down from upstairs. "Is someone here, Mom?"

She called out an answer. "It's Jackie, dear. Do you want to see her?"

"No. I...." Rachel's voice hesitated. "Yeah. I'd like to see her. Can you send her up?"

Mrs. Keller started to rise from her seat, but Jackie motioned her back. "I know the way."

Her father was muttering again as Jackie walked away.

Rachel's room hadn't changed much since the last time Jackie had seen it. The same pictures on the wall. Even the same comforter on the bed. Only it seemed smaller now, just a little corner of the world that had refused to change.

Rachel sat at the desk, hands folded in front of her.

Jackie stepped cautiously in. "You okay?"

"No. But there's not much I can do about that, is there?"

Jackie walked to the edge of the bed and sat down, leaning toward her friend. "If there's anything I can do.... Anything at all...."

"The only thing I want is for them to catch the bastard that killed Jeff."

"That won't bring him back, Rachel."

"I don't care." As Rachel turned, the light reflected in her eyes. It revealed a coldness Jackie had never seen before. It was like looking at a stranger. "I want him to suffer, Jackie. I want him to pay for every second of agony he brought to Jeff."

She turned away, her face shadowed once again. "And if there's any justice in the world, he *will* pay."

Chapter Forty-One: Friday, January 1, 2016

IT DIDN'T FEEL LIKE A NEW YEAR. TURNING a page on the calendar hadn't changed his life any. Same old problems, same old hassles. The only thing new was the date.

Daniel tried to sleep in - there wasn't any reason to get up that he could think of, anyway - but by eight o'clock he had showered and had breakfast and watched fifteen minutes of a talk show on television. That was about fourteen and-a-half minutes too many.

Rick was still asleep. Daniel hadn't heard his brother come in the night before, but he assumed it had been late. Or, rather, early.

Daniel considered waking Rick, just to have someone to talk to, then decided against it. He didn't feel like talking, anyway. All he wanted was to be alone.

Grabbing his coat, Daniel headed outside.

It had snowed overnight, a good inch-and-a-half that covered the neighborhood. A muffled silence seemed to envelope everything, as if a shroud had descended while mankind slept. No one was in sight. No birds chirped. No sign of life presented itself as Daniel stepped out of the house, feeling the sting of sub-freezing air against his face.

Walking out to his car he started the engine, pulled on his gloves, and stepped out to clean off the snow. He took his time; scraping the windows all around, brushing the headlights, even kicking off the ice that had accumulated behind each tire. The solitude was comforting, somehow. Peaceful. He wished it would never end.

By the time he climbed in, the car's interior felt like an oven.

Or like a foundry.

His mind wandered, recalling that fateful day. Had it really been only three weeks ago? He hadn't spoken with Michael Blake since the accident. Michael had been asleep on the one occasion when Daniel stopped in to visit at the hospital, and it had been too difficult to return.

Another thing to feel guilty about. Daniel knew he should visit Michael. He knew it was the right thing to do. But why was it so often that the right path to take was the hardest direction to follow?

The Blakes lived in a middle-class neighborhood a block from the intersection of Lewis and Laskey Avenues, a scattering of two-story homes that all looked to have been built at the same time. There was a certain uniformity to the setting, a pleasing symmetry that gave a comfortable feel to the area. The homes were well established, the type handed down from generation to generation, where a person could live his life within the same four walls, never venturing beyond the confines of the familiar.

Daniel pulled in the narrow driveway, shut off the engine, and waited.

Across the street a snow fort had been assembled. Two boys crouched behind the waist-high ramparts, while a third hid behind a tree, tossing an occasional snowball toward the fortifications. Their laughter, the causal excitement of youth, carried clearly to Daniel's car.

He switched the ignition to accessories and turned on the radio, drowning out the racket.

He had been sitting there for two minutes when he heard someone calling to him.

"Daniel? Is that you?"

The moment of truth had arrived. He forced himself from

the driver's seat. Amy Blake stood in the front entrance way to the house. Her face brightened at his approach.

"I thought that was you," she continued. "Mike will be so glad you stopped by."

"I hope I'm not intruding...."

"Of course not! The very idea. You're always welcome here. You should know that."

She held the door and he walked pass her into a hallway. Ahead was the kitchen. Daniel could see dishes on the table, and a stack of pancakes.

"Am I interrupting your breakfast? I can come back later...."

"No. No. We're all done. I just haven't got around to clearing things up yet. Seems like it takes me longer and longer all the time to get things done." She patted her belly and smiled. "I always blame it on my condition. Anyway, Mike's in the other room. Go on in."

Daniel hesitated, uncertain how to proceed. "How's he doing?"

"Oh, it's been an adjustment. For both of us. He can't go upstairs, of course, what with his...." She worried her lip, interrupting the words.

"I think he's getting stir-crazy," she continued, the words rushing forth, as though by hurrying over it she could deny the existence of the truth. "All he does is sit in the living room, watching TV. He gets around in the wheelchair, to come into the kitchen when he wants to. But it tires him out." She flashed a smile. "But we're managing."

Daniel made no response. He stood in the hallway, reluctant to enter further.

A hand touched his shoulder as Amy drew closer. "Go on. He knows you're here. He's waiting to see you."

Taking a step forward, Daniel noticed Amy turning away. "Aren't you coming in?"

"I'll be in in a minute. You two talk." She prodded him, then headed for the kitchen.

Michael sat on a recliner, an Afghan draped over him, watching television. He twisted in his seat as Daniel entered. A smile spread across his face.

"Hey, stranger. Where you been?" His voice sounded more exuberant than Daniel had expected.

Daniel, taken by surprise, stumbled for an answer. "I've been around. How 'bout you?"

"Been hanging in there." A lilting quality accompanied Michael's words, as though they were discussing the most trivial of events. "I've been meaning to work on the baby's room, but for some reason I can't seem to get myself upstairs." A laugh accompanied the words. "It's the darnedest thing. Guess I'm just not motivated, or something. I don't know."

The words hit Daniel like a shock wave. He halted where he stood, his eyes turning toward the floor. "God, Michael. I can't tell you how bad I feel about all this...."

Michael's tone turned serious. "Don't."

Daniel looked up.

"You don't have to feel bad, Daniel. You should feel great. I know I do."

"How can you say that? Look at you." Though he appeared in better shape than when Daniel had seen him last it was obvious the last three weeks had taken their toll on Michael. He was thinner than he should have been. His hair was cut short, almost in a buzz. It made him look older. More feeble. It reminded Daniel of pictures he had seen of concentration camp inmates. It was all he could do to keep his eyes on the figure in the chair.

Michael continued. "I tell you, Dan, I feel great. And I mean that. When this whole thing happened.... When I was standing there in the foundry, and heard that chain break.... You know what was on my mind?"

Daniel shook his head.

"It was the strangest thing. It happened so fast. So unexpected. I didn't even have time to move. Yet, at the same time, I could feel my mind racing. I was thinking, now I'll never get the chance to see my baby. I'll never see him - or her - grow old, and learn to ride a bike, and go on that first date, and a thousand-and-one other things I've been looking forward to so much. I'll never get to hold my wife again, and tell her how much I love her, and how much she means to me."

As he talked Amy entered the room. She approached the recliner and sat on the floor at his side, reaching to clasp his hand. For a moment Michael paused, as he and his wife locked eyes.

His voice trembled ever-so-slightly as he continued. "But that didn't happen, Dan. I made it through. I know I'm not the man I once was, but when you consider the alternative, I feel I'm damn lucky to even be here. And I wouldn't be here if it wasn't for you."

Amy spoke up. "We're both so very grateful for what you did. We can't thank you enough."

By now Daniel had made his way to the couch, and was sitting across from the couple. He felt their stares, and their open admiration, and a feeling of failure overwhelmed him.

"Damn it, Mike. It wasn't enough. I should have done more. I should have seen it coming. Or reacted quicker. Or something. I don't know. But whatever I did, it wasn't enough."

For thirty seconds no one spoke. At last Michael leaned forward as best he could. "I spoke to Teri Stone the other day. She says you haven't been back to the shop. Didn't even call to let them know what was going on."

"I couldn't go back there without thinking about...." He struggled for the words, but came up empty handed. "I just couldn't."

"So what are you going to do?"

"I don't know."

"And what's your wife have to say about all this?"

Daniel hesitated, wondering just how much he should tell them, and decided there was no point in denying what was going on. "I'm not staying at the house anymore. Becky asked me to leave."

"Because of this?"

"In part. Things haven't been good between us for a while. Maybe the accident was just the catalyst that brought things to a head. I don't know. I just have a lot of things to sort out."

"Oh, Daniel." Amy walked over, then sat down on the couch beside him. He found himself avoiding her eyes, wishing he had never decided to visit. He wasn't doing any of them any good by being there.

"You know," Michael began, drawing Daniel's attention away from his broodings, "there is something good about this whole accident."

"What could that be?" Daniel asked.

"Well, it's probably a good thing I can't get around anymore. Because if I still had my legs, I'd probably walk right across this room and beat the crap out of you."

Amy stood in shock. "Michael!"

Michael ignored his wife, anger flaring on his face. "Somebody should. Maybe that way he'd get some sense knocked into him. Look at him, sitting there, feeling all sorry for himself.

"I don't buy it, Daniel. You're just using this whole incident as an excuse to shirk your responsibilities. If you want to screw up your life, that's fine. It's your life to do with as you please. But don't be dragging me into this. Don't be using what happened to me as a reason for you to give up on life."

Feeling the need to defend himself, Daniel struggled with words. "You don't understand. You and Amy have your whole life in front of you. Things to look forward to. It's different with me."

"Bullshit!" Michael interrupted. "Maybe I did get a raw deal. And sure, things will never be the same again. But, damn it, I plan to enjoy life as much as I can. I think you'd do well to consider the same thing. Before you wake up some day and realize it's too late. When I think of all the time I wasted in my life.... All the things I could have done, but never took the time for...." His words trailed off as he drew into himself.

Amy reached over to touch Daniel's arm. Her voice sounded soft, almost a whisper, after her husband's outburst. "Think about it, Daniel. The things you do today will be the memories of your future. Will they be happy ones? Or will you regret them for the rest of your life?"

Chapter Forty-Two:

"SO WHAT DO YOU WANT TO TALK ABOUT, Daniel?" Her voice was cold. Emotionless.

"What kind of a greeting is that? Not even a 'How are you doing?'"

Becky took a deep breath. "So how are you doing?"

"Good, now that you ask. How about you?"

She took another deep breath, her exasperation obvious. "You know, Daniel, I have a million-and-one things I need to get done. Classes start next week. I have curriculum reports to prepare. I'm teaching three different courses this semester, and each needs its own syllabus. And that doesn't even take into account the housework I'm getting behind on. So if you just came to chit-chat...."

"I talked to Michael Blake this morning."

His announcement caught Becky by surprise. She instantly felt guilty, to think she had been so preoccupied with her own events when, after all, her problems were petty in comparison to what others had to put up with.

The anger drained from her voice. "So how's Michael doing?"

"Pretty good, actually."

Daniel looked around the hallway. He stood in the front entrance way, Becky effectively blocking ingress to the rest of the house. There was no mistaking her attitude. He had been around her long enough to know when she was angry. He really couldn't blame her for being so upset at seeing him, especially dropping in unannounced the way he had, though he had hoped for a different greeting.

"Listen," he began anew, in an attempt to get the conversation away from its shaky start, "can't we sit down in the kitchen or something? Just to talk?"

Becky hesitated. Her first impulse was to tell him to leave, but she couldn't do that to him. He deserved to be treated better. "Sure," she relented. "Come on in. Can I get you some coffee?"

"That would be great. I don't know what Rick puts in his machine, but it sure doesn't taste like coffee."

"What can you expect from a bachelor?"

He followed her into the kitchen. Daniel took off his coat and sat at the table. It felt comfortable sitting there, surrounded by the possessions they had accumulated together over the years. This was where he belonged. In his house. With his wife.

Becky sat down across from him a minute later, handing over a cup of coffee.

"So where are the kids?" Daniel asked.

She looked around, as though noticing their absence for the first time. "It is pretty quiet in here, isn't it?" She tried to force a smile but failed at the attempt. "Lisa stayed over at Melanie's last night. Jeff said he was going down the street, to play with Brian."

She waited, expecting Daniel to pick up the conversation, but he failed to do so. "So how is Michael?" she asked.

"Good. Really. He can't get around much, of course, but his spirits seem pretty high. It's like he's accepted things, and is doing whatever he has to in order to adjust."

"That's good."

"It's more than good. It's smart. You know, sitting there, talking to Michael, thinking about everything he's gone through the last month...." Daniel shook his head, hoping to clear his thoughts. He felt the words tumbling forth unchecked, fighting each other to be the first from his mouth.

He forced himself on. "It just made a lot of sense. And it

made me realize what an idiot I've been these last couple of weeks. How unfair I was to you and the kids."

Daniel paused, waiting for a reaction from Becky, but none was forthcoming. She sat immobile, staring at him, her face a blank expression.

"I decided to go back to work," he continued. "Get my life back in order."

"That's great, Daniel. Really. I'm happy for you."

Daniel noticed her tone of voice failed to match the enthusiasm the words conveyed.

He had been hoping she would make this easier for him - be more supportive - but that didn't seem to be the case. He blundered on. "Anyway, considering all that's going on, I was thinking, maybe we could...."

The scraping of the chair across the floor interrupted his next words. Becky pulled away from the table, coming up against the pantry closet door. "Don't say it, Daniel."

"Why not?" He stood, walking toward her. "I told you I'm ready to try again. To work things out."

"It's not that simple. I've been doing a lot of thinking myself in the last week. Something's happened between us, Dan. We've changed."

"So we'll change again."

She shook her head, denying the suggestion. "This isn't something that happened overnight. It's been a long time coming. I think we were both just so busy with our separate lives that we didn't see what it was doing to our life together. We never stopped to consider how much we've drifted apart."

She reached for his hand. Daniel found the touch to be uninspiring. It wasn't the touch of a lover, or even a friend. Just two strangers coming into contact with one another.

It was his turn now to pull away.

She leaned closer but made no more attempts to touch him. "You have to understand what I'm going through here," she explained. "Do you think this is easy? Asking you to leave was the hardest thing I ever did in my life. You can't imagine what a wreck I was the first day you were gone. Or how many times I wanted to call you up and beg you to come back. But it wouldn't do either of us any good. It wouldn't change what we've become."

"So what do we do about it? What do you suggest?"

"I think we need to take it slow for a while. You going back to work is a step in the right direction. Let's see how things go from there. Okay?"

"How about the kids? I'd still like to be able to see them."

"And they want to see you. But...."

He hung on her words, wondering what she was leading up to.

"This hasn't been easy for them, Daniel. They're confused right now. Uncertain where their loyalty lies."

"Loyalty? What's that supposed to mean?"

"Oh, you know."

"No. I don't know." His voice was beginning to rise. "Are you trying to turn them away from me?"

"Of course not. Damn it, Daniel, you should know me enough by now to not even ask a question like that. It's just that they're being pulled in two different directions. It's confusing to them. Let's not make it any worse than it is."

"So you won't let me see them?"

"I didn't say that. I won't stop you from seeing them. You are their father. I just wish you'd consider what they're going through. Give them time. That's all."

For a full minute he stared at her. Becky could feel her decisiveness wavering. She wanted to be strong. She needed to be strong. But it was hard with Daniel standing in front of her.

It would be so easy to take his hand, and lead him into the bedroom, and feel the closeness that had been denied them for too long now. But she knew that would only complicate matters. All she could do was wait, and hope Daniel made the right decisions.

She was expecting an outburst but it never came. Instead he reached past her, grabbing his coat, and headed toward the front door, all without uttering a word.

She followed him into the hallway. He stopped with his hand on the knob. "Tell the kids their father says hello," he called over his shoulder.

The next sound was the slamming of the door.

Becky walked to the front window and brushed the curtain aside. She watched as Daniel got in his car, backed onto the street, and pulled away through the sub-division. She continued to look out the window even after his car had disappeared from view.

Chapter Forty-Three:

DANIEL STORMS FROM THE HOUSE, NOT bothering to look around as he gets in his car. The vehicle roars to life, a cloud of vapor erupting from the tailpipe. Backing onto the street he pulls away, passing within inches of the blue Camaro, but he fails to register the vehicle's presence.

He fails also to detect the Camaro's occupant, slouched in the driver's seat.

Brad makes no attempt to start his engine, content to let the other car depart. He can always catch the trail again, like he did earlier this morning. For now, his interest is aroused by other matters.

He leans forward, wiping at the condensation on the inside of the windshield. His attention remains focused on the house just down the block, in particular the figure standing at the front window, brushing at the curtains. From a distance the woman is merely a blur, but Brad continues to watch, fascinated with even a glimpse.

When she finally retreats from sight Brad comes to life. Grabbing a pocket-sized notebook from the seat beside him, he opens it to a page with neatly lettered notations, a series of times and locations logged on intermittently since Sunday morning. He adds to the list the address of the house, underlining the data twice to show its importance. The smile on his face indicates his pleasure at acquiring this latest morsel of information.

He waits another ten minutes, detecting no further activity from across the street, and starts the Camaro.

As he pulls away he passes two teenage boys on the sidewalk. They stare in open admiration at the sports car. Brad presents a grin and a mock salute, though they fail to acknowledge the greeting, and then he is gone.

Chapter Forty-Four: Saturday, January 2, 2016

"SO WHAT DO WE HAVE SO FAR ON THE Black murder?" Captain Thomas Hulet's voice was, as ever, a low expression. His calm, calculated delivery was legendary around the squad room. Many people mistook his quiet demeanor as a sign of weakness, but it was a mistake they rarely made twice. Hulet lived the philosophy that actions speak louder than words, and therefore found it unnecessary to raise his voice when addressing others.

Tuppelo answered the Captain's query. "Not many surprises. Death by gunshot wound to the head. .45 caliber automatic, soft-nosed slug. We're still waiting for the full report from ballistics."

"Has time of death been established?"

"Approximately 1:30, Wednesday afternoon."

"Witnesses?"

"None. Nobody saw anything. Nobody heard anything. I guess that's to be expected. As cold as it's been, everybody must have been inside at the time."

"So what do we have to work with?"

"Not much. We've been over that place with a fine-toothed comb. There's no sign of breakage. No forced entry."

Hulet jumped to the logical conclusion. "Which implies that, whoever did this, was probably someone known to the deceased."

"Or at least someone he wouldn't hesitate to open the door to. Postal clerk. Delivery man."

"Are you presenting this as a theory?"

"No, Sir. Just don't want to dismiss any possibilities prematurely."

Fielding, who until now had remained silent, took over their end of the dialogue. "Nothing seems to be missing, as far as we can tell. The victim's parents - it happened at their house - were out of town at the time. It took us a while, but we finally got hold of them yesterday evening. Their plane's due in this afternoon. They should be able to give us a better account of the possessions."

Hulet nodded. "If nothing is missing, that pretty much rules out robbery as a motive."

"Unless," Tuppelo added, "the thief got scared, and ran away after the shooting."

Fielding presented his partner a quizzical look. "Another possibility?"

"We should consider everything," Tuppelo remarked, in defense of his words.

"Anything else?" Hulet asked.

Tuppelo continued. "Three distinct sets of recent fingerprints near the scene of the crime. One was the dead man's. One his fiance's, Rachel Keller."

"She the one that found the body?"

"That's right."

"And the third set?"

"A friend of Black's. Brad Wilkens."

"What do you have on them?"

"The Keller woman says she was at the mall, doing some last minute shopping. Nothing to substantiate her story one way or the other."

"And Wilkens?"

"We haven't spoken to him yet."

Hulet's eyebrows arched in surprise. "Why's that?"

"We're approaching this with the assumption he could be

responsible."

"You think he's the killer, then?"

"It's a possibility."

Fielding took over. "We ran Wilkens for priors. That's how we got his prints. A couple DUIs a few years back. He's been clean since then, but from what we've learned he has a pretty violent nature."

"'Bout a week ago," Tuppelo continued, "Wilkens threatened...." The detective paused to consult a notebook in his hand. "A Mr. Daniel Jameson. In the parking lot of a bar on Telegraph Road. *Papa Joe's*."

"I've seen the place," Hulet put in. "Never been in there, mind you, but I've seen it."

"Apparently he pulled a gun on Jameson, threatened to blow the guy's head off."

"Was it a .45?"

"Could be. He's registered CCW," which meant Wilkins had a permit for carrying a concealed weapon. "Whether it's a . 45 or not I couldn't say."

"So what was the beef about?"

"Seems Jameson was making the moves on Wilkens' girl," Fielding provided. "Which wasn't the brightest thing to be doing."

"So you haven't talked to Wilkens yet," Hulet summed up. "But I assume you've been checking him out?"

Tuppelo and Fielding answered a simultaneous "Yes, Sir."

"Have his whereabouts been determined for the time of the murder?"

"From what we've learned," Fielding said, "he had planned to meet Jeff Black at the bar that afternoon."

"That would be *Papa Joe's*?"

"That's right. Lots of people say he was there, but no one can substantiate what time he arrived."

Tuppelo leaned toward his partner, whispering loud enough so the Captain would be certain to hear. "Don't forget the message."

Hulet turned to Tuppelo. "Message?"

Tuppelo continued. "A call came through on Jeff Black's cellphone at 1:45. From Wilkens. Said he was calling from the bar."

"Message could have been faked," Fielding pointed out.

Tuppelo shrugged. "The bartender verifies Wilkens was there. Could be legit."

"Or not," Captain Hulet added. "If he did commit the murder, he could have been using the call as a way to set-up an alibi."

"Pretty tough to verify, either way," Tuppelo pointed out.

"How about motive," Hulet asked. "Either Wilkens or the Keller woman have a reason for killing Black?"

"Nothing's come to light, yet."

"You want to know what I think?" Fielding asked no one in particular. "This Wilkens is the killer. Plain and simple. All we need to do is get a search warrant for the gun and run a ballistics test. Bingo! We got him."

"On what grounds are you going to get a warrant?"

"Well, if he does have a .45...."

"We don't know that for a fact," Tuppelo reminded.

"Hell, I have a .45," Hulet pointed out. "Does that make me a killer?"

"No. But your fingerprints aren't all over the place."

"Nothing strange about that, Fielding. You said they were friends. Hell, I'd be more surprised if his prints weren't at the house. We need some solid ground, Fielding. Not supposition."

Hulet faced Tuppelo again. "What do you think?"

"If Wilkens is the killer, I hate to lose him by rushing things. I'd like to have things locked-down better before we make a move."

Hulet nodded. "I agree. It's too soon to go after a warrant. No judge in his right mind is going to let you invade this guy's privacy on supposition."

"So what do we do next?" Fielding asked.

"Keep digging. Something's bound to come up. Just be

sure to let me know when it does."

Chapter Forty-Five:

THE PHONE WAS RINGING WHEN BECKY stepped out of the shower. The dual tone carried through the bathroom door, first the shrill rattle of the old set on the nightstand beside her bed, followed immediately by the electronic pulse from the phone in the kitchen. They almost seemed to be calling out to one another - dueling telephones.

She wondered to herself - not for the first time - why they even bothered keeping the landline now that she and Daniel had cellphones. It made more sense to her to get the kids their own phones and do away with the home line completely. But Daniel always had been slow to accept new technology, and this was a battle she had never convinced him to relinquish.

"Can someone grab that?" she yelled out.

Becky's only answer was the repeated chiming of the phones.

She dragged a towel through her hair, then wound the cloth around herself to maintain at least a modicum of decency as she stepped into the bedroom. The air felt cold against her damp skin, raising a row of goose bumps down her arm, and she snuggled as best she could into the towel's warmth as she plopped down on the bed.

"Hello?"

"Hi. Mrs. Jameson?" It was a young woman's voice. Probably either a phone survey or somebody trying to sell replacement windows.

"Yes?"

"I hope I'm not calling at a bad time...."

Becky bent over, wiping at her soaked hair with a flap of the towel. "Well, actually you are. I just got out of the shower."

"I'm sorry. I can call back later if you'd like."

Becky never did have the patience for phone solicitations. The last thing she wanted was to have them calling back. "Look, I don't know what you're selling, but I'm really not interested."

Laughter from the other end of the line cut off the rest of the words. "Oh, Mrs. Jameson. I guess you didn't recognize me."

Becky paused. The voice had sounded familiar, though Becky couldn't place it. "Who is this?"

"It's Carole. Carole Rosetti. From The Community College."

"Of course! I'm sorry, Carole. I didn't realize it was you."

"That's okay. Listen, I can call back if you'd like."

"No. That's all right. I'm out of the bathroom now, anyway. So what can I do for you?"

"Well, you know this is my last semester at Monroe. Anyway, I've been applying to some other schools. To finish my degree. And I'm having a little trouble."

"What kind of trouble?"

"Well, I've got these forms to fill out. Some essay questions, really, asking about my background, my aspirations. You know. The usual stuff. And I just want to make certain everything sounds right."

"And you'd like me to look them over?"

"Could you? I'd really appreciate it."

"No problem. If you want, we can get together next weekend on it. How would that be?"

"Well...." Disappointment was obvious in her voice. "I know I should have called earlier, but I've been kind of busy and all...."

"When do you need them?"

"I have to turn them in by Thursday," Carole admitted.

"Oh. That doesn't give us much time." Becky considered.

"Listen. I'm booked up for the weekend. And I still have a ton of things to prepare for Monday's classes."

"I understand. Thanks anyway."

"Now don't give up so quickly. Tell you what. I don't have any classes Tuesday afternoon. I should be home by 11:30. If you'd like, we can get together then. We'll have a few hours to look things over before my kids get home from school. How would that work?"

"That would be great!"

"All right, then. See you Tuesday."

Becky hung up the phone, wondering if agreeing to meet with Carole had been the right thing to do. The last thing she needed right now was something else tugging at her. She really did have a lot to do, preparing for next week's classes.

On the other hand, it was always a pleasure to spend time with a student as enthusiastic as Carole. And maybe this would take her mind off other things.

The more she thought about it, the more she was looking forward to Tuesday afternoon.

Chapter Forty-Six:

"MAYBE I SHOULDN'T HAVE STOPPED over." Daniel shifted position on the couch, but failed to get more comfortable. "If you want me to leave...."

"No." Jackie leaned over, her hand touching his arm. "I'm glad you stopped, Daniel. I feel...." She paused, struggling in her mind for the words she was searching for. "Safe, I guess, when you're around."

"Safe from what?"

She made no reply.

Daniel clasped her hand in his. "From Brad?" he asked.

"Yeah. I guess that must be it." She withdrew her hand and shifted away, an expression approaching embarrassment on her face.

"What's wrong? Has Brad done something to you?"

"Oh, nothing. Lately. I haven't even heard from him since that scene at the bar. I just can't help wondering what he's up to."

"What makes you think he's up to something?"

"Because I know Brad. I've seen the way he operates, though for a long time I guess I really didn't pay any attention to it. Once he gets his mind set on something, he won't let anything stand in his way."

"Maybe I scared him off," Daniel suggested in jest.

"Oh, yeah." She chuckled at the thought. "I'm sure that must be it."

"Let's just forget about Brad. Okay?"

"Believe me. I'd like to." She took a deep breath. For a

moment her mind wandered, recalling all the good times she and Brad had shared together. They had so much in common. So many of the same interests. It almost made her forget the other times.

"So how's your friend doing?" Daniel asked.

"Rachel?"

He nodded.

Jackie shrugged. "As well as to be expected. She still won't leave the house. Doesn't want to see other people. I suppose I wouldn't be any different if I was in her place."

"Have the police learned anything yet?"

"Not that I've heard. God, it's so frustrating. Just wondering and all."

Daniel paused, uncertain how far he should proceed with the conversation, and decided at last to continue with what was on his mind. "The police asked me to come down to the station. For questioning."

Jackie's face revealed her surprise at the announcement. "You?"

He nodded. "I went down yesterday afternoon."

"I don't understand. Why would they want to talk to you? You didn't even know Jeff."

"Mostly they were asking about Brad. What happened at *Papa Joe's*. Why he pulled a gun on me."

Jackie felt suddenly defensive. "What did you tell them?"

"What could I tell them? The truth, of course."

"Great!"

"What could I do? They'd learn it all from somebody else anyway. Besides, I'm certainly not going to protect him. Not after what he did to me."

Conflicting emotions were beginning to cloud Jackie's mind. Her affection for Brad, which was still real, struggled with her fear of what the man was capable of. "So how'd the police react?" she finally managed.

"It's hard to say. They didn't say much. I got the impression they were just fishing for information."

She made no reply.

Daniel leaned closer. "Anyway, I just wanted to let you know." He reached for her hand. "You're not mad, are you?"

"No." She forced a smile. Daniel thought he detected a trace of moisture in her eyes, but it was hard to say for certain with the lighting in the room. "You did what you had to do. And like you said, they would have found out anyway."

Daniel, still holding Jackie's hand, moved closer to her, his free hand coming to rest on her knee. For a moment their eyes locked.

Then she pulled away, standing up to face him. "You know, I'm really hungry. How about you?"

The abruptness of the remark surprised him. He had to stop and consider a moment. "I guess I could eat."

Jackie continued, barely allowing Daniel time to complete his response. "I know this real good Mexican place. Makes the best fajitas. How's that sound?"

He rose and walked over to her. His hand gravitated to her shoulder. "I'm not really that hungry."

"Oh, but I am." She pulled away once more, headed for the closet, and rummaged through to find her coat. She managed to avoid looking at Daniel's face the entire time. "I'm starving! So what do you say?"

Daniel, doing his best to disguise his disappointment, grabbed his coat from where he had flung it over a chair in the next room. "Sure. Mexican sounds fine."

"Great."

He followed her down the stairs. It occurred to Daniel that Jackie seemed to be doing her best to avoid eye contact with him.

Chapter Forty-Seven: Tuesday, January 5, 2016

IT WAS AMAZING HOW FAMILIAR everything seemed to him, even after a month's absence. Daniel leaned back in his chair, pulling his eyes away from the computer monitor, and surveyed the office. Nothing had changed at CONSOLIDATED since the day of Michael Blake's accident. The same drab desks crammed the room. The same piles of paperwork, or at least identical piles of paperwork, littered the desktops. The same people performed the same routines they had been busy with a month ago, and would undoubtedly be busy with for years to come.

On the other hand, there was a certain amount of comfort in the old routine, a feeling of safety in not having to tread unfamiliar water.

Monday had been worse. Everyone walking through the office had made it a point to stop at Daniel's desk and express their sympathy at what had happened to Michael, while at the same time praising Daniel's courage and quick thinking. Like he had done something special. They all talked to him as though he was some kind of hero.

Daniel knew otherwise. Instinct, plain and simple. That's all it had been. If he had stopped to think, Daniel was certain he would have reacted differently. It was a good thing, for Michael Blake's sake, that he hadn't considered his actions in more detail.

At the same time, Daniel couldn't help wondering how

different things would have been, in his own life, had the chain of events followed a different path.

"How are you doing, Dan?"

The voice was Daniel's first indication that someone was standing beside him. He looked up at Teri Stone, who smiled before grabbing an empty chair from the next desk.

"Hello, Teri."

She sat down, casting a quick glance around the room before continuing. "I'm sorry I didn't get the chance to stop by sooner to talk."

"That's okay. I've had plenty of people to talk to."

"So I noticed." She leaned closer, her voice lowering. "So how are you?"

He gave the question no consideration before replying. "Okay, I guess."

She shook her head. "That's not what I mean. I know you're going through a bad time here. It's obvious just by looking at you."

"Hey. I'm okay. Really."

For thirty seconds nothing was said, as Teri studied Daniel's face, searching for a sign of weakness. Behind his eyes a weariness lay, an indication of trouble, but it was the only sign he gave that things were bothering him.

Teri stood. "I guess there's nothing else to say, then. Is there?" She made no attempt to disguise the sarcasm in her voice. "I'll see you later, Daniel."

She took a step away before Daniel spoke up. "Teri?"

Making no reply, she turned toward him once more.

"I'm sorry. I appreciate your concern. Really."

Teri moved closer. "Do you want to talk about it?"

"Not right now. Maybe later. Anyway, things really are going better. I'm back at work now, if you can call that a good sign, and things are looking up."

"I hope you're not just saying that."

"I'm not. I really think the worst is over now."

Chapter Forty-Eight:

THE ANGEL OF DEATH GREETED TUPPELO as he entered the squad room.

"This can't be good," Tuppelo prophesied, as Garry Benson approached.

Benson managed to look dumbfounded and exuberant at the same time. "Why are you always so damn pessimistic about things?"

"I'm not pessimistic about things, Garry. I'm pessimistic about *you*." It seemed every time Benson got involved in one of Tuppelo's cases things took a turn for the worse. And it wasn't only Tuppelo who took note of the fact. Everyone in the squad room felt the same way. It would be hard to pinpoint who first started using the sobriquet Angel Of Death, but by now it was in common usage among the detectives.

Sometimes it seemed Benson was almost proud of the nickname, like he had earned it through some act of distinction that set him apart from those around him.

"Boy, and here I thought you'd be glad to see me." Benson waved the air with the folder in his hand. "'Specially considering the info I've got for you."

By now they had reached Tuppelo's desk. The detective sat down, propped his feet up on the desktop, and leaned back in his chair. "So let's have it."

Benson handed over the information. "The ballistics on the .45 used in the Black homicide."

His attention distracted by the report, Tuppelo mumbled a

reply as he scanned the papers. "Anything of interest?"

"How's this for starters. Ever hear of Zak Tyler?"

"Nope."

"I'm not surprised. Young kid, worked in a convenience store near South Bend, Indiana. Shot to death the morning of December 7th."

The announcement caused Tuppelo to lift his head toward Benson, though he said nothing, waiting for the other to continue.

"Ballistics ran a routine check through The Crime Lab and hit pay dirt. Seems the same .45 that killed Jeff Black did the Tyler kid."

A new voice interrupted, as Fielding wandered over to the desk. "So we have a multiple killer on our hands." He paused, considering the ramifications. "That's bad, right?"

"Not necessarily," Tuppelo answered. "So far we've drawn a blank with Black's murder. Maybe this other one will give us a break."

He finished his rapid perusal of the ballistics report, gleaming no new information, then turned to Fielding. "See what you can dig up concerning Brad Wilkens' whereabouts from, say, the 6th to the 8th. Who knows? Maybe we'll be lucky."

"Gotcha. And you?"

"Think I'll contact the authorities in Indiana. See what they can give us on this Tyler killing."

"What about me?" Benson asked.

Tuppelo answered as he reached for the phone. "You've got the most important job of all. And I'm only giving it to you because I know you won't let us down."

Benson's posture straightened as he considered his new found importance. "Just name it. You can count on me."

"Two coffees. I'll take mine with cream and sugar. Harry?"

Fielding didn't miss a beat. "Sugar only."

"Up yours!" Benson turned away, mumbling under his

breath. "Damn detectives."

Fielding laughed all the way to his desk.

Chapter Forty-Nine:

JACKIE STARED AT THE PICTURE, HER MIND flashing back to the trip she and Brad had taken several months earlier, during a stifling August that had been steamy in more ways than one. They had driven into Kentucky for three days, on the way down stopping off at an amusement park just outside of Cincinnati. It had been a whim to have the photo taken, at one of those kiosks where they dress you in old clothes and pose you in the type of stiff seating that she refused to believe was ever popular. It had all been so ridiculous and yet, at the same time, enchantingly romantic.

She had dressed in a blue and white evening gown for the occasion, with yards and yards of material swirling about her legs. A costume worthy of Vivien Leigh. Brad stood stiff behind her in a uniform of gray, plastic rifle held ramrod straight at his side. Their expressions were so serious she couldn't help but laugh at the sight.

It had been a fleeting moment, captured for posterity, harkening back to what had truly been an enjoyable trip. One she knew she would never forget.

Jackie had been apprehensive at the hotel, the first time she had ever spent the night with a man, but Brad was quick to put her at ease. He had been so gentle. So caring. Moving with a preciseness of motion that seemed nearly rehearsed, he had shown nothing but concern for Jackie and her feelings, treating her with respect and understanding.

It was the only time she had enjoyed - really enjoyed -

their love making.

It proved there was a side to Brad that most people didn't see. A side he kept locked away, reserved for only the most special of occasions. If he could be that way once, then there was no reason he couldn't be that way more often. If only she could coax that inner gentleness from him.

But she knew she couldn't. His behavior had changed since then, growing ever more coarse, ever more violent. She couldn't remember the last time he had given any concern to what Jackie wanted to do.

Still, was it really his fault? He couldn't help his attitudes. Maybe what he needed was for her to call him, to attempt a reconciliation. Then maybe things would return to the way they had been four months ago.

As she reached for the phone, Jackie's eyes caught sight of the slip of paper on the counter. The single word CONSOLIDATED was written on the page, followed by a phone number.

It took a moment to recall the significance of the information. Daniel had left his work extension number with her Saturday evening, saying she should call him if she needed anything during the week.

Jackie paused, her mind distracted. Not for the first time, she found herself questioning her feelings concerning Daniel Jameson. There was no denying she felt safe when he was around. It wasn't even a matter of personal safety so much, but rather an emotional freedom. She could be herself, be at ease, and never wonder what demands were expected of her next. She was enjoying this new-found experience, and hoped it would never end.

It was unlike anything she had ever shared with Brad.

She grabbed her cellphone and punched in the number on the slip of paper. Seconds later she heard the familiar voice.

"Daniel Jameson."

"Hi, Dan. It's me. Jackie."

"Jackie?" Was it her imagination, or did his voice become

more quiet after that? "Is something wrong?"

"No. What makes you think something's wrong?"

"I guess I didn't expect to hear from you again." Once more the pause intruded, as though he was uncertain how to proceed. Or maybe it was simpler than that. Perhaps there were other people nearby, and Daniel was afraid of being overheard? "You seemed so distant the last time I saw you."

"That's part of why I called. I wanted to apologize."

"For what?"

"For the way I was on Saturday. I guess I'm still reeling from everything that's going on. I never should have snapped at you the way I did. I'd like to make it up to you. How 'bout I fix you some supper tonight?"

"You don't owe me anything, Jackie. You don't have to do anything for me."

"But I want to. I really do."

He paused. For a moment, Jackie wandered if they had become disconnected.

"Sure," Daniel put in at last. "I'd love to join you for supper."

"Good. What time do you leave work?"

"I should be out of here by four o'clock. Can probably make it to your place by five. Sound all right?"

"Five o'clock is fine. I just hope you like spaghetti."

"Spaghetti sounds great."

Jackie smiled. It felt good to be able to please someone. "So I'll see you this evening."

"Count on it. Bye, Jackie."

"Bye, Dan."

She listened as the line was disconnected. As she replaced the phone in her purse she caught sight of the photo of her with Brad. She picked the picture up off the table, holding it closer for a better inspection. She noticed, for the first time, how cheap the material of her gown was, and how tarnished the buttons were on the jacket Brad wore. Even the background was nothing more than a cheap cardboard backdrop, poorly illustrated and rudely colored. The photograph stood out for what it truly was. A sham. A fabrication of the truth. A make-believe moment in a relationship that hadn't ever been there, except in the fertile ground of Jackie's imagination.

For several minutes all was silent in her apartment.

The picture ripped easier than she had expected. Placing the two halves together, she tore it once again down the middle, then repeated the process one more time, ending up with eight ragged portions. The pieces were deposited into the kitchen garbage can.

She gave the matter no further thought as she began rummaging through the cupboards for the spaghetti sauce.

Chapter Fifty:

"SHIT."

Becky glanced at her in-dash clock for the fifth time since leaving the college. 11:10. The traffic ahead continued to crawl. She had made good time across Dunbar, and the first five minutes heading down Telegraph Road had been decent, considering the snow and occasional patches of ice on the pavement.

But then traffic had screeched to a halt. Movement became a slow crawl, as the line of cars ahead inched down the road. There was no sense trying to get around them. If she tried the back roads she would probably just end up getting lost, and being even later getting home.

All she could do was wait it out.

She looked again at the clock. 11:12.

"Shit."

Well, maybe Carole would be late.

Chapter Fifty-One:

HE HOLDS THE AUTOMATIC LOVINGLY, wiping the blue-steel of the barrel with a cloth until it shines. He is particular with the task, taking his time, savoring the moment, buffing off each speck or blemish that might otherwise mar the gun's appearance.

His eyes contain a faraway gleam, as though imagining great things to come, as he reaches for the can of Budweiser on the table. He takes a quick swallow then sets the can down, his thirst abated, and returns to the automatic.

His spiral notebook sits on the table. It is open, as it has been for the past two days, to a particular page. He looks again at the address he wrote nearly a week ago. He silently mouths the suburban location, even though he has already committed it to memory.

Finally the preparations are complete. The moment is announced in a flurry of movement, as he stands from the chair, places the Smith & Wesson .45 automatic, spare clips, and notebook in his coat pocket, and heads for the door.

He catches sight of himself in the bathroom mirror as he moves down the hallway. He smiles, admiring the image, flinging back an errant strand of hair before brushing away a wrinkle in his coat.

Silence fills the room following his departure.

Chapter Fifty-Two:

"WE'VE GOT HIM! I CAN FEEL IT!" Excitement was obvious in the detective's tone.

"I don't know." Hulet shook his head. "Still sounds circumstantial to me."

"Circumstantial my ass." Fielding continued to pace the room. His fedora, clenched in his fist, endured a steady caressing that managed to add to the spiderweb of wrinkles already covering the fabric. "Brad Wilkens is our man. I'd bet my life on it."

"We don't do things by speculation around here," Hulet pointed out. "We need facts, Fielding. You know that."

Tuppelo, standing in the doorway watching the conversation between the two men, smiled in spite of himself. He had seen the routine before of Hulet playing the role of devil's advocate, forcing his men to examine every bit of evidence from all perspectives. It was a good technique, and had saved the department on more than one occasion from blundering into an embarrassing situation.

Remaining silent, Tuppelo watched as his partner presented the information they had accumulated.

"All right, Captain. Let's look at the facts. The Tyler kid was murdered the morning of December 7th. We know Wilkens was in the general vicinity at the same time.

"First...." Fielding paused, extended a beefy finger to stress his point. "The body shop he works at verified that Wilkens was in South Bend that day, picking up some custom-made auto parts. He arrived the afternoon of the 6th, but since the order wasn't ready yet, he had to stay overnight.

"Second...." Another finger beckoned. "I talked to the desk clerk at the Howard Johnson in Roseland, where Wilkens stayed when he was in town. The place is less than five minutes from the convenience store where the kid was shot. What does that tell you?"

"Coincidence. Simple coincidence."

Fielding waved the matter off as he continued. "How about the car? The state police told us there were reports of a blue Camaro at the scene just before the body was discovered. Wilkens drives a blue Camaro."

Tuppelo spoke for the first time since entering the Captain's office. "All they said was a blue sports car. They couldn't verify the make."

"Doesn't matter. With everything else we've got, how can it not be Wilkens? He had opportunity for both killings, and we know he owns a handgun. I say we bring him in."

Hulet placed both hands together on his desk top as he considered. For a moment it almost seemed as though he had forgotten the two detectives in the room with him. "What do you think, Ben?"

Tuppelo answered immediately. "I agree with Harry. It all seems to fit."

"But are we forcing it? Does it fit because we want it to fit? Let's not have The Department overlooking something obvious because we're all fixated on Wilkens as the killer."

Fielding remained silent as Tuppelo continued the presentation. "There's no guarantee we're on the right track, Captain. You know that. But I will tell you this. It may not be a good idea to wait any longer on this."

"What makes you say that?"

"Everything we've learned about Wilkens points to a disaster waiting to happen. He's got a short fuse that's forever going off. And assuming he is the murderer, something prompted him into killing Jeff Black. I still don't understand what. They were best of friends, after all."

"What are you getting at?"

"Just this, Captain. The Tyler kid looks like a simple case. Armed robbery, plain and simple. Wilkens planned on taking the cash and getting out of there, but something went wrong. Tyler apparently drew a gun. Wilkens shoots first, and the kid is dead.

"Black's murder was something else. Something more personal. Something pushing the killer to the point where he doesn't care anymore. Frankly, the thought scares me. If Wilkens is far enough gone to kill his best friend, there's no telling what he'll do next."

Hulet nodded in agreement. "Good point. Do you know where he's at?"

"That's another problem," Fielding answered. "Wilkens hasn't been back to work since before Christmas. Place he works at tried calling him, but didn't get any answer. They claim he's always been reliable in the past, so they were concerned something out of the ordinary may have happened."

"Can you track him through his cellphone?"

"We've tried the number Jackie Somerset gave us," Tuppelo supplied. "We can't pick up a signal, so he must have the phone turned off."

"Which is pretty suspicious in itself," Fielding offered.

"Keep a tab on that number," the Captain directed, "and continue to scour any of his hang-outs. We better find him before things escalate further. Bring him in for questioning. See what we can get out of him."

"You got it, Captain." Fielding shoved his hand in his hat, reforming the proper crease, then headed for the door, placing the fedora proudly on his head.

Tuppelo was just turning to follow when Hulet spoke again. "One more thing."

"Yes, Captain?"

"Don't take any chances. If Wilkens is the man were after, he's killed twice already. I don't want anyone added to that list. Especially not one of my detectives. Got it?"

"Got it."

Albert Brooker leaned closer. His eyes squinted behind the bifocals as he examined the badge. "My. That shore is a purty one."

Fielding rolled his eyes. Tuppelo shook his head, urging his companion to silence, and replaced the identification in his pocket. "We appreciate you taking time to talk with us, Mr. Brooker."

"Always glad to help the poo-lice. Though, don't know as I can help you much."

"What can you tell us about your neighbor? Mr. Wilkens?"

Brooker considered a moment. "Quiet kid. Keeps to himself. Never been no trouble to no one, far as I know."

"We understand he hasn't been at work lately. Any idea why?"

"Nope. Come to think of it, I have seen him around bit more than usual, last couple, three days. Still, we didn't have much to do with one 'nother."

"Of course not."

Fielding stepped forward. "Did you happen to notice whether Mr. Wilkens was here at all today?"

"Well...." Brooker scratched his head in contemplation. "I seen his car in the parkin' lot. This mornin', must of been, when I was fetchin' the newspaper."

"What time was that?"

"'Bout 10:00, 10:30. Didn't see or hear nothin' since then. Sure wish I could do more to help you fellas out."

"You're doing fine, Mr. Brooker," Tuppelo assured him. The detective removed a business card from an inside pocket. He wrote HARRISON FIELDING next to his own name and handed the card over. "It's very important that we find Mr. Wilkens. If you can think of anything that might help us. Anything at all. Don't hesitate to call. You can contact either me or Detective Fielding at this number."

"Well, I'll be sure to tell Brad you was lookin' for him."

"Actually, we'd prefer that you didn't tell him we were here. Just call us, and we'll do the rest."

"Oh. I get it." Brooker winked knowingly, as though he was privy to an important secret.

"So what do we do now?" Fielding asked, as the car pulled away from the curb, leaving behind the apartment complex where Brad Wilkens lived.

"Keep looking," Tuppelo answered. "And hope we find Wilkens before something else turns up."

Chapter Fifty-Three:

"MRS. JAMESON?"

"Yes?" Becky stands in the doorway, looking out at the man on her doorstep. The sun reflects off the snow in the front yard, forcing her to squint as she stares into the glare.

He smiles. His eyes rove down her body. He nods, making no attempt to conceal the fact that he's satisfied with what he sees. His gaze remains on her legs as he continues. "You're much better looking than I expected." He looks up. "Close up, that is."

"I beg your pardon?"

"First time I saw you, I was parked down the street." He throws a casual glance across his shoulder. "Over there. Didn't get a good look at you, though."

Becky's voice cracks with approaching concern. "I don't know what's going on here....."

"You know," he interrupts, "I think your husband's a damn fool. Why he wants to mess around when he's got something this nice at home, I'll never understand. What's he want with a girl half his age, anyway?"

The door, in the act of closing, stops, as Becky hesitates. "What do you know about my husband?"

He smiles, a youthful grin, his countenance the picture of innocence. "Hell, me and Dan go way back. We're quite close, you know." He looks around. "Tell you what. It's damn cold out here. What say you let me in and we'll talk some more."

"I don't think that's a good idea."

The panel swings forward to close but he moves faster than her, blocking the motion. His hand lifts, revealing the .45 automatic.

His voice is cold. Demanding. "Let me put this another way. I'm coming in."

He brushes against her, closing the door behind him and leaning against it. Becky steps away, her lower lip quivering as she struggles to control herself. "What do you want?"

For a moment he stands. Listening. The house is quiet - no radio, no television, no voices from another room. "We need to talk," he explains. "That's all. A heart-to-heart chat. Fill you in on what old Danny boy's been up to."

"Who are you?"

He smiles, seemingly oblivious to her growing panic. "Now that's better. Sure. Why not observe the.... How should I put it? Social niceties? Yeah. My name's Brad. And you're...?"

Becky turns away but says nothing.

His free hand reaches out, cupping her chin and forcing her to look his direction. The gun lifts the slightest amount. Just enough to catch her attention. "I asked you your name."

"Becky." The word is barely a whisper. "My name's Becky."

He releases her, and she instantly backs a step further away. "Now see there, Becky. That wasn't that bad. There's no reason me and you can't be friends, now is there?"

"What are you doing here?"

"Your husband owes me something. I came to collect."

For thirty seconds nothing else is said as they stare at one another. Brad smiles once more, walks past her to look around the room. "Nice place you got here." He nods his head in satisfaction. "Your hubby must have a pretty good job."

Becky makes no reply. He turns, the smile vanishing, the cold intensity in his eyes increasing. "I asked you a question."

"I don't understand...."

Brad grabs her arm just above the elbow, squeezing hard. "Your husband has a pretty good job. Makes a good living.

Don't he?"

She nods and stumbles with the answer. "We do okay."

"Damn right you do okay. Nice neighborhood. Nice house." The gun hand reaches out, the .45's barrel catching the edge of her skirt, brushing the material aside to reveal her upper thigh. "Nice wife."

Becky attempts to move away, but his grip is too strong. Fear is obvious in her voice. "I don't know what you want. But if it's money, then take whatever you can find. I don't care. I'll get my purse, and...."

"I'm not interested in money. Your husband took something from me. I think I have the right to return the favor. I want...."

The rest of the sentence is interrupted with the crunching of snow from the driveway, announcing a car's arrival.

Brad manhandles Becky to the front window, peeking out the curtain.

"Who's that?" Brad whispers.

"I.... I was expecting someone when you arrived. Her name's Carole. She's a student. From the school where I teach."

"Damn." His composure slips for a moment in his confusion, but the moment passes on the instant. "Get rid of her."

Brad's hand comes to rest against her chest, the .45 smacking against her right breast. Pressure is applied.

"I'll.... I'll try."

The doorbell rings, the chiming disturbing the silence of the room.

Her steps none too steady, Becky moves to the door as Brad backs away. When the door opens he is out of sight, though the conversation is clearly heard from his position.

Becky forces her voice into a semblance of normalcy. "Hello, Carole."

"Hi, Mrs. Jameson. I really appreciate you taking the time to see me today."

Becky glances toward Brad, who holds the gun to his lips like a finger, his mouth forming a silent "shh-hh."

"You know, Carole, maybe this isn't such a good time to get together."

"But I need your help," Carole pleads. "These applications have to get in by this week."

"I'm sorry, Carole, but...." Becky's voice cracks. "But something's come up. Unexpected." She tilts her head, looking away. "I'm sorry."

For several seconds nothing is said. When Carole resumes, her concern is obvious. "Is something wrong, Mrs. Jameson?"

"No, Carole. Nothing's wrong. Why would you think that?"

"You just seem so...." She stops, the word eluding her. "If there's anything I can do...."

"No. No. I think you should just leave." Becky's voice grows stronger. "Right now. Please. Just get out of here!"

Brad lunges forward, pushing the door open as he forces Becky aside, a look of disapproval cast her direction. His hand raises, the gun leveled at Carole's chest. "Get in here, sister. Right now!"

Carole can do little but follow his orders. She shuffles forward, the door slamming shut behind her. Watching them out of the corner of his eye, Brad latches the chain, then turns to face the two women.

Becky leans against the wall, her hands covering her mouth, tears forming in her eyes. "I'm sorry, Carole," she mumbles, the words forcing their way through her grief. "I'm sorry."

"Save it," Brad commands. "Where's the bedroom?"

Becky shakes her head. "I don't understand...."

Brad raises the gun. The barrel moves toward Carole, coming to rest against the young girl's temple. Her lips quiver, her eyes locked pleadingly on Becky.

"I'm not in the mood for games," Brad says.

"It's in back!" Becky shouts the words out. Her arm points down the hall. "There. Back there."

Brad pulls the weapon away, a smile spreading across his face. "See? Wasn't that easy? I do believe you're getting the hang of this." He motions with the gun. "Both of you. In back."

He follows them down the hallway to the bedroom. Brad stops in the doorway, surveying the room. The barrel of the gun points. "The shades. Close them."

Becky does as ordered, plunging the room into a dismal half-light. Only then does Brad enter the room, closing the door behind him.

"Got a bathrobe?"

Becky nods.

"Get it."

She opens the sliding door of the closet. Her hands tremble as she pushes aside dresses and skirts and blouses until finally coming up with the object of her search, a dark blue terry-cloth affair with a heavy cord hanging around the waist.

"Perfect." Brad steps forward, pulling the cord free of the loops. He tugs on it, testing the strength. "This will work fine."

He motions toward Carole. "You. Against the far wall."

She does as ordered.

"And you, Becky...." He recites the name as he would speak to a close friend. Then he smiles. "On the bed. I think.... Yes, on your back. Definitely on your back."

Becky forces herself forward, her eyes closed as she lays down. Brad bends over her, tying one end of the bathrobe's cord around her left wrist, then winding the cord around the support on the headboard.

As he reaches for her right arm Becky lunges off the bed, grabbing his gun hand. Her voice screams out. "Run, Carole! Get out of here!"

The two struggle as Carole hesitates, uncertain what to do. In two seconds she decides, throwing open the door and running down the hallway.

"You stupid bitch!" Brad spits the words out. His hand pulls free, and with a swipe the gun slashes toward Becky's face. The barrel catches the side of her chin, a horrid grinding sound emanating as metal scrapes across flesh.

Brad steps into the hallway as Carole reaches the front door. Panic slows her movements. She yanks at the knob, pulling hard. The door opens two inches and comes to a stop, held securely by the chain.

"That's not a good idea." Brad is calm now. His voice cold. He takes a casual step nearer. "Close the door."

The door closes. Carole turns to face him, tears in her eyes. "Please don't hurt me. Please."

A pained expression crosses his face. "You think I'm going to hurt you? Now why would I do that?" He steps forward, reaching out, his fingers brushing gently against her hair, stroking the strands.

She attempts to pull away, but has no place to go, and can do little but turn her face away from him.

"I don't want to hurt you," he assures her. "Believe me. It's not you I'm after. But I can't let you out of here until Becky and I are done with our little discussion. Now can I?" He steps back and motions with the gun. "In the back."

She leads him down the hallway. The sound of Becky's tears can be heard as they near the bedroom. Carole moves for the doorway, but Brad shakes his head.

"Not there." He motions to an opened door beckoning from across the hallway. "This way."

They enter another bedroom. Plastic models line the shelves, a football blanket adorns the bed.

"Now I want you to stay put," Brad tells her. "Understand?"

Carole nods her head.

He starts to leave, then appears to change his mind. He turns to face her. "But how do I know you won't try to get away again?"

"I won't." Her voice quivers. "I promise."

"Yeah." He nods in understanding. "I know you won't."

The blast from the automatic shatters the still silence of the room. Carole collapses to the floor. The ragged tear in her left leg flows crimson onto the carpet. Her teeth clench in pain as she stares up at her attacker.

Brad steps forward and the gun barks once again.

"What did you do to her?!" The tears are gone from Becky's face, a fiery intensity overwhelming her eyes. She seems oblivious of the blood seeping from her bruised chin, staining the top of her sweater. "Where's Carole?"

"Let's just say she won't be bothering us anymore."

Brad leans over, winding the cord around Becky's free wrist and tying it securely.

The panic is gone from her voice, replaced now with anger. "Why are you doing this? What have we ever done to you?"

Brad sits down on the edge of the bed. His hand gravitates toward her, the gun moving in a slow circle across her breasts, a gentle motion that barely disturbs the material.

"Do you have any idea what your husband's been up to?"

Becky shakes her head.

"He didn't tell you 'bout Jackie, did he?"

"No. Who's Jackie?"

"Jackie's my girlfriend."

The automatic continues to roam. It forces Becky's sweater up, revealing her bra. His eyes linger on the pale white flesh above the black lace.

Brad speaks, his voice lacking all emotion. "Jackie's the girl your husband's been fucking for the past week."

Becky's eyes open wide with a combination of shock and anger.

He smiles. "That's right. He's been staying at her apartment at night. I know. I've seen them."

The gun skims across her stomach, the barrel finding the hem of her skirt.

"Oh, he's fucking her all right. Why wouldn't he? She's young. She's available. And she's a real hellcat in bed. Believe me."

The barrel of the .45 disappears beneath Becky's panties. Brad rotates his hand, forcing the gun forward even as she struggles to keep her legs clenched together.

"And that's why I'm here. If old Dan can have his way with my girl, I think it's only fitting I get a crack at his. Don't you think?"

He smiles, a look of total pleasure, and Becky's tears begin once again as she shuts her eyes tight.

Chapter Fifty-Four:

CAPTAIN HULET STOOD AT THE DESK, waiting for Tuppelo to finish his telephone call. When at last the detective replaced the phone in the receiver the expression on his face was one of disappointment.

"Well?"

Tuppelo shrugged. "No sign of Wilkens. No one at work has seen him. He hasn't returned to his apartment." He shrugged again. "You want us to put out an APB on him?"

Hulet shook his head. "No. We still haven't determined he's guilty of anything. The Department doesn't need a harassment charge hanging over it. Check things out some more. Maybe he's at that bar. What was the name of the place?"

"*Papa Joe's*."

"That's the one. You and Fielding head over there. Talk to some of the regulars. Maybe they can point you in the right direction."

Hulet, mumbling under his breath, headed back to his office. "If it's not one damn thing it's another." The slamming of the door cut off anything further he had to add.

Chapter Fifty-Five:

"EVERYTHING SMELLS DELICIOUS." Daniel breathed deeply, taking in the aroma of the simmering spaghetti sauce. A white linen cloth covered the small table in the dining room, two red candles flickering in the center. "What's the occasion?"

"It's nothing fancy," Jackie protested, as she took his coat from him. "I just wanted things to look nice for you. That's all. I hope you like it."

"Everything looks great."

"Thanks." She motioned toward the couch. "Do you want to sit down for a bit? The sauce has to cook a little more yet, anyway."

"Sure."

He sat down, leaning back against the cushion, while she remained standing.

"Aren't you going to sit down?" Daniel asked.

"Yeah. But...." She paused, unsure what to say, and embarrassed with the fact that she was having such a difficult time with the words. She couldn't understand it. She had rehearsed the lines all afternoon in her mind. What she would say to him, and all his possible replies. But it had been so much easier when he wasn't there. When she didn't have to actually face him.

Might as well just get it over with it, she finally decided. "I just want to apologize," she blurted out.

"We were over this already. When you called me at work.

There's nothing to apologize for, Jackie."

"Yes there is. Last time you were here, I was so.... Distant, I suppose. It wasn't fair to you. I should have considered your feelings more."

He shook his head. "Look. You've been honest with me. You've told me how you feel about things. If you want to just be friends, that's fine with me. I know I can use all the friends I can get right about now."

"But it's not enough. Is it?"

Daniel considered her question. Had he been asked a week ago, he would have admitted he was at rock bottom. Life couldn't have looked any worse to him. He had needed something in his life, and Jackie had been there for him.

But things had changed since then. Talking to Michael Blake, then returning to work, had done something. He looked at things differently than he had a week ago. Though still not happy with where his life was headed he had grown to accept things more. His complacency remained, but it was no longer a depression to him. It was more of a wait-and-see attitude. Things would get better. He realized that now.

Jackie leaned closer. "Well?"

"Well what?" he asked.

"Don't make me spell it out, Dan. You know you were expecting more the last time you were here. And I knew it, too. I guess I was just too afraid. Or too selfish. To be there for you."

"It doesn't matter. It that's what you want...."

"But that's not what I want." She approached the couch and sat on the edge, her body close to his. It felt warmer with her next to him.

"I've done a lot of thinking today, Dan. About my life. My relationship with Brad. All the mistakes I've made."

"We all make mistakes. Believe me. I could write a book about all the stupid things I've done lately."

"But I don't want to make another one. You're the best thing that's ever happened to me."

"What are you trying to say?"

Time seemed to slow, as Jackie's mind flashed to her imaginings of how the evening would proceed. How did it go? Following a plan she'd rehearsed in her mind her hand reached for her blouse and began unfastening the buttons. Her eyes remained on his face - the cut of his chin, the faint trace of the scar across the bridge of his nose - as though taking a mental photograph of the image to store away for future reference.

"I want tonight to be special, Dan. For both of us."

Moments later the blouse slipped from her arms, sliding off her skin, coming to rest on the carpet at her feet. Her breasts, naked and firm, pointed at him invitingly as she leaned closer. She reached for Daniel's arm. Her touch was warm and delicate. Soft and gentle.

Her voice, as inviting as her actions, whispered to him. "Do you like what you see?"

Daniel felt sweat on his palms. He nodded, his lips forming a single word. "Yes."

"I'm glad." She drew closer. Her lips found his. Daniel wrapped his arms around her shoulders, in invitation, and she fell against him.

Chapter Fifty-Six:

"MOM?! IS SOMETHING BURNING?"

Lisa slams the door, drops a pile of books onto the floor, and heads for the kitchen, where the smell seems to be stronger.

"Mom?"

She stops in the doorway, a concerned look crossing her face. "Who are you?"

Brad, half-turned in the chair, smiles over at her. A Marlboro dangles from his mouth, the smoke curling lazily toward the ceiling. He withdraws the cigarette to casually exhale a puff of blue. "So you must be Becky's little girl."

"Where's my mother?"

"She's sort of tied up right now."

Lisa casts hurried glances about, then turns around in the doorway. "Mom?!"

Brad is at her side before she takes three steps. From behind his left hand wraps around her waist, while the right holds the automatic against her cheek. She flinches from contact with the cold metal as he draws her up against him. He leans down, his lips inches from her ear, his smoky breath against her face.

"You're not going anywhere, girlie."

He spins her around, to face the kitchen, then motions with the gun. "In there."

She marches obediently forward. Brad follows, returning to the chair he has just vacated.

"You might as well sit down," he suggests.

"I prefer to stand."

"Sit!"

Lisa pulls out a chair and sits.

"Now isn't that better?"

"Where's my mother?"

He tosses his hand in a casual aside. "Oh, she's around here. Somewhere."

"What have you done with her?"

Brad reaches for the Coca-Cola on the table, finishes what's left in the can, then crumples the container and sends it sailing toward the garbage can in the corner. It clatters as it hits the floor, six inches short of its target. "Damn it. Never could make baskets."

Lisa's eyes have remained on his face the entire while. "What have you done with my mother?"

"You don't want to know." He shakes his head, making a tsk-tsk sound. "Believe me. You don't want to know." He takes a drag from his cigarette. "Don't you have any beer around here?"

She hesitates. "I think there might be some in the garage. If you want me to check...."

"That's a good one. You figure I'll let you go to get it, but you'll slip out the door. Right?"

She shrugs.

"What's your name?"

"Lisa." She snaps back the reply, defiance in her eyes. "What's yours'?"

"Brad. Where's your brother?"

"I don't have a brother."

He reaches for the automatic on the table, spinning it in a half-circle in a slow, lazy manner. Somehow, he manages to make the gesture a threatening one. "Don't lie to me, Lisa. I know you have a brother."

She looks at the clock. "He gets out of school later than me. He should be home in about ten minutes."

"Ten minutes. Not much time." He stands up and walks behind her. His hand comes to rest on her shoulder. Lisa flinches, but her gaze remains steady, as his fingers play with her hair. "You sure look a lot like your mother. You know that?"

She makes no reply.

"Yeah. You sure do." Brad tugs on the hair, drawing it toward his face, the maneuver forcing Lisa to lean her head backward. He sniffs. "And you know what else? You smell good, too. I like that."

A fling of his hand releases her as he pulls away. Heading for the refrigerator, he removes another can of Coke and returns to his chair. Lisa breathes a sigh of relief as Brad sits down.

For ninety seconds, the only sound in the room is a soft whirring from the electric clock on the stove. Brad seems disinterested in everything around him. He leans back in his chair, closing his eyes.

"So now what do we do?" Lisa asks.

"We wait. For your brother."

"Then what?"

"Then?" He pauses, as though considering the question for the first time. "Then, the three of us take a little ride. Wouldn't you like to go for a ride?"

"Not with you, I wouldn't."

He laughs, straightening up and opening his eyes. "That's a good one. You got spirit, girlie. I like that." His eyes narrow, focusing on her face. "You know, I think you and me could learn to be good friends."

"I don't think so."

"I do." He takes a swig of the drink, his eyes never wavering from her face. "It's amazing what a person will do." Then, as an afterthought: "Especially with the proper incentive."

He laughs again - a cold, emotionless outburst - and Lisa shifts in her seat, attempting to draw further away from him.

Chapter Fifty-Seven:

HER EYES OPEN WITH AN INFINITESIMAL slowness, pain shooting through her with even such a simple effort. Something has awakened her, dragged her from the shock and the agony, disturbing her into an uncomfortable state of consciousness. She steadies her labored breathing, straining her ears for recognizable sounds.

Voices beckon from somewhere. Close by, yet far away, as though something separates them.

She forces herself off the floor, grabbing the edge of the bed, dragging herself to a sitting position. For some reason she fails to comprehend her right arm refuses to cooperate in the task, the labor falling to the left arm alone. She manages the procedure at last, then slumps back against the wall, knocking a plastic airplane off the dresser. The craft glides to the floor, shattering as it hits the carpet.

The voices are louder now, and she realizes they come from outside the house.

Carole stands, a distant part of her wondering how she can manage the effort, and lurches forward. She feels no pain from her shattered leg. In truth, she feels no sensation at all from the limb.

Her shoulder is another story. The slug from the .45 lodged in the bone burns. Her hand reaches for the pain. It pulls away, dripping red.

The voices continue.

Carole reaches toward the window, depositing a trail of

red fingerprints that treks across the curtain, then dribbles across the glass. She looks out the window, catching a glimpse of the speakers. There are three of them. The young boy has just climbed in the back seat of the Camaro. Then the girl gets in the front seat on the passenger's side. Their fear, their panic, is obvious, even from a distance, even through the hurt blurring her vision.

"No!" She pounds against the pane, the effort making as much noise as a falling feather on a bed of snow.

Brad looks about before walking around the car and sliding in behind the steering wheel. The engine rumbles to life. The car pulls away.

Carole feels her body slumping, fatigue overcoming her. Images whirl. Words float, unbidden, into her subconscious. *To sleep; perchance to dream....* The phrases entice her. Taunt her. Mesmerize her.

Don't do it, girl. Don't give up.

She makes her way through the room, lurching from the bed to the dresser to the doorway, refusing to surrender. She knows she is fighting for more than just her own life. She knows she can't afford to be weak. She doesn't stop to consider the horror of the situation, the bizarre set of circumstances that brought her to her predicament.

Crossing the hallway seems an impossibility. Carole falls, gasping for breath, wondering how she can go on, until the simple answer strikes her. Using only her right arm - her left is utterly useless from the agonizing wound - she claws at the floor, dragging her tortured limbs across the carpeting, leaving a trail of her life's blood with the passage.

A seeming eternity later she makes it to the side of the bed. She pulls herself up, falling against the inert form still lashed to the bedpost.

"Mrs. Jameson!" The words tumble out with the tears. "Please! Speak to me."

No answer comes.

Carole's head slumps against Becky's naked chest. Her eyes close in a useless attempt to block out the pain.

This can't be happening. I must be imagining it. But it all feels so real. So vivid. If only I could open my eyes and have everything return to the way it should be.

But such is not the case. The reality of the moment invades her senses, flooding her emotions, letting loose a torrent of tears that shakes her fragile frame.

It takes a full five minutes for the panic to abate; for the tears to still. Only then does she become aware of the rhythmic motion beneath her, the shallow breathing disturbing her.

Carole's eyes sparkle as her head lifts. "Thank God. Thank God!"

She can detect now the life signs - the flicker of an eyelid, the heaving of the breasts, the soft whisper of air through the partially open mouth.

It is an effort to stand once more, but she ignores the pain coursing through her frame to perform the deed. She looks about the room, her gaze lingering on the telephone on the dresser. Hope lies there. Salvation.

"Thank God!"

A lurch takes her to the dresser. Her hand gropes - it is difficult to see through the tears and the pain and the redness welling up in her eyes - and she finds the receiver. It takes all her concentration to dial the simple three digits.

The task completed, she feels her determination drain away. She has no strength left. Her energy has evaporated, leaving a shattered shell in its wake.

As she collapses to the floor a voice fills the room.

"Crisis control. Can I help you?"

No answer comes.

"Hello? Is someone there? Hello?"

Carole Rosetti makes no answer. Carole is beyond answering anyone. Ever again.

Chapter Fifty-Eight:

"HOW WAS IT?" JACKIE HAD TO TILT HER head slightly to see him, finally settling on the glimpse afforded between the flickering candles.

Daniel set his fork down, then dabbed at his mouth with the paper napkin. "Everything was great."

Jackie smiled, a knowing smile, the type of look that conceals a secret between two conspirators. "Everything?"

Daniel pushed his chair back from the table, rose, and walked over to her. His arms wrapped around her waist as he bent down to deliver a kiss on the cheek. "Everything."

"I'm glad." She set her glass down, twisted in her seat to more directly face him. "So what do you want to do now?"

"I don't know. See a movie?"

"Maybe." By stretching she was able to reach his neck, her lips delicately caressing the skin. Her mouth felt warm against him, a warmness he relished.

"Or shopping?" he suggested.

Her mouth journeyed across his chin, planting kisses along the way. "Shopping might be nice," she agreed, in a dreamy sort of voice.

"Of course, we could always just stay here."

She drew away, her expression one of surprise, though the glow in her eyes betrayed her emotions. "Now what would we do here?"

Daniel shrugged. "I'm sure we'd find something."

"Yeah. I'm sure we would." He leaned closer. Their lips

met, and no further words were exchanged.

A pounding on the door at the foot of the stairs interrupted the moment. The two retreated from one another, exchanging startled looks.

"I wonder who that could be?" Jackie asked.

"Whoever it is, he sure sounds excited."

A worried look crossed Jackie's face. "You don't suppose it's Brad, do you?"

Before Daniel could answer a voice called, muffled with distance. "Daniel?! Are you there, Dan?"

"That sounds like my brother." Daniel released his hold on Jackie and headed down the stairs.

Rick stormed in the instant the door was opened, panic on his face. "You have to come with me, Dan." He grabbed his older brother by the arm. "Right now!"

"Hold on! What's wrong with you, anyway?. You'd think somebody died or something...."

"Somebody did."

The announcement brought a sudden silence to the room.

"What?" Daniel couldn't help wondering for a moment if he had heard his brother correctly. "What are you talking about?"

Rick gasped for breath, struggling to bring himself under control. "A college student. Named Carole Rosetti. She's dead, Dan. Dead."

"I don't understand...?"

"They found her at your house. She was murdered."

"What?! My house?" Countless unanswered questions instantly flooded through his head. "Where's Becky?"

"She's in the hospital."

"God." Daniel felt himself losing control as he slumped to a sitting position on the stairs. His legs, his arms, everything about him felt useless, heavy and sluggish, pulling him down with their weight. He lifted his head, his eyes searching Rick's face. "What happened?"

"It's pretty sketchy right now. Looks like somebody broke into the house, shot the girl, and...." The words caught in Rick's throat.

Daniel stood, grabbing his brother on the shoulders. "Becky. What about Becky?"

Rick averted his eyes. "She's in bad shape, Dan. They found her in the bedroom. Whoever did it wasn't gentle with her."

"Where is she now?"

"They took her to Toledo Hospital. The police have been trying to find you for the last half hour to let you know what was going on. We've been calling your cellphone but there was no answer." Rick looked up, his eyes locking on Daniel's. "Christ, Dan, what have you been up to, anyway?"

Guilt assailed him as he looked at Jackie. "I was here. My phone was turned off. We were just...." His shame forced the words into a whisper. "I was here."

For several seconds no one spoke. Forcing himself into motion, Daniel bounded up the stairs. "Let me get my coat," he called down to Rick. "Think you can drive me to the hospital?"

"Sure. No problem."

Daniel halted. Something about his brother's tone caught his attention. He turned, saying nothing.

"There's more," Rick admitted.

"What? What else could go wrong?"

"It's Lisa and Jeff. The police haven't been able to locate them. They talked to the neighbors. Some of the kids in the neighborhood. Nobody knows where they're at." Rick swallowed, failing to ease the dryness in his throat. "The police think whoever did this.... Well, they may have taken the kids with them. I'm sorry, Daniel. I'm sorry."

"Yeah. Yeah. I know you are."

Daniel grabbed his coat. He was nearly down the steps before he remembered Jackie. She stood at the top of the stairs. Their eyes met, but she said nothing.

"I'll call you," he said.

She nodded, forcing back the tears. "Just go on. Your wife needs you."

Daniel followed Rick out the door. Jackie listened for the sounds of their departure - the footsteps on the front porch, the car springing to life, the crunch of snow as they drove off. With a sigh she returned to the table and sat down. With all her preparations, all the imaginings her mind had rehearsed, nothing had prepared her for this.

Picking up her fork she poked at the spaghetti, swirling the pasta around the plate, making designs in the bright red sauce.

Her eyes lighted on the half-full wine bottle. "What the hell."

She dragged the bottle toward her and filled her glass.

Chapter Fifty-Nine:

ONCE AGAIN DANIEL JAMESON FOUND himself visiting a hospital. As he walked the unheated corridor leading from the parking garage his mind flashed back to Michael Blake, laying shriveled and weak in the midst of recuperating. Daniel had been sick with the sight, sick with grief over what his friend was going through, and sick to think how things had turned out following the accident at the foundry. Even so, there was a certain detachment to the visit. A separation existed between the principals.

This time was different. This time, it wasn't a co-worker in the hospital bed. This time it was his wife.

Becky was sleeping when he arrived. He paused in the doorway, taking in her features. An ugly bruise adorned her right cheek, just below the eye. Her chin was bandaged, the edges of the dressing pink with dried blood. The hospital gown she wore fit loosely on her shoulders. Where the material draped, he could just make out another patch of gauze, the tape wrapped around her shoulder to disappear beneath the gown.

He didn't want to think about what she had gone through. How frightened she must have been. But it was difficult to look at her without considering how she had arrived at the condition.

Daniel entered as quietly as he could, pulling a chair over to the side of the bed. Becky's arm lay flung to the side. He couldn't resist the urge to touch her. To feel her softness. Her skin was warm, almost as though she was feverish. He caressed her hand as he stared into space, his thoughts a lifetime away.

"Daniel?"

The whisper nearly escaped his notice. Had it not been so quiet in the room he would have missed it.

Daniel stood, refusing to relinquish the grip on his wife's hand, and moved into her line of vision.

"I'm here, Becky. I'm here for you."

"It hurts, Daniel. It hurts all over."

A feeling of helplessness washed over him. "You want me to get the nurse? See if you can have a pain pill or something?"

"No." She shook her head, closed her eyes, and took a deep breath. Daniel was beginning to think she had fallen asleep again when her eyes popped open. "Carole? How is she? Is she...?"

"She didn't make it. She managed, somehow, to call 911, but by the time the authorities arrived...." Unable to complete the words, his voice trailed away to nothing.

"That poor girl. It should have never happened. If only she hadn't been there." The words trailed away, replaced by tears, as Becky shut her eyes. Daniel said nothing, allowing her time to compose herself.

"Who's Jackie?" she asked at last.

"What?"

"Who's Jackie?"

"I don't know what you're talking about."

She pulled her hand away and attempted to sit up. It was obvious from her expression that even such a simple effort caused her pain. Her voice, soft from fatigue, still managed to convey anger. "Damn it, Daniel. Don't lie to me. Not now. Not after what I've been through. I deserve better than that."

She turned away.

"Jackie's a friend of mine," he finally managed. "That's all."

She faced him once more, a look of disbelief on her face. "Just a friend?"

"Yeah."

"Her boyfriend didn't think so."

"What do you mean?"

"Her boyfriend. You know. Brad."

"You mean, he's the one who...." The words caught in his throat.

Becky nodded.

"I had no idea, Becky. Honest. I never imagined he would do anything like this."

"Are you sleeping with her?"

Daniel turned away.

Becky sighed, closing her eyes. "Why, Daniel? Why would you do this to me?"

He sat, considering his reply, while she waited in silence.

"I don't know," he admitted at last. "It just seemed something was missing from my life."

"Did you find it in her?"

He shook his head.

"I should have been the one you came to, Daniel. I should have been the one you relied on."

She turned to hide the approaching tears. "I'm tired. I need my sleep. Please leave me alone."

He stood and, for a full two minutes, watched her quivering back, listening to the muffled sound of crying. He wanted desperately to reach out and grab her. To bring her to him. To tell her how much she meant to him. How much she had always meant to him.

But it was foolish to even think such thoughts, and he realized as much. Especially considering what he still had to tell her.

"There's more," he managed at last.

She rolled over in bed to face him. "What else could you do to me, Dan? Haven't I been through enough already?"

His eyes locked on the floor. "The kids are gone."

"What?" Her eyes glowed fierceness. "What are you saying?"

"They didn't want to tell you, when you first arrived.

They didn't think you could handle the shock. But no one knows where Lisa and Jeff are."

"No. No!" Her head began a rapid back and forth motion. She grabbed at her forehead, as though she could block out the pain.

Daniel continued. "They think...." The words caught in his throat. "They think Brad may have taken them with him."

"Why? Why would he do this to me? To Carole? Why would he hurt my children?"

"We don't know for a fact that he's hurt them. We only know...."

"Damn you, Daniel Jameson! This is all your fault!" Somehow she found the strength to lurch forward, her fists pounding ineffectually against his chest. "How could you do this to us?"

"I'm sorry."

"It's not enough. It will never be enough. Just get out of here! Get out!" She groped around, searching for anything, coming up at last with the pillow from her bed. She threw it at him, but it landed at his feet.

Becky failed to notice as she plopped back on the bed. She lay there, staring at the ceiling, muttering through the tears. "My babies! My babies!"

He left her to her sorrow. There was little else he could do.

Chapter Sixty:

THE SOUND OF WHIMPERING, BARELY audible above the car's racing engine, comes from the back seat.

Brad looks to Lisa. "What the hell's the matter back there?"

She sits leaning against the door, as far removed from him as the cramped space permits. Her eyes lock on his face. A stiffness dominates her body, betraying her fear, but her voice is firm. "Do you have to swear?"

"Just tell him to stop."

"He can't help it. He's scared."

Brad glances at the rear view mirror. "Hey kid. Kid!"

Jeff wipes his eyes with the back of his hand but makes no reply.

"What's your name, kid?"

"His name's Jeff," Lisa answers, when it becomes obvious her brother doesn't want to talk.

"Really?" Brad smiles with what appears to be genuine sincerity. "I used to have a friend named Jeff. We were like that." He holds his hand out, two fingers crossed to indicate closeness. "We had some good times together." He pauses, a faraway look in his eyes. "I sure miss him."

"What happened to him?" The question originates from the back seat.

Brad shrugs. "He got in my way one day. So I shot him." He chuckles at the thought. "Bang. No more Jeff."

A silence invades the car, punctuated only by whistling

wind as the Camaro hurtles down the road.

Brad nods his head. "Yeah. I sure do miss him."

"You're kidding. Right?"

No reply. Jeff looks from Brad to his sister for an answer. "He's kidding. Isn't he?"

Lisa's eyes have remained on Brad for the entire exchange. Her voice is emotionless. Empty. "I don't think so."

Brad smiles once more at the two children, who do their best to shrink further from him.

Chapter Sixty-One:

A DOZEN EYES STARED AT DANIEL. THEY were frightening in their intensity, demanding in their perseverance. The demeanor of each of the six men was the same - that of stolid determination.

The man who had introduced himself as Alan Murdoch did most of the talking for the group. "We can only help you if you help us, Mr. Jameson. Understand?"

"Look. I told you everything I know. I only met Wilkens once."

"Yet the man forced his way into your house. Raped your wife. Kidnapped your children...."

"I know what he did." Daniel felt his anger growing. He didn't like this man. He didn't like his cold attitude. He didn't like his ruthless efficiency that treated people as if they were objects. "You don't have to remind me what Wilkens did. It's been on my mind constantly for the last five hours."

"Don't you think these are pretty extreme actions from a person you only met once?"

"I don't think extreme is a strong enough term."

"Then how do you explain it?"

"I don't know. Why don't you talk to his girlfriend about it?"

"We've already talked to Miss Somerset."

"Then talk to her again."

Murdoch made to answer, but Daniel cut him off. "What are we sitting here talking for, anyway? Why aren't you looking for my children? Why aren't you after the no good bastard that put my wife in the hospital and sent that poor girl to the morgue?"

"We're doing everything we can...."

"It's not enough. Look at you. You're the FBI. You're a Federal agency, for heaven's sake. You must have all sorts of resources at your command. Use them. Find my children."

"That's what we're trying to do. But until then...."

"Until then," Daniel interrupted, weary of the delays, "you're wasting my time. And your time."

Murdoch sighed. "I already explained this once, Mr. Jameson. We need to determine everything we can about Wilkens before we act. We need to be prepared. Know how he might act. What we can expect him to do."

"Then why talk to me? Why not talk to him?" Daniel pointed at the tall bulk of a man across the room. "What was your name? Tuppelo, wasn't it?"

Tuppelo nodded. "That's correct, Mr. Jameson."

"Then you tell them. You questioned me the other day about Wilkens. You probably have a file a half-a-mile long on the guy."

"That's true, but...."

Murdoch waved the detective to silence. "Detective Tuppelo is here as a courtesy only. He works for The Toledo Police Department. This incident with your wife and children is out of his jurisdiction. He's agreed to help us, for which we're grateful, but otherwise he has no purpose for being here."

"How about Jeff Black's murder? He's involved with that, isn't he? Doesn't that make him involved with Brad Wilkens?"

The federal agent chose his words carefully. "There's every possibility that Brad Wilkens may have been responsible for the death of Jeff Black."

"Then why wasn't he arrested?"

"Because the police....."

"No." Daniel sprang from his seat, crossing the room to face Tuppelo directly. After spending the last hour and a half in a useless round of questions and answers, Daniel had taken about as much as he could handle. "I want to hear it from you. Why wasn't Wilkens arrested? Why was he allowed to roam free? To do what he did. If you had done your job right, my wife wouldn't be in the hospital right now. My children wouldn't be who-knows-where with some kind of maniac."

"Mr. Jameson...."

Before Murdoch could proceed further Tuppelo motioned him to silence. The Toledo detective's voice was calm. Rational. "This isn't television, Mr. Jameson. We can't arrest somebody because we think he might have committed a crime. I understand you're upset. But that doesn't help the situation at all. The best thing to do is cooperate."

"But I have cooperated."

"We're well aware of that, Mr. Jameson. And we appreciate it. All we want is the same thing you want. We want your children returned safely home. We want the man responsible for what happened to your wife to be held accountable for it. He's killed three people already. We'd like to see it stopped. Now. Before someone else gets hurt."

Daniel's shoulders sagged. "So what can we do?"

"We go over everything again, on the off chance that there may be something you're forgetting that may help us. All right?"

Daniel nodded and turned to the FBI agent. "Okay. What do you want to know?"

Murdoch made a point of scowling at Tuppelo before focusing his attention on Daniel. "Let's take it again. From the beginning. When did you first meet Brad Wilkens?"

"It was a Saturday night. The Saturday between Christmas and New Year's."

"That would be the 26th."

"If you say so."

"And you never met him before?"

"That's right."

"Tell us again what happened."

"Not much to tell. The whole night was one big mistake.

It started when I went to *Papa Joe's* that night."

Chapter Sixty-Two:

THE HOUSE WAS DARK WHEN DANIEL drove up. He forced himself to the door, let himself in with the key his brother had given him, and entered the living room. Sinking onto the couch he allowed the cushions to overwhelm him.

Footsteps approached.

"Are you okay?" Rick asked.

Daniel stared at the floor as he stared at his hands. "It's not me I'm worried about."

Rick approached, sitting opposite his brother. "How's Becky doing?"

"Mostly sleeping. They've got her pumped full of pain killers and who knows what else. God, it must have been terrible. What she went through...."

"Don't even think about it, Dan. There was nothing you could have done to prevent it."

"Yes there was. I could have done *everything* to prevent it. I never should have gone to see Jackie that night. It only made a bad situation that much worse."

"But how were you to know?"

The logic refused to agree with Daniel. "It doesn't matter. I shouldn't have done it."

He lapsed into silence.

Rick felt the need to keep the conversation going. To keep Daniel talking, before he dragged himself further into the depths of depression. Before he was so overcome with remorse that there would be no chance of ever rescuing him.

"Jackie's been calling, by the way. To see what's going on. I don't know why she can't just leave you alone and...."

"No, Rick. Don't say that." Daniel surprised himself with his calmness. "It's not Jackie's fault what's going on. She's a victim. Just like Becky. Just like Carole Rosetti."

Daniel stood. He walked over to stare out the front window. It was beginning to snow, fat flakes that drifted lazily down in the still night air, adding an infinitesimal layer to the blanket of white covering the landscape.

"I've really screwed things up good this time."

"Now, Daniel...."

"No, Rick. I have. I've made mistakes before in my life. I guess we all do. But this time...."

His mind wandered as he spoke, images from the past flashing before his eyes. "I had it all, Rick. The perfect life. Loving family. Two beautiful kids. House in the suburbs.

"Sounds corny, doesn't it? But it wasn't. It was everything I could have ever expected from life. Hell, it's more than a lot of people get. Why couldn't I have accepted things the way they were?"

"It's like you said before. We all make mistakes."

"Not like this." Daniel shook his head, his voice dropping down to a whisper. "Not like this."

He turned from the window, the light reflecting the tears in his eyes. "I appreciate your concern, Rick. But I just can't think straight anymore. I think if I could just lay down for a while...."

Rick rose. "Sure. I know it's been a rough day for you."

He trudged from the room, stopping in the hallway, turning back at the last moment to look back at his older brother. "Are you sure you're all right?"

"Yeah. I'm just great." Daniel walked to the couch and stretched out on the cushions, his eyes locked on empty space. "I think I'll just try to get some sleep. You'll let me know if anyone calls?"

"Sure, Dan. Don't worry 'bout it. Just get yourself some rest."

"Thanks."

Rick's footsteps faded away, the sounds of night filling the emptiness; the ticking of a clock, the electric whir of the refrigerator in the kitchen, light traffic noises from outside, the occasional wail of a freight train speeding along somewhere off in the distance.

The sounds accompanied Daniel throughout the long evening.

Chapter Sixty-Three:

"I'M COLD." JEFF'S VOICE SOUNDS FROM the darkness.

"So what?" Brad - sitting in a wooden rocker, can of Budweiser in his hand - stares at the huddled form of the two children on the worn couch. "What do you expect me to do about it?"

"You could turn up the heat," Lisa suggests, in a matter-of-fact tone of voice.

"I already told you. This is a summer cottage that belongs to my old man. They got the heat shut off for the winter."

"Aren't there any extra blankets?"

"Quit your moaning and get to sleep."

For five minutes all is quiet, until once again Jeff disturbs the silence. "I wish my father was here."

"Don't worry, kid. You'll see him tomorrow." Brad holds up the .45 automatic. "Count on it."

Chapter Sixty-Four: Wednesday, January 6, 2016

"BRAD CALLED."

"What?" Jackie had his attention immediately, his drowsiness banished. Rick stared at her in the doorway as he stumbled for a reply. "When did this happen?."

"This morning. He has a message for Dan." She tried to look past him, to see into the house, but Rick effectively blocked the doorway. "Where is he?"

"He's...."

"Right here." Daniel stepped up behind his brother.

His eyes locked on Jackie. A look of determination, infused with a smoldering intensity, burned beneath his features. It was a look she had only ever seen before in one person.

And that person was Brad.

Jackie struggled to hold back the shivers as a chill swept over her body.

"He told me where he is," Jackie informed them. Then, speaking directly to Daniel: "He wants you to go see him."

"And my children?"

"He says they'll be fine. As long as you do like he says. He says if you tell the police where he's at, or lead them to him, he'll...." The words caught in her throat. "Just don't bring the police. Okay?"

There was no need to deliberate on the issue. Daniel decided on the instant. "Then I have to get going."

He moved for the door.

Rick stopped Daniel with a hand on his shoulder. "What do you think you're doing?"

"I'm going to get my kids."

"Are you crazy?! Let the police handle this. That's their job."

Daniel shook his head. "You heard what she said. I can't let anything happen to Lisa and Jeff."

"But this guy is nuts, Daniel. If you go after him, you're liable to not make it back."

"That's a chance I'll have to take."

For ten seconds they glared at one another, until finally Rick backed down. "All right, Dan. If that's the way it's going to be. But I'm coming with you."

"It's not your problem."

"Hell, Daniel. Now's a lousy time to be playing big brother. Quit trying to run my life for me. I'm not a little kid anymore. I can make my own decisions. Just give me a minute to get something we might need."

Rick disappeared to the back of the house. He returned minutes later, zipping on his coat as he headed for the door. Daniel shot him a quizzical look, but Rick offered no explanation.

"So what are we waiting for?" Rick asked. "Where's he at, anyway?"

"Up in the Irish Hills," Jackie informed them.

Daniel and Rick both knew the Southern Michigan locale. About two hours drive north of Toledo, it was known for its summer recreation, offering parks for camping, hiking, and boating. Largely undeveloped, the area was a minor tourist attraction. Along with the natural splendor of the location the area was interspersed with the typical fare of miniature golf and fast food restaurants.

It was a summer haven for those wishing to escape the city for a spell, though at this time of year the chances were the area would be pretty deserted.

Jackie continued. "Brad says he's at a cottage on Sand Lake. I wrote down the directions for how to get there."

Daniel and Rick stepped outside. The snow continued to fall, several inches having coated the ground since the night before. Daniel's face betrayed his concern. "I wonder what the roads are like?"

"No problem." Rick grinned. "We'll take the Bronco."

Rick and Daniel took the seats in front, Jackie climbing in back. Daniel turned to face her once the car was in motion. "I think we should drop you off at your place."

"No way." Jackie fought to control the approaching shivers. "I won't lie to you. If you don't think I'm scared, you're crazy. I know Brad better than anyone. I've seen what he's capable of. And I know - now - the type of person he really is."

She took a deep breath. "But I have to do this, or I'll never be able to live with myself. Besides...." She forced a smile. "Maybe I can reason with him."

"I wouldn't count on it." Daniel offered.

"Doesn't matter. I'm going anyway."

"Suit yourself." Daniel turned to Rick. "There's one stop we have to make first."

"Now?"

"Now." Daniel's face showed no indication of flexibility.

Rick shrugged his shoulders. "You're the boss. Just tell me where to go."

Chapter Sixty-Five:

"I KNOW WHERE THE CHILDREN ARE."

Becky showed interest with the revelation, forcing herself to a sitting position. Her voice was stronger than it had been the day before. "How'd you find *that* out?"

"From...." Daniel hesitated with his reply. His intention in stopping at the hospital wasn't to upset Becky further. He finally managed a reply. "From a friend."

"Jackie?"

He nodded.

She displayed no reaction to the admission. "Where are they? Where are my children?"

He hesitated, wondering how much he should tell her. While she had every right to know where her children were there was no sense in burdening her with too much information. It was enough for her to know that he would be bringing them back to her. Then maybe their lives could get back on track.

He purposely avoided her question. "I'm going after them, Becky."

"By yourself?"

"Jackie's coming along."

"Oh?! That's just great, Daniel. I'm sure you'll have a nice time together."

He chose to ignore the sarcasm. "Rick's coming along as well," he was quick to add.

"So now you're dragging your brother into this mess."

"I'm not forcing him to come. He volunteered."

She closed her eyes. "So why are you here? Why did you bother to stop? Why not just get going? Jackie's waiting for you, isn't she?"

"Because I thought you should know. Just in case.... In case something happened."

She turned away. "Maybe you better be on your way."

"Yeah. Right."

He turned toward the door and stopped. Nagging doubts attacked him. There was a good chance he wouldn't be coming back. That he would never see Becky again. But what could he do? What could he say, to make up for what he had done to her?

He took two steps and she called out.

"Daniel?"

"Yes?" Expectation dominated his features as he faced her.

"I want my children back, Daniel. Do you understand?"

"Of course."

"I just want you to be clear on that point. If you can't bring Lisa and Jeff back...." The words caught in her throat. She turned away, coughed once, then faced him again.

Her eyes blazed with renewed energy. "If you can't bring Lisa and Jeff back, then don't bother coming back yourself. Ever. Understand?"

Daniel nodded, then left the hospital room.

Chapter Sixty-Six:

THE BUILDING WAS A CAVERNOUS AFFAIR, nothing more than a large utility shed, the front wall sheathed in aluminum. A cluttered conglomeration filled the place; the motor from a boat, dry-docked on a pair of sawhorses - a snowmobile - water skis - tools and other gear. A solitary window adorned one wall, high up toward the ceiling. It provided a minimum of light in addition to the sliver of illumination bordering the single door.

"I'm scared, Lisa."

"I am too, Jeff." She hugged him in the darkness, feeling his shivering. "But we can't let it get to us. We have to get out of here."

"But how? He's got a gun!"

She released him, to begin feeling her way through the gloom. "There's lots of stuff in here. If we can find something...." Her mind considered the possibilities.

Returning to her brother she grabbed him by the shoulders, shaking him gently to focus his attention. "You've got to listen to me, Jeff. This is real important."

He nodded. "All right. I'm listening."

"When he comes back I'll distract him."

"How you gonna do that?"

"Don't worry 'bout it. I'll find a way. But when it does happen, I want you to run. Get away from here as fast as you can. Go get help."

"But what will happen to you?"

"That's why you have to get help. I'm counting on you."

"But I'm scared!"

"So am I." She hugged him once again, fighting back the tears. "So am I."

Chapter Sixty-Seven:

"SO WHAT DO YOU THINK OF MURDOCH?"

Tuppelo shrugged. "About the same as any other Fed, I suppose. Just doing his job."

"The guy's an asshole." Fielding took a bite from his corned beef sandwich. "Comes in here like he owns the place, but what's he done so far? Nothing. Zilch. Nada." He took another bite. "What a jerk."

Tuppelo sat back in his seat, watching his partner. "So you just about done with that, or do I have to sit here all day watching you eat?"

"What's your rush? You that anxious to go back to the office and sit on your butt?"

"I was thinking...."

"That's your first mistake."

He ignored Fielding's attempt at humor. "Maybe we should go talk to Becky Jameson."

"The wife?"

Tuppelo nodded.

"What good will that do? Last time we were there she was pretty out of it."

"That's just it. Maybe she's doing better now. And maybe she can remember something Wilkens said. Something that might give us an idea what he's up to."

"I suppose it's worth a shot." Fielding finished his drink and grabbed his fedora from the seat beside him. "Give me a chance to check out the nurses on the day shift."

*****

The room was dark. Tuppelo stood in the doorway, hesitating, wondering what to do.

Becky's voice called out. "Who's there?"

"Detective Benjamin Tuppelo, Mrs. Jameson. With the Toledo Police Department. I was wondering if I might have a word with you."

She made no reply. As the detective took a step into the room the muffled sound of crying reached his ears. "Are you all right, Mrs. Jameson?"

He grew more bold, stepping up to her bedside. It was obvious she was fighting her emotions, trying desperately to hold back the tears.

"Mrs. Jameson? Are you in pain? Should I call for a nurse?"

"No." She shook her head. "No. It's.... It's my husband."

Tuppelo stole a quick glance around, thinking someone else was in the room, but it was just the two of them.

"Your husband isn't here."

"I know. He's gone."

"Gone?"

She nodded.

Interest was growing. "Where did he go? Mrs. Jameson? Where did your husband go."

"He went to find the man who has our children."

"Brad Wilkens? Your husband's going after Brad Wilkens?"

"Yes."

"How can he do that? How would he know where to go?"

"He called her. That woman. He called that woman."

"Jackie Somerset?"

Becky's eyes closed, as if trying to shut out the pain. "Yes." The word was quiet. Barely a whisper. "Yes. That woman."

"So your husband called Jackie Somerset...."

"No!" She shook her head violently back and forth as her eyes snapped open. "He called. The man who did this to me."

"Brad Wilkens called Jackie Somerset?"

"That's right."

"Damn."

Fielding was deep in conversation with the nurse at the desk when Tuppelo rushed over. "Was Daniel Jameson here today, visiting his wife?"

She stopped to consider the question. "Yeah. I guess he was."

"When?"

"I don't know. Why?"

Tuppelo leaned against the desk, his face etched in determination. "When was he here?" Tuppelo asked once again, his voice booming off the corridor walls.

"I don't know. An hour ago. Maybe longer. But I don't see what...."

"Damn it!" Tuppelo's fist smashed against the counter. He grabbed Fielding by the sleeve and hauled him toward the elevator. "Come on, partner. We've got places to go."

Chapter Sixty-Eight:

FOOTSTEPS SOUND FROM SOMEWHERE outside. A cough follows.

Lisa leans toward her brother and whispers. "Are you ready?"

He nods.

"Just remember what I told you and we'll be okay." She pounds on the door. "Mister! You out there, Mister?"

"What do you want?"

"We have to go to the bathroom."

"Wait."

"But we REALLY have to go."

Silence answers, followed by the sound of a key in a lock. Brad mumbles as he opens the door. "Damn kids."

Light floods into the shed. Jeff blinks as he walks, stiff-legged, into the open. He stares at Brad, then looks at the cottage.

"Go on," Brad commands, pointing. "You know where the shitter is."

Jeff begins to walk away, while Brad waits in the doorway. No further sound comes from within the shed.

"Where you at, girlie?" He steps inside to look around. "Hey, girl...."

The two-by-four catches him on the right shoulder, knocking him to the ground. Lisa makes no attempt to avoid stepping on him as she rushes past.

"Run, Jeff! Run!"

Her voice carries through the clear winter air. She searches around for her brother, then spies him on the other side of the building. He looks back, panic on his face, before disappearing into a grove of trees. Lisa turns the other direction and begins to run.

She manages four steps before an arm reaches out. Brad grabs her and pulls her off her feet. The .45 flashes before her eyes.

"That was a stupid thing to do, Lisa." His voice is calm. Quiet. It's the expression in his eyes that screams out at her. "A real stupid thing."

He looks around, sees the footprints, and follows them to the tree line. He raises his voice to a shout. "You better come back, kid! I got your sister!"

After thirty seconds of silence he turns away. "Damn it!"

Brad faces Lisa. She smiles, as though she's scored a major victory.

"You'll pay for this, girlie."

She offers little resistance as he drags her back to the shed. Brad stands in the doorway, taking a quick inventory of the clutter. Reaching a decision, he grabs a length of oily rope and wraps it around Lisa's arms. The other end he ties to one of the building's uprights.

"That should hold you."

Lisa begins to shake, fighting back the tears, but she says nothing.

It takes twenty minutes to haul the snowmobile outside and get it ready to start. The most difficult thing is finding the fuel. He finally locates the gasoline in a smaller, auxiliary shed, not much more than a lean-to, that's attached to the back of the main structure. Metal cans, each clearly marked, line a shelf on the wall: GASOLINE - PAINT THINNER - ALCOHOL.

Brad stands up from the vehicle once the preparations are complete. He walks to the still opened door of the shed, glaring in at Lisa. "I hope you don't get lonely, girlie."

He laughs as he slams the door.

The sound of a lock snapping shut reaches in to her, followed shortly after by the snowmobile's engine kicking into life. It idles for a few minutes, warming up, then the sound fades into nothingness as Brad leaves the vicinity.

It is difficult to do, but Lisa manages to slump to the floor. The rope strains against her, but she appears not to notice. With a sigh she leans her head forward. It's no longer possible to hold back the tears.

Chapter Sixty-Nine:

JEFF'S FINGERS WERE STARTING TO BURN. He really didn't understand why. *You would think, with all the snow around, that they would feel cold, not hot.* It just didn't make any sense to him.

From time to time he would stick his hands in his coat pockets. The warmth felt good at first, until the snow and ice on his fingers began to melt. Then the moisture made things even worse.

He pulled his hands back out, rubbing them together until they felt dry and at least a little more like they should, and continued trudging through the woods. It was slow going. The snow seeped into his boots every time he stepped into a deep patch of the stuff. He had fallen twice, tripping on unseen objects buried in the field of white. Each time he picked himself up, brushed the snow off his face as best he could, and continued on.

He felt like finding a warm place to lie down, but he knew he couldn't give up. He had to keep going. Lisa was counting on him.

A sound reached his ears, and Jeff stopped to listen better. It was a whining sound, a high-pitched squeal that fluctuated from time to time. A motor, maybe. He wasn't sure what it meant, but since it came from behind him, from the place he was trying to get away from, he didn't want to find out what it was. It only urged him to continue onward.

He had started off by running, to get as much distance

between him and the man with the gun as he could, but his legs soon gave way and he tired of the exertion. More rested now, he began to run once again.

He soon found himself gasping for breath. His lungs hurt each time he gulped in the cold air. His cheeks felt dry and chapped.

Up ahead he saw a break in the trees. It looked like it could be a road. He paused for a moment, deliberating what to do next. He felt safer in the woods, where he could duck behind a tree to hide if he had to.

On the other hand, it made sense to follow the road. It might lead him to a house. Or maybe a car, with somebody in it. Then he could get away.

His mind made up, he took a step forward.

He felt the snow give way as he lost his footing. The next thing he knew he was sliding down an embankment.

Snow blinded his eyes as he rolled along. Trying desperately to stop his motion his arms flailed about, grabbing for anything but finding nothing. His momentum halted only when he came to rest against an oak tree.

Jeff heard the snap of his arm as he came to a stop. He screamed in pain, biting his lip, fighting back the tears. He lay there for several minutes, hoping the agony would go away, but it refused to cooperate.

Somehow he managed to stand, holding the injured limb against him, trying to keep it from shaking too much. It hurt each time it shook. His eyes clouded. He felt weak. Dizzy.

Forcing himself on, Jeff began a methodical march along the side of the road. He fell once, and lay there a moment to catch his breath, then forced himself to continue. His legs felt like they weighed a ton, the snow sticking to his clothes pulling down against him.

And his hands still burned. It was worse now, like sticking his fingers into a fire. They tingled constantly, no matter what he did, no matter how hard he tried to keep them dry. If only he had his gloves.

He found himself slowing down even as he urged himself to continue. When he finally fell again, his weakness overtook him. He lay in the snow, gasping for breath, and closed his eyes. Sleep relieved him of his agony.

Chapter Seventy:

THE SQUAD ROOM WAS A HUSTLE OF activity. The commotion centered around Tuppelo's desk, where the beefy detective coordinated his team's efforts. The scene had erupted with movement as the police force scrambled to determine the location of Daniel Jameson.

Above the bustle a voice called from across the room. "We've located the cellphone."

"Jameson's?"

"No. The Somerset girl."

"About time." Tuppelo strode over to the computer terminal. "Where is she?"

"Northwest of here, about forty miles. Nearing Adrian Michigan."

"You think she's with Jameson?" Fielding inquired.

"That would be my guess," Tuppelo speculated, "that the two of them are heading somewhere together. More than likely to make contact with Wilkens."

The detective grabbed his coat and made for the door, Fielding joining him. "Contact the Michigan State Police," he called behind him to no one in particular. "Advise them of the situation."

Captain Hulet, standing in his office doorway, shot an intimidating glance toward the duo. "And where are you two off to?"

They halted, as if brought short by an invisible wall, but neither said a word.

Hulet continued. "Michigan's out of our jurisdiction, boys. You know that."

Neither replied. Neither moved from their location, poised to exit the room.

Hulet sighed deeply in resignation. "So what are you waiting for?" The Captain returned to his office, mumbling under his breath. "About time we catch that son-of-a-bitch."

Chapter Seventy-One:

"OH MY GOD!"

Daniel rushed to the still form at the side of the road. He picked his son up with the utmost of care. It was obvious, from the position of the boy's arm, that he had broken the limb.

Daniel laid him on the back seat of the Bronco. Rick grabbed some blankets from the rear of the vehicle, covering the child.

"We've got to get him to a doctor," Daniel remarked.

Jackie stepped closer. "What about your daughter?"

"I don't know." Daniel looked down the road, wondering what waited beyond. "But I can't leave him like this. I have to do something to help him."

Rick placed a hand on Daniel's shoulder. "It shouldn't be far. You can probably walk from here. I'll take Jeff into town, then come back for you."

Daniel nodded. "Yes. That's probably the best idea."

Rick reached into his coat. "Here. Take this." He held out his hand. In the palm sat a Browning 9mm handgun.

"Where'd that come from?"

"Remember a few year's back? When my neighbors got their house broken into? It seemed a good idea to get some protection, so I bought this."

Daniel made no attempt to grab the weapon. "I can't take that."

"You damn right *better* take it. You don't think that maniac you're walking up there to meet has a gun on him?"

"I still can't take it. I wouldn't know what to do."

"Release the safety, aim, and shoot. There's nothing to it."

He hesitated. "I just don't know...."

"I'll take it." Jackie reached over, grabbing the automatic.

Rick looked at the two of them, shook his head, and walked over to the driver's door of the Bronco. "I'll be back as soon as I can. You two be careful."

Daniel and Jackie watched as he executed a three-point turn around and headed back in the direction they had come. Without a word between them they started to walk, following the footprints leading along the side of the road.

Jeff had come from that direction. It was only logical to assume that following the trail would lead them to where Jeff had been. And where Lisa still was.

And where a crazy maniac of a person with the death of three people on his hands was waiting for their arrival.

Chapter Seventy-Two:

THE SNOWMOBILE SITS ATOP A LOW HILL, the engine silent. Brad stands fifteen feet away. By watching through a break in the trees he can observe the activity in the near distance. He watches as the boy's still form is loaded in the Bronco and as the three figures converse for several minutes.

They appear to be arguing, but the words fail to carry to his position. Eventually they seem to reach a decision and the vehicle drives away. Left behind are two forms that begin a slow trek down the road.

Brad returns to the snowmobile. He seems relaxed, his motions calm, his manner assured. Withdrawing a cigarette from his coat pocket, he takes the time to enjoy a smoke, his eyes never wavering from the duo headed his way. The air whistles through the trees, the cold breeze picking up particles of snow - a fine dust of white - that whips against the silent figure. Brad exhibits no reaction to the element's onslaught.

When the cigarette is done he throws the smoldering butt off to the side. The engine kicks on with no hesitation. Executing a sharp turn, he heads back toward the cottage.

Chapter Seventy-Three:

DANIEL AND JACKIE KNEEL BEHIND A LOW mound of snow, taking note of the surroundings. The Camaro sits in front of a small weather-beaten structure. Several inches of snow coat the vehicle, attesting to the fact that it hasn't been moved since the night before. No sound comes from the building. A lamp shines in one of the windows, throwing a rectangle of light on the porch fronting the cottage, but otherwise there are no signs of activity. Nothing to indicate that anyone is around.

"Do you see anything?" Jackie whispers, holding her lips inches from Daniel's ear.

He surveys the scene. "No." He points across the clearing. "See that?"

"Looks like a shed. I suppose for somebody's boat. What about it?"

"Look around it. What do you see?"

"Snow." She peers more intently, shakes her head and shrugs. "All I see is snow."

Daniel stands up and begins moving forward. "Footprints," he says. "Lots of footprints. And they definitely look fresh. Think I'll check it out."

She grabs his arm, slowing his progress. "Are you crazy? What if Brad sees you?"

"I came here to get my children. I knew I was going to have to face Brad sooner or later. Might as well get it over with."

He walks into the clearing, his path never wavering as he

heads for the utility shed. He reaches the door, peers at the Master lock on the hasp, and bends closer to listen. The expression on his face changes as muffled sounds reach out to him from inside.

"Lisa? Is that you?"

The reply is instantaneous. "Daddy?!"

"Yes, Lisa. It's Daddy. Are you okay?"

"Just scared, that's all. But I'm worried 'bout Jeff. He ran away, and I don't know what happened to him."

The smile on Daniel's face grows. "Your brother's just fine. He's with Uncle Rick."

"I want to go home, Daddy." Crying distorts the words. "Can I please go home?"

"I'm working on it, Princess."

By now Jackie has made her way across the clearing. She holds the automatic at her side as she scans for signs of activity around them. She seems painfully aware of their vulnerability as they stand out in the open.

"Where's Brad?" she whispers.

"How would I know?"

She tilts her head, motioning to the utility shed. "Ask her."

Daniel raises his voice enough to be heard through the door. "Where's Brad, Lisa? Where's the man with the gun?"

"He left. On a snowmobile. He was trying to catch Jeff."

"Then we're in luck. Maybe we can get out of here before he makes it back."

Daniel grabs the lock securing the door, yanking on it. It only takes one attempt to demonstrate the futility of the effort. He turns to Jackie. "We need to find something to pry this open. A crowbar, maybe. Look around."

He starts to move away. Lisa's voice - loud with panic - calls out to him. "Don't leave me, Daddy! Don't go away!"

"I'm not leaving you, Princess. But I have to find something to get you out of there. Just hang on. I'll be right back. Count on it."

A clattering sounds, from around the side of the building. Daniel follows the noise to the lean-to built on the side of the shed and finds Jackie rummaging around inside.

"Do you have to make so much noise?"

"Do you want to get your daughter out of there or not?" She pushes against a shelf, dislodging several cans that crash down, spilling paint onto the cement floor. "I didn't think you'd be so damn particular about things." She steps back, hands on her hips, surveying the contents of the shed. "There's got to be something in here we can use."

While she looks in one portion of the little room Daniel attacks another part. Three minutes of searching yields nothing better than a rusted screwdriver and an old brick.

Jackie's expression declares her astonishment. "What good is that gonna do?"

"Let's find out."

They step out of the building. Both instantly come to a stop, aware of a new sound from off in the distance.

"What's that?" Jackie asks.

For a moment Daniel freezes, but only for a moment. There is no time to waste. Saying nothing, his pace quickens as he heads for the locked door.

Jackie follows close behind. "Is that a snowmobile?" Panic taints her voice. Her eyes dart around them, attempting to isolate the approaching sound. Echoes distort the noise, making it impossible to judge where it comes from. "It sounds like a snowmobile, doesn't it?"

"Of *course* it's a snowmobile," Daniel answers, not bothering to look her way. "It means Brad's getting closer."

"Hurry up. Hurry up!"

"I'm moving as fast as I can."

Daniel jams the screwdriver into the lock, below the hasp. Wedging the blade against the door, he pulls down with his left hand to apply tension, then lifts the brick. His eyes find Jackie. "Wish me luck."

"Good luck." The words squeak out.

Daniel's hand lowers. The brick sideswipes the handle on the way down, catching the side of Daniel's arm. He drops both tools, grabbing his sleeve.

"Damn it!"

"Are you okay?"

He continues to hold his sleeve, applying pressure, pain etching his face.

Jackie moves closer. "Let me see."

"I'm okay." He takes a step backwards. "Really."

"Don't be such a baby."

Reluctantly, he pulls his hand away. She rolls back the coat sleeve, exposing his arm. The skin is scraped raw just above the wrist. Blood seeps through to discolor his coat.

Her hands begin to shake. "Christ, Dan! That looks awful!"

He pulls away from her. "It feels even worse. Believe me."

"Daddy!" Lisa's voice is raised in alarm. "I hear something, Daddy!"

"Don't worry, Princess. You'll be out any minute now."

Daniel retrieves the screwdriver and brick to repeat the procedure. He takes more care this time, backing off to the side so his arm isn't as close. The brick hurtles down, smashes into the screwdriver, and explodes into a shower of fragmented stone.

"Oh, great." Jackie turns away in frustration, turns back, and turns away once more. "That's just great. Now what are we gonna do?"

"There's got to be something else we can use. All we have to do is...."

The snowmobile bursts into the clearing, the revving of the engine drowning out further conversation. There is no denying the sound, vibrations pounding against the shed and echoing off the trees.

Brad throttles the motor, bearing down on them. His eyes lock on Daniel and Jackie. A grin crosses his face.

Daniel takes a step away from the shed as he sizes up the situation. He has seconds only to react as the machine hurtles toward them. Even as he turns to move away he pushes Jackie, forcing her away from him.

"Get out of here!" He has to yell to make his voice heard. "Find cover!"

Four steps take Daniel away from the shed. The snow hinders his progress, making his best effort appear little more than baby steps. It's a plodding gait, agonizing in its slowness, that covers little distance.

Brad leans into the turn, swerving the snowmobile, aiming for his quarry. Daniel jumps at the last moment. The fiberglass body of the vehicle catches his leg as it speeds past. Momentum spins him while still in the air.

His landing is anything but graceful. A thud sounds as he falls on his side, rolling twice, snow filling his nose and mouth as he tumbles across the clearing. He pushes himself off the ground the instant he comes to a stop. Coughing, shaking his head, he searches for Brad.

The snowmobile vaults over a small mound of snow, taking to the air for a second, then settles down to execute a sharp turn. Brad pauses, standing on the runner, reconnoitering.

Jackie has disappeared around the side of the shed. Daniel scrambles to his feet, stepping awkwardly through the snow, desperately seeking to put more distance between himself and his attacker.

The engine throttles once more and Brad is moving again. There is no question concerning his intent.

As Daniel continues, he reaches a spot where the snow has blown clear. He makes better time now, managing to sprint. He chances a look behind him.

The action proves to be a mistake. His wild panic has taken Daniel to the edge of the lake. His foot slips on the bank and he falls once more. He lands hard on the ice, his body spinning in lazy circles through the slush and snow covering the frozen water. The coldness soaks into his coat and jeans as he struggles to stop his careening motion.

The snowmobile lurches off the bank and onto the ice, bearing down on Daniel. At the last moment Brad swerves purposely, sending a spray of ice into Daniel's face as the machine glides by only inches away. Brad's laughter fills the air, expressing anything but humor.

As the snowmobile executes a slow turn on the iced surface Daniel reaches his feet. A dozen steps take him to the lean-to at the side of the shed. He disappears from view within the structure. His hands reach out - groping, searching.

Mere seconds later Daniel steps back out into the open. He has moments only to react, the snowmobile aiming for him once more.

In the five seconds before Brad reaches him, Daniel manages to tear off the lid of the container in his hand. A pungent smell assaults his nostrils. Turpentine, thinner, it's impossible to say what it is. But it doesn't matter. In a single motion he jumps to the side and tosses the can.

Brad swerves wildly, in an attempt to avoid the projectile, but in his haste misjudges the maneuver. The snowmobile lists to the side and smashes against the side of the large utility shed, tearing through the thin aluminum sheathing even as it throws its driver to the ground.

As Brad falls, the dirty liquid from the can tossed at him splashes on the side of his face. The fumes attack him, instantly bringing him to tears. He has time only to claw at his eyes as a scream of agony leaves his throat.

With his hands no longer on the handlebars, the snowmobile's engine dies. All is silent for exactly three seconds.

Like an outtake of a giant's breath a WHOOSH announces the flames as they burst into life, erupting from the belly of the doomed vehicle, bursting in seconds into a full-fledged conflagration. Snow and ice sizzle as the fire attacks the side of the building, the orange-red tendrils reaching for the heavens. The glare forces Daniel to turn away.

Jackie is at his side, grabbing his arm. "Your daughter!"

"Oh my God!"

They run to the door. Lisa's screams can be plainly heard. "Daddy! Help me, Daddy!"

"I'm coming, Princess." He pounds on the door. "Hang on, Lisa!"

"I can see the flames, Daddy! I can see them! They're coming closer!"

"Goddamn it!" Daniel spins around, panic on his face. "There's got to be something! There's got to be...."

He grabs Jackie.

"The gun! Where's the gun?!"

It takes a second for her to catch on. "I dropped it. Here, somewhere, when Brad was coming."

She falls to her knees in the snow, her fingers searching. Daniel does likewise, as Lisa continues to scream from inside the building.

"I got it!" Daniel jumps to his feet. "I got it!"

He fumbles with the mechanism, finally managing to figure out the safety. "Look out, Lisa! I'm going to shoot the lock!"

"Hurry, Daddy! Please! Hurry!"

He misses completely, the shot striking the ground. Grabbing the Browning with both hands, he steadies himself, takes careful aim, and pulls the trigger twice, the shots sounding as a single terrific explosion in the still coldness of the scene.

The lock remains intact despite the onslaught. The wood around the hasp, however, splinters and tears. Daniel drops the gun, grabs at the door, and pulls.

A moment later the door is open and he hurtles inside.

Chapter Seventy-Four:

SMOKE FILLS THE SHED, BILLOWING CLOUDS of black and gray and white that hang everywhere. Smoke, and an eerie red glow.

"Daddy! I'm over here!"

He follows the sound of her voice and seconds later Daniel is at his daughter's side. Blood drips from Lisa's wrists, resulting from her struggles against her bindings. Daniel grabs the rope, straining with his arms to part the strands, but it refuses to yield. He backs away, his eyes searching.

"Don't leave me, Daddy!"

It is growing warmer now. There isn't much time left. Daniel rushes over to a workbench and rummages through a pile of rusted tools. When he returns to Lisa's side he holds a utility knife.

"We're almost there, Princess."

He smiles at her. She attempts to return the gesture, but panic works against her.

It takes only twenty seconds to slice through the rope. Daniel grabs his daughter, pulling her to him, hugging her before turning to head for the door.

A crash sounds to their left as the wall on that side collapses. Daniel ducks down to avoid the flaming embers, shielding Lisa from the falling debris. Smoke fills their lungs, causing shared coughing that abates only after the fumes clear through the now open wall.

Daniel straightens up, takes two steps toward the door,

and comes to a stop.

Brad Wilkens stands in the newly opened wall of the building. His clothes are torn, and black with ash. Stains on his pants are a suspicious red in color, the blood running in tiny rivulets that course down his legs and color the snow at his feet. A gash on his forehead leaks fat drops of blood, the stream flowing down the left side of his face. The right side is blistered and raw. His eyes are red.

He is obviously hurting, yet his demeanor fails to reveal the fact. He stands ramrod straight. He never flinches.

The Smith and Wesson .45 in his hand is leveled at Daniel's chest.

His voice is rough. He practically coughs the words out. "It's payback time."

Daniel blinks in astonishment. "You stupid bastard." He looks around at the encroaching flames. "Let us out. Before it's too late."

"It's already too late. It was too late from the second you started messin' with Jackie."

Brad takes a step forward. His eyes close, his body shivering as if through a great effort. The moment passes, and his attention returns to Daniel. "I've been waiting a long time for this."

Daniel sets Lisa down. Fear has deprived her of voice as she stares mutely at Brad.

"Let the girl go, Brad. She hasn't done anything to you. Please."

"Begging for mercy? I love it." Brad shakes his head. "But it's too late."

He advances a step.

From somewhere outside the shed a voice calls out.

"Brad!"

All eyes turn to face Jackie. She stands behind and to the left of Brad. She holds Rick's gun, pointed at him. "Don't make me shoot you, Brad."

He laughs, a twinkle in his eyes. "That's a joke. You haven't got enough balls to do it, Jackie, and you know it." He faces Daniel again. "Stupid bitch," he mutters under his breath.

"Please, Brad." Jackie takes a step closer. "Don't force me to do something I'll regret."

He doesn't even bother to look her way. "You won't do it, Jackie. And you know why?" Now he turns around, a smug expression on his face. "Because you love me."

Tears are in her eyes. "You're right, Brad. I do love you."

The three shots follow one another in rapid succession. The first smashes into Brad's chest, jerking him a step backward. The next two complete the job and he collapses to the ground. No movement comes from where his body lays, save for the red flow that oozes into the snow around him.

Daniel buries Lisa's face in his coat. Picking her up, he hurries away. "Let's get out of here."

Jackie drops the gun. A moment later she falls to her knees. The tears shake her body as she covers her eyes.

Chapter Seventy-Five:

THE THREE OF THEM WERE SITTING AT A folding table in the front room of the cottage when the cars pulled into the clearing. There were two cruisers, Michigan State Police emblazoned on the sides, and a familiar truck. Lisa ran to the window, flinging back the curtain. Her eyes lit up when her uncle stepped out from behind the steering wheel of the Bronco.

"Uncle Rick!"

She stopped at the door to look back at her father and Jackie. "Aren't you coming?"

"We'll be right out," Daniel told her.

Lisa stormed out the door.

Jackie sighed and slid her chair back from the table. "Guess it's time to face the music."

"Wait." Daniel placed his hand on her arm, restraining her. "We might not have time later, and I wanted to thank you."

"For what?"

"For saving my life."

"You don't have to thank me. It was something that had to be done. I guess, in a way, it was something I had to do." She took a deep breath. "There's no turning back now, is there?"

"I guess not."

They both continued to sit there, each reluctant to move, each hesitant to say anything. It was Jackie who broke the silence.

"So what happens now, Dan?"

"I don't know. But I can tell you this. Seeing my wife in

the hospital, then finding out my children had been taken from me, made me think. For the first time in a long while, I realize what's important to me.

"I don't know if Becky will take me back. I can only hope she will. But if she doesn't...."

He stopped a moment to consider.

"She'll have to," he decided. "I won't take no for an answer. It may take some convincing, but I know what I'm fighting for now. And I won't give up."

"Your wife's a lucky woman."

"I doubt if she'd agree with you right now. But in time, I hope she feels the same way."

He stood up.

"What about you, Jackie? What will you do?"

She waved the matter off, as though unimportant. "Don't worry 'bout me. I'm a survivor. This thing won't keep me down. I'll just.... I'll just...."

Jackie stopped abruptly, the words sticking in her throat. They stared at one another until Daniel, too uncomfortable to speak, walked to the door. He stopped, but didn't look back.

"Goodbye, Jackie Somerset."

"Goodbye, Daniel Jameson."

He tried to ignore her tears as he walked out the door.

Detective Benjamin Tuppelo, surrounded by a trio of state troopers, stood staring at the destruction at the edge of the lake. The flames still burned, volumes of black smoke pouring from the empty shell that was the utility shed. Nearby pine trees stood green against the skyline, their limbs denuded of snow and ice from the heat of the fire.

"Damn." Tuppelo whispered the word under his breath as he shielded his eyes from the glare. "Damn."

Lisa stood holding Rick's hand. "What are you doing here?" she asked him.

"I thought I was here to help. Looks like I'm too late."

"Is Jeff okay?" Daniel asked, as he stepped off the porch

and walked over to them.

Tuppelo answered. "Fielding took him to the hospital in Adrian. I'm sure he's doing just fine. Where's Wilkens?"

Without a word Daniel led the police officer around the wreckage of the building. The blackened carcass of the snowmobile lay silent in the snow. Beside it sprawled the still form of Brad Wilkens.

Tuppelo took out a notebook. "What happened?"

"It's a long story. Let's just say I wouldn't be here right now if it wasn't for Jackie."

"Where is Miss Somerset?"

Daniel pointed to the cottage. "Inside. Listen, I'd really like to see my son. Is there any way...?"

"Sure. I'll have one of the officers take you there." Tuppelo paused, as if seeing Daniel for the first time. "I hate to tell you this, Mr. Jameson, but you look like hell. Are you all right?"

Daniel forced a smile. "Well, I've had better days, believe me."

His eyes lighted on his daughter. Lisa was still chatting with Rick. Though the words were indistinguishable from their distance, her face sparkled.

"Then again," Daniel added, "things are looking a whole lot better than they were a day ago."

A smile lit his face as he headed back to his daughter.

The End

Author Bio

Originally from Erie Pennsylvania, Keith has lived in the Toledo Ohio area since 1982, where he and his wife raised their two boys. The children live now in Missouri and Kentucky while Keith and Colleen reside just north of Toledo, across the border in Southern Michigan.

www.KeithJulius.com